ONLY THE GOOD DIE YOUNG

"Do you remember a girl called Alicia Doyle, Mr. Hollister?" Thanet asked the retired classics master.

"Of course I do," snapped Hollister. "I am far from senile yet, Thanet. She was that little trollop Paul Leyton was running about with. If it hadn't been for her, he would never have killed himself."

His venom startled Thanet and he wondered, could he by chance have stumbled across Alicia's murderer? That Hollister should speak with such passion after all these years astonished him.

"You may not have heard, sir, but Alicia Parnell—Alicia Doyle, as you knew her—was found dead in the Black Swan on Sunday morning. She had been strangled."

Hollister didn't even blink. "Doesn't surprise me. A fitting end, I should think."

Bantam Books offers the finest in classic and modern British murder mysteries.
Ask your bookseller for the books you have missed.

Agatha Christie

Death on the Nile
A Holiday for Murder
The Mousetrap and Other Plays
The Mysterious Affair at Styles
Poirot Investigates
Postern of Fate
The Secret Adversary
The Seven Dials Mystery
Sleeping Murder

Dorothy Simpson

Last Seen Alive
The Night She Died
Puppet for a Corpse
Six Feet Under
Close Her Eyes
coming soon: Element of Doubt

Sheila Radley

The Chief Inspector's Daughter
Death in the Morning
Fate Worse Than Death
Who Saw Him Die?

Elizabeth George

A Great Deliverance
coming soon: A Payment in Blood

Colin Dexter

Last Bus to Woodstock
The Riddle of the Third Mile
The Silent World of Nicholas Quinn
Service of All the Dead
The Dead of Jericho
The Secret of Annexe 3
Last Seen Wearing

John Greenwood

The Mind of Mr. Mosley
The Missing Mr. Mosley
Mosley by Moonlight
Murder, Mr. Mosley
Mists Over Mosley
What, Me, Mr. Mosley?

Ruth Rendell

A Dark-Adapted Eye
  (writing as Barbara Vine)
A Fatal Inversion
  (writing as Barbara Vine)

Marian Babson

Death in Fashion
Reel Murder
Murder, Murder Little Star
Murder on a Mystery Tour
Murder Sails at Midnight

Christianna Brand

Suddenly at His Residence
Heads You Lose

Dorothy Cannell

The Widows Club
coming soon: Down the Garden Path

Michael Dibdin

Ratking

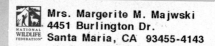
LAST SEEN ALIVE

A LUKE THANET MYSTERY

Dorothy Simpson

BANTAM BOOKS

TORONTO · NEW YORK · LONDON · SYDNEY · AUCKLAND

LAST SEEN ALIVE

A Bantam Book / published by arrangement with
Charles Scribner's Sons

PRINTING HISTORY

Charles Scribner's edition published September 1985

Bantam edition / October 1986
3 printings through March 1989

ISBN 0-553-27773-1

Published simultaneously in the United States and Canada

Bantam Books are published by Bantam Books, a division of Bantam
Doubleday Dell Publishing Group, Inc. Its trademark, consisting of the
words ''Bantam Books'' and the portrayal of a rooster, is Registered
in U.S. Patent and Trademark Office and in other countries. Marca
Registrada. Bantam Books, 666 Fifth Avenue, New York, New York 10103.

PRINTED IN THE UNITED STATES OF AMERICA

O   12 11 10 9 8 7 6 5 4 3

To Hazel

Reviens, reviens,
Ma bien aimée. . . .

Berlioz, *Nuits d'été.*

ONE

Even before Thanet had closed the front door behind him Bridget was hurtling down the stairs, face radiant and long hair flying.

'She spoke to me, Daddy! She spoke to me!'

'She did?'

Thanet smiled indulgently as Bridget flung her arms around him. No need to ask who 'she' was. Like countless other young girls the world over, twelve-year-old Bridget was an ardent admirer of the Princess of Wales. Ever since that fairy-tale vision had floated up the aisle of St Paul's Cathedral, capturing the hearts and imagination of millions, Bridget had taken an avid interest in anything and everything to do with Princess Diana. Her bedroom was crammed with posters, books, commemoration china and bulging scrapbooks and she had been looking forward to today's royal visit for months.

When it had been suggested that the Princess should be asked to open the new children's orthopaedic unit at Sturrenden General Hospital, nobody had really expected her to say yes. But she had, and the small country town had been in a fever of anticipation ever since.

Thanet had been somewhat less enthusiastic. For the police, a royal visit means weeks of planning, a crescendo of detailed organisation culminating in a day of hectic activity and high tension, especially when the visitor is as universally popular as Princess Diana. But now it was all over and they could breathe a sigh of relief that nothing had gone wrong. The enormous crowds had dispersed without serious incident, the support groups drafted in from Canterbury had departed and traffic signs had been cleared away from the route. Most important of all, the Princess had gone and others were responsible for her safety. Thanet did not envy them their job.

'How exciting! What did she say to you?'

'She asked me how long I'd been waiting, and I said, since eight o'clock this morning.'

'And?'

'She pulled a little face and said, what a long time.'

'And that was it?'

'Yes. I was really *close* to her, Daddy. I could have put out my hand and touched her! I didn't, of course, but oh, she's so beautiful, she really is, far more beautiful than all the pictures of her . . .'

Thanet put an arm around Bridget's shoulders and they moved towards the kitchen as she chattered enthusiastically on. Thanet put his head around the living room door as they went by. 'Hullo Ben.'

'Hi, Dad.' Ben scarcely turned his head. He was deep in 'Doctor Who.'

In the kitchen Joan was shaking the water out of lettuce. She looked up, smiled and came to kiss him. 'It all went off well, I gather.'

'You weren't there? I thought you were going with Sprig.'

Joan shook her head. 'Mary took her, with Belinda. I had an emergency call.' Joan was a probation officer. 'Sprig, go and lay the table, will you?'

'Oh, but I haven't finished telling Daddy about . . .'

'Later, poppet.'

'But I wanted to . . .'

'I said, later. Go along.' Joan scooped up a handful of cutlery and pressed it into her daughter's reluctant hands. 'Go *on*.' She waited until Bridget had left the room. 'It was Tracey Lindop — you remember, the persistent shop-lifter? Well, she's pregnant, apparently, and by her stepfather. When her mother found out, she just threw her out. I had to find her somewhere to stay. She's only fourteen. Just think, Luke, that's only two years older than Sprig. And, what's more, she's saying she's not only going to have the baby, she's going to keep it.'

'She might well change her mind, as time goes on.'

Joan shook her head. 'I doubt it. She seems pretty set on the idea. Honestly, she has absolutely no idea of the difficulties involved. How on earth is she going to manage? She has no qualifications, she'll never get a job . . .'

'She'll scrape along on social security, I expect.'

'Yes, but what sort of permanent prospect is that? She says, if she keeps the baby, at least she'll have someone to love who'll love her. . . . I can just see the whole cycle starting up again. Sooner or later the baby'll begin to get on her nerves and she'll probably batter it just as her own mother battered her. . . . The whole business is so depressing.'

Thanet gave her a brief, wordless hug.

'Honestly, I sometimes wonder if I'm achieving anything, anything at all . . .'

'Are these ready, Mum?' Bridget had returned and picked up two of the plates on the table.

'Yes. Come on, we'll eat.'

Bridget, still fizzing with excitement, chattered on through most of supper. Thanet and Joan listened benevolently and it was some time before Thanet noticed that Ben was unusally subdued and was only picking at his food.

'What's the matter, Ben? Aren't you hungry?'

Ben shook his head and mumbled something about having eaten a large tea at Peter's house.

Thanet raised his eyebrows at Joan, who gave a little shrug, but said nothing. Thanet, following her cue, let the matter drop.

After supper they all settled down to watch a family quiz show. Thanet felt in the mood to spend the entire evening mindlessly in front of the television set, then have an early night. It was good to have the prospect of a free Sunday ahead tomorrow, his first for some time. He hoped that nothing would crop up at work to spoil it. He lit his pipe and relaxed into the comfortable depths of his armchair. They'd get up late, he thought contentedly, go to church together, enjoy Sunday lunch at home, and in the afternoon they'd take the children to the sea . . .

The call came while they were still at breakfast next morning. Resignedly, he replaced the receiver and returned to the kitchen. Just as well he hadn't mentioned the beach to Bridget and Ben.

'Oh, no,' said Joan, after one glance at his face.

'I'm afraid so.'

'Couldn't someone else go, just for once?'

'Not possible, love. I'm sorry.' He gave a 'not in front of the children' glance at Ben and Bridget. He needn't have bothered.

'Is it murder, Dad?' Ben, whose uncharacteristically quiet mood seemed to have lasted the night, was at last showing signs of animation.

'Could be.' Almost certainly was, by the sound of it.

'Where?' Ben was on his feet, following Thanet and Joan into the hall.

Thanet ruffled his son's hair. 'Don't be a ghoul. You'll read all about it in good time, I daresay.'

'Oh, *Dad*. What's the point of having a police inspector for a father, if you don't hear all the juicy bits before anyone else?'

'That's enough, Ben,' snapped Thanet. 'Murder is not supposed to be a source of entertainment.'

Ben returned to the kitchen, scowling, and Thanet kissed Joan goodbye. 'Not sure when I'll be back.'

'You don't have to tell me. . . . Take care.'

To add insult to injury, it looked as though it was going to be another lovely day, he thought gloomily as he drove through the deserted streets. It was now the end of July, and so far it had been a truly glorious summer, one golden day following another in a seemingly endless procession. It was really galling to have this one snatched away from him at the eleventh hour. With difficulty, he forced himself to stop dwelling on his disappointment and concentrate on the scanty information he had been given.

The dead woman's name was Alicia Parnell and she had arrived in Sturrenden the previous day. She had been a guest at the Black Swan, the oldest and most luxurious hotel in the town. For centuries it had been a coaching inn, much frequented by travellers on their way to Canterbury, but with the advent of the motor car its fortunes had declined and the beautiful old building had become more and more delapidated. Then, in the late nineteen-fifties, when the country was gradually recovering from the bleak austerity of the post-war years, it had been bought by a man called Jarman, an ex-R.A.F.

Wing-Commander who had recognised its potential and had accurately predicted the tourist boom. Now it was a thriving business, run by his son.

Thanet turned in through the arched opening in the black and white façade and parked in the cobbled yard alongside two other police cars and Detective-Sergeant Lineham's Ford Escort.

Lineham was in the foyer, talking to the proprietor. Thanet knew most of the prominent people in Sturrenden and Jarman was no exception.

'Ah, there you are, Inspector.' Jarman came hurrying across, looking harrassed. He was in his early forties, his well-cut suit almost, but not quite, hiding his growing paunch. The Swan had a superb chef.

'This is terrible. I don't know what to say. It's just . . . unthinkable. I keep wondering if I'll wake up and find it's all a nightmare.' He mopped at his forehead and moved closer, lowering his voice. 'Look, do you think we could . . . The other guests . . . My office, perhaps?'

'Not just yet. I must go upstairs, first. There's no need for you to come with us, I'm sure you must have a lot to attend to down here. Sergeant, have you had time to talk to any of the staff yet?'

'Only the chambermaid who found the body, sir.'

'In that case, Mr Jarman, perhaps you could have a discreet word with your members of staff, find out if any of them saw the woman at any time since her arrival yesterday. When did she get here?'

'So far as we can tell from the register, some time between four and four-thirty yesterday afternoon.'

'She was alone?'

'Yes.'

'Right, well, if you could do that, then . . . Oh, and make sure none of the other guests checks out until we've been able to talk to them.'

Jarman closed his eyes in despair. 'If it's absolutely necessary . . .'

'Come, Mr Jarman, you must see that it is.'

Jarman gave a resigned shrug and Thanet followed

Lineham to the lift, trying to ignore the cramp-like sensation in his stomach. No one could have guessed from his calm, business-like demeanour just how much he was dreading the next few minutes. Even Joan, with whom he shared almost all his secret hopes, fears and aspirations, was unaware of this one most private weakness, his inability to look upon the newly-dead with equanimity. For years he had hoped that he would overcome it, that custom would dull the edge of his sensibility, but gradually he had had to accept that this wasn't going to happen. Now he tried to meet the experience with the same stoicism with which he faced the dentist's drill: endure, and the pain will soon be over. And it always was, thank God. It was just that first sight of the corpse . . .

'What did the chambermaid have to say, Mike?'

'Nothing much. She found the body when she went to make the bed this morning. She wasn't on duty last night, so she hadn't seen the woman before.'

'What do we know about this Mrs Parnell?'

'Very little. She's in her late thirties, I'd say. Pretty well-off, nicely dressed — well, you'll see for yourself. She's been strangled, manually by the look of it.'

'Dead long?'

'Late last night, I should think. Rigor is pretty well-established.'

'Is the SOCO here?'

The Scenes-of-Crime Officer is an essential part of any murder investigation. It is his job to find and preserve the forensic evidence which, however microscopic, may succeed in establishing the vital link between murderer and victim.

'Arrived shortly before you, sir. The SOCO sergeant has come along too.'

'What about Doc Mallard?'

Lineham grinned. 'On his way. Not too pleased about having his Sunday morning disturbed, though.'

'He's not the only one.' But Thanet's tone was mild. He was too preoccupied with bracing himself against the next few minutes to resurrect his sense of grievance.

'Here we are.'

The lift had stopped at the third floor. A corridor stretched right and left, with rooms on either side. The carpet was thick, the wallpaper expensive, and there were orginal prints on the wall.

'Stairs?'

'There's a flight at each end of the corridor, I'm afraid.'

Lineham turned left and Thanet followed him. Strangled. Sir Sydney Smith's description of a strangler's victim flitted through his mind. '. . . *Not a pretty sight . . . Bluish or purple lips and ears, change of colour of the nails, froth and possibly blood-staining about the nose or mouth, the tongue forced outwards, the hands clenched . . .*'

They had arrived. Lineham opened the door and Thanet preceded him into the room, automatically returning the greetings of the SOCOs, who were still busy taking photographs. They stood back as he approached the body. Grimly, without touching her, he silently confirmed Lineham's diagnosis, forcing himself to note the details as the roaring in his ears faded to a hum and his stomach settled. She was half-lying on the bed, her short, softly-waved dark hair framing that hideous parody of a face, the bulging brown eyes fixed in that blank, motionless stare which instantly proclaims the absence of life. Her black dress and high-heeled sandals were clearly expensive, and a heavy gold chain bracelet encircled her right wrist, a cocktail watch her left. She also wore a chased platinum wedding ring and an engagement ring, a sapphire and diamond cluster. Somebody's wife, then, probably somebody's mother. Thanet was filled with the familiar anger at the waste of a life, with all its attendant suffering for a shocked and grieving family.

'Robbery certainly wasn't the motive, anyway,' said Lineham's voice, close beside him.

'Nor a sexual assault, by the look of it.' Thanet stepped back. 'Carry on,' he said to the photographers.

He looked around. There were no signs of a struggle. The Black Swan certainly did its customers proud, he thought. It was a beautiful room, more like a room in a private house than a hotel bedroom, with leaded casement windows and sloping ceilings striped with ancient beams. The bed on which the woman was lying was an authentic four-poster, with chintz

15

hangings and bedspread in delicate shades of cream, lilac and pink. Ruched blinds of matching chintz hung at the dormer windows and the fitted carpet was lilac. The bedside table and the chest of drawers were genuine antiques. The adjoining bathroom was equally luxurious, with an oval lilac bath, thick cream carpet and built-in dressing-table. Alicia Parnell's cosmetics — all expensive — were neatly ranged upon it.

In the bedroom a cream silk jacket was lying across an armchair. It looked as though she might have tossed it there when she came in. Had she been out, Thanet wondered, curiosity beginning to work in him like yeast. And if so, where had she gone, and with whom? What had she been like, this woman? He spotted a photograph in a silver frame on the bedside table and bent to examine it. A man and a woman — Mrs Parnell and her husband? — smiled up at him, the man seated and invisible from the chest downwards, Mrs Parnell standing behind him with her hands on his shoulders. Thanet frowned. Surely . . .

It looked as though the frame had already been dusted for prints, but he checked before picking it up and examining the picture more closely. Yes, he was sure, now. Alicia . . .

Image after long-forgotten image began to race through his mind: Alicia, hair streaming behind her in the wind as she and the others sailed past in Oliver Bassett's open-topped sports car . . . Alicia on the tennis court, her sensational legs golden beneath the flare of her brief white skirt . . . Alicia cycling past in the usual noisy, laughing group, her straw school hat pushed back at a forbidden angle, her face tilted provocatively up at the boy beside her. . . .

Thanet glanced at the body on the bed and his grip on the photograph frame tightened.

Lineham had noticed the look on his face.

'What is it, sir?'

Thanet put the photograph carefully back on the table. 'I knew her, Mike, long ago, when we were at school.'

'Well?'

Thanet shook his head. 'Oh no, not well. But she . . . she was stunning, then. She was a couple of years older than me, and I don't suppose she even noticed my existence, but half the school was in love with her, or claimed to be.'

'She was at the Girls' Grammar?'

'Yes. She and another girl — I can't remember her name, but she had red hair, that I do remember — used to go around with a group of sixth formers from the Boys' Grammar . . .' Thanet shook his head. 'I can hardly believe it.'

'You're sure it's her?'

'Certain.' Thanet picked up the photograph and held it out. 'Look at her.'

Alicia Parnell had had the sort of face which, once seen, is not easily forgotten. The chin was too pointed, the nose too tip-tilted for beauty, but combined with huge dark eyes and high, classically-rounded cheekbones, they created an individuality which had not become blurred over the years. Looking at the snapshot over Lineham's shoulder Thanet could clearly visualise the softer, more rounded adolescent Alicia beneath the mature face in the photograph.

'I see what you mean,' said Lineham.

'I'd have recognised her anywhere, though I hadn't seen her in years. Not since . . .' He stopped, remembering.

'Not since what?'

There was a knock at the door and Doctor Mallard appeared, escorted by Jarman, who took one brief, hunted glance around the room and withdrew. Thanet crossed to meet the little police surgeon.

Mallard, as usual, looked irritable, but Thanet ignored this. The loss of his dearly-loved wife, many years before, had left Mallard at odds with the world. Thanet sympathised with his inability to come to terms with his grief and tended to treat him as if he were still the good-humoured old friend Thanet remembered so well.

'What have we got this time?' said Mallard, frowning over his half-moon spectacles at the photographer who was obscuring his view of the body.

'Nearly finished, Bates?' said Thanet.

'Yes, sir. Just one or two more.'

'Hurry it up, then, will you?'

Mallard's examination of the body did not take long. When he had finished he rose stiffly to his feet, pointedly ignoring

17

Lineham's outstretched hand. 'No need to tell you how she died. Any dunderhead can see that for himself.'

'Manual strangulation?'

'Yes. The bruises are clearly visible, as you've no doubt noted. No scratch marks on the neck, though. Of course, her nails are very short . . .'

'What about time of death?'

Mallard hesitated, considering. 'Taking all the various factors into consideration, I'd say between ten and eleven last night. That's only a guess, mind.'

'Of course,' said Thanet, trying not to grin. Mallard was rarely wrong in such 'guesses'.

Mallard gave him a severe glance over his spectacles. 'I mean it.' He picked up his bag. 'Well, if the guardians of law and order are satisfied, perhaps I may now be allowed to return home and go to church, like a civilised human being. Don't bother to come down with me.'

'I've got to have a word with the manager anyway.'

While they waited for the lift Thanet said, 'She was a local girl, you know.'

'Local? What makes you think that?'

'I recognised her. From years back. . . . There was a photograph on the bedside table,' he explained as Mallard opened his mouth to protest that nobody could possibly have made such an indentification from that distorted face. 'She hadn't changed much — scarcely at all, in fact.'

'What was her name?'

'Her maiden name was Doyle. Alicia Doyle.'

'Doyle . . . Doyle . . . Let me see, didn't she go around with one of the Rain boys for a while?'

'Yes. Nicholas Rain. The violinist.'

'Don't treat me like an idiot! I know he's the violinist. As a matter of fact I was quite close to the Rain family at one time. His father and I were friends for years, good friends, up until the time of his death. I've followed Nicholas's career with great interest, right from the start. He was playing in Sturrenden last night, you know. I went to the concert.'

'Ah, yes, I'd forgotten. We've been so tied up with the royal visit . . .'

18

'Bach's double violin concerto. With that young girl he's just become engaged to. A fine performance they gave, too . . . though a bit too sensual for my taste.'

'I wonder if that was why she was here — Mrs Parnell, I mean. For the concert.'

'Could be.'

They had reached the ground floor and they parted. Thanet knocked on the door of Jarman's office.

'Come in.'

Jarman was sitting at his desk, head in hands.

'Sit down, Inspector. Have you finished, upstairs?'

'Not quite. In any case, I'm afraid it will be some time before the room is available to you.'

'When do you think you'll be able to get around to dealing with the guests? I've got three couples who are all packed and ready to go, and they're not too pleased at being held up, I can tell you.'

'Very soon. In most cases it'll just be a question of taking a brief statement and making sure we have their names and addresses.'

'Good. Oh, by the way, I'm afraid two couples had already left, before the . . . before the crime was discovered.'

'Which floors were they on?'

'One was on the third, two doors from Mrs Parnell. And the other was on the second.'

'How long had they been here?'

'The first couple came a week ago, the second the day before yesterday. They were all on holiday and booked some time ago.'

'And Mrs Parnell?'

'Booked a fortnight ago, just for the one night.'

'I'd like their addresses, and a quiet room where we can question the other guests.'

'There's a small lounge on the first floor. Would that do?'

'Fine. Thank you. Have you had an opportunity to question the staff yet?'

'Some of them. Of course, a number of those who were on duty last night are not here this morning. The chambermaid, for instance, and she's not on the phone. . . . There were two

19

points you might find interesting. The first is that Mrs Parnell made a local call, soon after she checked in.'

'Do you have the number she rang?'

'Sorry, no. She just asked for an outside line, around four-thirty.'

'And the other point?'

'My receptionist saw her in the foyer at about seven o'clock, talking to some local people, a Mr and Mrs Leyton.'

'Would that be Mr Richard Leyton, the fruit farmer?' Thanet hadn't seen him in years.

'That's right. There was a Rotary Club Ladies' Night here last night, in the Fletcher Hall. My receptionist recognised Mr Leyton because he'd been involved in organising it.'

Thanet groaned inwardly. The place must have been crawling with people between ten and eleven last night. 'You have the Leytons' address?'

'Their telephone number,' said Jarman unhappily. He handed Thanet a slip of paper. 'I've written it down for you. I don't like doing this, but I see that I must. Anyway, apparently this was only a brief conversation and then Mrs Parnell left the hotel. She hadn't had dinner here, we don't start serving until seven-thirty.'

'And she didn't mention where she was going, to your receptionist?'

'No.'

There was a knock on the door. The ambulance was here to remove the body. With Jarman hovering in the background, anxious to ensure that maximum discretion was observed, Alicia Parnell's mortal remains were discreetly removed via back stairs and rear entrance.

While Thanet had been talking to Jarman, Lineham had been getting on with the search.

'Found anything, Mike?'

Lineham shook his head. 'Apart from the contents of her handbag, there's nothing interesting at all. She'd brought very little with her, just a nightdress, a change of underwear and her toilet things.'

And the photograph, thought Thanet. Why had she brought it, on such a brief trip? And where was her husband — if the man in the photograph was her husband . . .

'What was in her bag?'

'Just the usual stuff — oh, and a rosary.' Lineham held it up.

'She was a Catholic then.' Thanet took it from him and ran the beads through his fingers. How often had Alicia handled them in just this way? Thousands, hundreds of thousands of times, perhaps?

'Where did she live?'

'Fulham. Runs an employment agency, by the look of it.' Lineham handed over a business card.

Alicia had a partner, it seemed, a Jessica Ross. Both their names were on the card, together with the address of the agency in the Fulham Road.

'No home address?'

'No. Perhaps she lived over the shop, so to speak.'

Thanet remembered Alicia's expensive clothes and jewellery. 'Unlikely, I would have thought. I wonder if Jarman's got a London directory.'

He had, and Lineham's guess proved correct. Alicia was listed as A. Parnell, with a different telephone number from the agency, but the same address. There was no reply, when they tried ringing.

'We'd better go and take a look,' said Thanet.

It took a little while to get clearance for the trip from the Metropolitan Police and while they were waiting Thanet organised the work to be done in their absence: the hotel staff and guests were to be questioned and the Leytons were to be interviewed.

Then he and Lineham headed for the M20 and London.

TWO

The Sunday morning traffic was light, and they were soon on the motorway. The London-bound carriageway was virtually empty, but on the other side of the crash barrier a steady stream of cars was speeding towards the coast, crammed with families heading for their weekly dose of sun, sea and sand. For a while both men were silent, thinking back over the events of the morning. Eventually, 'Since what?' said Lineham.

'Mmm?' It took a moment or two for Thanet to register the question, but when he did he had no problem in knowing what Lineham meant. He and the sergeant had been working together for so long that they were well-attuned to each other's thought processes.

'Oh . . . I'd been going to say, not since just after the inquest.'

Lineham, who was driving, shot Thanet a quick, interested glance: 'What inquest?'

'Odd, isn't it? You don't think about someone or some period of your life for years and then suddenly, something triggers off that particular memory chain and the images come so thick and fast, so vividly, that you wonder how on earth you could have forgotten them.'

'Inquest on who?'

'Whom,' corrected Thanet. 'A boy called Paul Leyton. It was a real tragedy. He was one of those who seemed to have everything. He was brilliant, for a start, all set to become a fine classical scholar. But he was also a first-rate sportsman — captain of cricket, of rugger, you name it, he could do it better than anyone else.'

'I can't stand people like that.'

Thanet cast an amused glance at his sergeant. Obviously, Lineham did not enjoy being reminded of his own inadequacies.

'For us younger boys he had an almost god-like quality. He looked like one, for that matter — the sort of profile you see on Greek coins, golden curls . . .'

'Ugh.'

'. . . the lot. And whatever you say, it didn't seem to stop his contemporaries liking him. I was a couple of years younger than he — he was the same age as Alicia — but I know he was immensely popular with his year. And the masters liked him too.'

'So what happened to this paragon?'

'He killed himself.'

'What?'

Lineham was genuinely shocked, a little ashamed, too, Thanet thought, of his sneering tone of a moment ago.

'But why? The way you were talking, it sounds as though he had everything to live for.'

'That's what everybody said. But at the inquest it came out that he had been very much in love with Alicia — yes, the same Alicia — that his work had been falling off because things hadn't been going too well between them, and that on the day he committed suicide she had finally broken off with him. The whole thing caused a bit of a furore at the time because Paul had been so universally popular. Alicia and her parents left the area shortly afterwards.'

'Just a minute,' said Lineham, with a note of excitement, 'did you say Paul *Leyton*? Wasn't that a Richard Leyton who was seen talking to Mrs Parnell in the foyer last night?'

'Paul's younger brother.'

'Interesting.'

'Very.'

'You don't think . . .'

'At the moment I'm not thinking anything. We've only been on the case five minutes and it would be a waste of time.'

They were both silent for a while. They had switched to the M2 at Dartford and were now coming into the outskirts of London. Lineham gestured at a For Sale sign.

'Louise and I had hoped to go and look at some more houses today.'

The Linehams were still living in the tiny terraced house they had bought when they were first married. Their son, Richard, was now eighteen months old and they were beginning to think of a second child. This was the time, they felt, to try to find somewhere with a little more space — a third bedroom, and a larger garden, perhaps. They had begun by putting their own house on the market, and had been delighted if somewhat disconcerted when it had found a buyer within a week. They had plunged at once into an intensive search for the kind of property they wanted, so far without success. Now, completion was only a matter of weeks away and the matter was becoming urgent.

'Too bad. Anything promising?'

'There was one. A Victorian semi-detached in Frittenden Road. I think Louise is going to go over it tomorrow.'

Frittenden Road would have the merit of being further away from Mrs Lineham senior, Thanet noted. The Linehams' present house was only five minutes' walk from hers. For years the sergeant's life had been complicated and bedevilled by the unreasonable demands of his possessive mother. Widowed young, she had had to bring up her son alone, and for Lineham, emerging into adulthood, life seemed to have been one major battle after another — first to enter upon his chosen career in the police force, then to marry the girl of his choice, Louise. For the first couple of years of his married life he seemed to have been perpetually caught in the cross-fire between wife and mother, constantly trying to placate both and succeeding in pleasing neither. Then, with Richard's birth, things had changed. Mrs Lineham senior, with a new focus for her attention, had begun to channel her devotion towards her grandson. This had created a whole new set of problems for Louise, but had at least had the merit of taking the pressure off Lineham. Thanet couldn't help admiring his sergeant's determination to make his own choices and fulfil his obligations as he saw them, despite the pressure of two dominating women. Many men, he felt, would have gone under long ago and it was good to see Lineham in calm waters at last, if only temporarily. Though Thanet couldn't help feeling that if the young couple did move to the other side of town, it wouldn't be long before Mrs Lineham senior followed them. In any case she certainly wasn't going to allow it to happen without giving them a bad time first.

'I'm not sure of the way from here, sir. Could you keep an eye on the map and the road signs, now?'

'I think it'll be fairly straightforward so long as we don't hit too many one-way streets.'

Alicia Parnell's employment agency was called Jobline and appeared to be thriving. The single-storey premises were freshly painted in black and cream and the shop front was full of advertisements for jobs, some on display boards, others on slowly-revolving columns. The plate glass was clean and when Thanet peered in he could see that the office was close-carpeted and attractively furnished with sleek desks, leather chairs and flourishing pot plants. In the back wall was an inner door.

'There's no upstairs.' said Lineham. 'If she does live here she wouldn't want to go through the office every time she goes in and out. This'll be her front door, don't you think?'

Alongside the entrance to the shop was a solid, panelled wooden door without a number, unobtrusively painted black to match. Cunningly concealed in a fold of the moulding was a spyhole. Alicia, then, had been security-conscious. Had she lived here alone? If so, at night she would have been pretty isolated. To the left of Jobline was a small boutique called Annie's, to the right a shoe-repair shop.

'Must be,' he agreed. 'We'd better ring, first, in case her husband's at home.'

There was no answer, but they rang twice more and waited several minutes before Thanet took Alicia's keys from his pocket. The second fitted perfectly, turning twice in the lock before the catch was released.

They found themselves in a long, wide corridor which obviously ran the depth of the shop. It was carpeted in a soft, leaf green. When Lineham found the light switch they saw that the wallpaper was cream, with a tiny, geometric scribbled design in green, and that there were green-framed abstract prints evenly spaced along the left-hand wall. The door at the far end led to a surprisingly spacious ground-floor flat.

'I should think this runs along behind the agency and both

the shops on either side,' said Lineham. 'Pretty plush, isn't it?'

The sitting room was large, with ceiling-height patio doors leading into a tiny walled garden with climbing plants on the walls and white, wrought-iron chairs and table. Apart from a thick creamy rug in front of the long, low settee upholstered in soft, blond leather, the floor of polished, golden wood blocks was bare. There was one matching armchair, a low coffee table and, near the hatch leading into the kitchen, a dining table of smoky glass and four cream tulip-shaped dining chairs. The long, abstract painting in creams, browns and misty blue which hung above the settee was the only decorative object in the room apart from a six-foot tree with feathery leaves which stood in a huge cream ceramic pot near the patio doors. The effect was light, airy, yet austere, the taste of a woman given more to understatement than to exaggeration.

The main bedroom displayed the same restrained elegance, this time in blue and white. On the wall above the bed hung a crucifix, further evidence of Alicia's devotion to her faith. Interestingly enough, although one half of the long, fitted wardrobe contained men's clothing, there was no other sign of Parnell's presence in the flat. The double bed had only two pillows, one on top of the other in the centre of the bed, and one of the two bedside tables was bare. In the bathroom there was no shaving cream or aftershave lotion, no male deodorant, nothing to show that anyone but Alicia had lived here.

'Perhaps he's dead,' suggested Lineham. 'He'd hardly have left all his clothes here if they were divorced or separated.'

Alongside the mirror on the built-in dressing table was a larger, studio portrait of the man in the photograph they had seen in Sturrenden. Thanet picked it up. Parnell — if it was Parnell — had been in his early thirties when this was taken. It was a thin, sensitive face with deeply-etched lines around the mouth. Lines of pain? Thanet wondered. Something had been nagging at him ever since they had entered the flat and now he suddenly realised what it was.

'Have you noticed the doors, Mike?'

'What about them?' Lineham walked across and studied the bedroom door. 'Ah, I see what you mean. Unusually wide, isn't it?'

Thanet joined him. 'At least four feet, wouldn't you say? And custom-made, without a doubt.'

'You think Parnell was in a wheel-chair?'

'Seems likely, don't you think? There's no sign of children. And all the doorways are the same. If Parnell was crippled, it would explain why they built this place on behind the agency. No stairs, convenient for the office . . . Well, come on, we'd better get down to details. We'll start with the desk in the bedroom. That looks the most promising.'

Alicia's bank statements revealed that if she hadn't been exactly a wealthy woman, she at least had had no financial worries. But apart from a bundle of letters from her father and an address book, there was little else of interest.

'No mention of her mother,' said Lineham, skimming quickly through the former. 'Looks as though she might be dead, too.' He made a quick note of Mr Doyle's address. 'I suppose we'll have to contact him, to tell him the bad news.'

'Where does he live?'

'Manchester.'

'We'll see to it as soon as we get back. We'll take the address book with us.'

'Odd that there are no legal documents, isn't it, sir?'

'She may have kept them in the office safe, as it's so close.'

'Are we going to take a look around the agency before we go back?'

'I don't think we can do that until we've talked to Miss Ross. Come to think about it, it might be an idea to try and see her while we're up here. I expect her address is in here.'

It was. Jessica Ross lived not far away, in a block of modern flats on a side street off the Fulham Road. Unfortunately, according to a neighbour, she was away for the weekend.

'Where, do you know?'

The woman squinted up at him. She was elderly, with wispy white hair and skin like tissue paper which has been scrumpled up and then smoothed out again.

'Sorry, no idea.'

'When did she go?'

She shrugged. 'I saw her go off to work on Saturday morning and I haven't seen her since. Usually, when she's at home, I can hear noises through the walls.' Her mouth twisted with disgust. 'These modern places are all the same. Blown together, that's what they are. And flimsy. . . . You can't clean your teeth without other people hearing.'

'She was carrying a suitcase?'

'No. Just one of those squashy bags.'

'But she did tell you, that she was going away?'

The old woman was becoming exasperated by Thanet's persistence. 'Not in so many words, no. But I've got my eyes and my ears and there's nothing wrong with either, and I told you, I haven't heard a sound since early Saturday morning. So it stands to reason she's away, doesn't it?'

Thanet gave up. There was nothing for them here, at present.

'Looks as though we'll have to come up to town again tomorrow,' he said, as they walked back to the car.

'What a bore.'

'I agree, but there's nothing we can do about it.'

'Been a wasted journey, really,' grumbled Lineham.

'Not quite, I think. Not quite.'

All the same, he was anxious now to get back to Sturrenden.

THREE

Thanet and Lineham went straight to the Black Swan. In their absence, much had been accomplished. Bentley and Carson had accelerated the initial questioning of the fifty-eight hotel guests by dividing them into two groups and conducting interviews simultaneously. Only five now remained to be seen, all of whom had left the hotel early to go out for the day. Nothing of interest had emerged, however. One couple, who had signed in immediately after Alicia, had fixed her time of arrival more precisely — four-twenty — and another woman remembered travelling down in the lift with her at around seven o'clock. Apart from that, nothing.

'You've taken all their names and addresses?'

'Yes, sir.' Bentley was big, burly, painstaking. 'And verified them by checking driving licences and so on.'

'Good.'

'Some of them are getting a bit restive, sir.'

'I can imagine.' Thanet sighed. 'Well, we don't want a riot on our hands. . . . So long as we can get in touch with them if necessary, I think they can be told that they're free to carry on with their plans.'

'Right, sir. I'll see to that straight away.'

'Just a moment. What about the staff?'

'Bates and Warren interviewed them, sir.'

'Have they finished?'

They had, but once again nothing of significance had surfaced.

'Is DC Sparks back yet?'

Sparks had been sent to do the outside interviews. A new recruit to Thanet's team, he was an A-level entrant, thin and dark, with a quick grasp of new disciplines and a degree of ambition which did not endear him to his more pedestrian fellows. Thanet didn't think that he would be with them long, he would be off, up and away.

'Yes. Came in about ten minutes ago, sir.'

'Find him for me, will you?'

Sparks looked pleased with himself.

'Nothing new from the receptionist who was on duty last night, sir, nor from the chambermaid. She went in to turn Mrs Parnell's bed down at about eight-thirty pm and everything was in order then.'

'So? Come on, out with it, man.'

'Well, sir, it did occur to me that Mrs Parnell might possibly have ordered a pot of tea or a drink, and no one had thought it important enough to mention, so I checked and she had. I managed to track down the waitress who took afternoon tea up to her at about five o'clock, and she told me that when Mrs Parnell let her in there was a red folder lying on the bed. She noticed it because it was a splash of colour against all those pastels. . . . Well, I hope you don't mind, sir, but I had a quick check around Mrs Parnell's room, and there's no sign of any folder, red or otherwise, so unless you took it away earlier . . .'

'I didn't,' said Thanet thoughtfully. 'Well done, Sparks. You might have another word with both the chambermaids, ask if either of them saw it.'

'I have, sir, and they didn't.'

He might have guessed. Sparks was always one jump ahead.

'Interesting . . . And what about Mr and Mrs Leyton?' Thanet had hesitated before sending Sparks to see the Leytons. As an old friend of Alicia Parnell's, Richard Leyton might well turn out to be a suspect. But Thanet knew that opportunities for conducting potentially important interviews were thin on the ground for keen young detective-constables and was well aware, too, that it is always a temptation to keep the really significant interviews for oneself. He had decided to risk it and give Sparks a chance to show what he could do. 'Did you manage to see them?'

'Yes. They were pretty shaken when I told them what had happened. Apparently they both knew Mrs Parnell years ago, when they were at school. She used to live here, and they were all in the same crowd.'

'Just a minute,' said Thanet. 'Has Mrs Leyton got red hair?'

'Yes, sir.' Sparks grinned. 'And plenty of it.'

Prompted, Thanet's unconscious came up with the name he had been trying to remember. 'Vivienne,' he said. 'Her name is Vivienne.'

'That's right, sir.' Sparks paused, to see if Thanet had anything to add.

Thanet shook his head. 'Go on.'

'Well as you know, they ran into Mrs Parnell in the foyer, but they didn't talk for long because Mr Leyton had things to do in connection with the Ladies' Night and Mrs Parnell was on her way to a concert.'

'The Nicholas Rain concert?'

'Yes, sir. Anyway, they had one of those "Fancy meeting you here after all these years" conversations — they both said they were amazed how little she'd changed, that they'd have known her anywhere. And she said how surprising it was that she'd only been in Sturrenden five minutes, so to speak, and she'd already bumped into three of her old friends.'

'Three?'

'Apparently, on the way to the hotel from the station, she'd met another man from their old crowd, a Mr Oliver Bassett. She said he was going to the concert that evening too.'

'Was he, indeed. With her?'

'That wasn't the impression I got, sir.'

'Anything else?'

'Not really.'

'But?'

Sparks hesitated, for the first time. 'It was just an impression, sir, but I had the feeling they hadn't really been pleased to see Mrs Parnell. I mean, they were full of how surprised they were to run into her and so on, but I had the impression that the surprise had been one they could well have done without. On Mrs Leyton's part, anyway.'

'Really. And they didn't see her later on, when she came back to the hotel after the concert?'

'They said not, sir.'

'But you didn't believe them?'

Again, Sparks hesitated. 'I'm not sure, sir. I think Mrs Leyton was holding back on something . . .'

'On what?'

'I couldn't make up my mind, sir. Sorry.'

'You've done well, Sparks.'

Lineham had been following all this with interest and when Sparks had gone Thanet said, 'Well, Mike, what do you think?'

'Sounds as though we ought to see the Leytons ourselves.'

'I agree. But we'll leave them to stew for a while, I think. Meanwhile . . .'

'A visit to Mr Oliver Bassett?'

'Yes. Get his address from the telephone directory, then ring, find out if he's in.'

He was, and could see them whenever they wished. Lineham arranged that they would go along right away.

'One advantage of it being a Sunday,' he said, putting the phone down. 'Most people are at home. Though I could think of better ways of spending it, myself.'

'I know. I'd hoped to take the children to the sea. It would have been a perfect day for it.'

It was now four-thirty and the sun was still hot, the sky cloudless. Bassett lived in one of the sidestreets off the far end of the High Street. It wasn't far, and they decided to walk.

Sturrenden is a busy market town in the heart of the Garden of England, as Kent is often called. It is best avoided on Tuesdays and Fridays. On the former, market traders from far and wide converge on the large open space which on Fridays become the cattle market, and on both days parking spaces in the town are virtually impossible to find. The Town Council has tried to solve the problem by introducing a one-way system and providing free parking on the edge of the town, but with little success. Today, however, it was empty of any but sightseers enjoying its picturesque High Street, admiring the higgledy-piggledy conglomeration of ancient façades and lingering in front of the antique shops which dotted its length.

Mill Street was quiet, elegant, its terraced Georgian houses raised slightly above ground level. Each front door, with semi-circular fanlight above, had its own short flight of steps edged by curving wrought-iron railings. The door of number fifteen was painted a glossy purple.

'Looks prosperous,' commented Lineham as they awaited an answer to their knock.

'I should think he's fairly well-off. He's the Bassett of Wylie, Bassett and Protheroe.'

'The solicitors in the High Street?'

'That's right. What's more, he's a bachelor, so he doesn't have a wife and family to support. I knew him at school,' Thanet added hurriedly as the door began to open.

'Ah, Thanet. Do come in. And this is . . .?'

'Detective-Sergeant Lineham.'

Bassett was tall and well-built, with a beaky nose, high forehead and a small, pursed mouth which gave him a curiously prim, old-maidish look. Although he was presumably spending a quiet Sunday afternoon at home, he was formally dressed in what was obviously a tailor-made suit in fine, brown herringbone tweed, tattersall-check shirt and slub silk tie. His highly-polished brogues were the colour of ripe chestnuts.

'This way.'

He led them through a spacious hall with curving staircase into a drawing room overlooking the garden at the back of the house. The atmosphere was one of restrained opulence, a combination of deep, muted colours, genuine antique furniture, carefully-arranged bric-a-brac and richly-textured soft furnishings. The effect was as impressive and as impersonal as a photograph in a glossy magazine.

'I was having tea when you telephoned, so I made a fresh pot. Will you join me?'

It would have been churlish to refuse. Thanet sat down on a Victorian tub chair upholstered in jade-green velvet and accepted the proffered porcelain cup and saucer with a murmur of thanks.

'Well then,' said Bassett, when he had served them both. 'How can I help you?'

'I believe you ran into an old friend in the High Street yesterday afternoon?' Thanet drank off his tea, which had been only luke-warm, and carefully put his cup and saucer

33

down on a tiny mahogany table beside his chair.

'An old . . .' Briefly, Bassett had looked puzzled, then his face cleared. 'Oh, you mean Alicia Doyle — or Alicia Parnell, as she now is.' He gave a little half-laugh. 'But of what possible interest could such an encounter be to you, Inspector?'

Inspector now, not *Thanet*, Thanet noted.

'You obviously haven't heard the news.'

Bassett frowned. 'What news?'

Thanet saw no reason to cushion the blow. 'That she was found murdered this morning.'

Bassett's eyes opened wide with shock. 'Murdered? *Alicia*? Where?'

'In her room at the Black Swan.'

'My God!' Bassett heaved himself jerkily out of his chair and went to stand for a few moments with his back to them, looking out into the garden. Then he swung around. 'I can hardly believe it. But as I certainly can't think that you are playing some kind of charade, I suppose I must. Well . . . Alicia . . .' He shook his head, returned slowly to his seat. 'So how can I help you?'

'I'll be frank with you. At the moment, we have very little to go on. Mrs Parnell lived in London, where she ran a small business, and so far we haven't found anyone who knows anything about her. No one knows if she had arranged to meet anyone down here during the weekend.'

'Except that she was obviously seen talking to me,' said Bassett with a hint of displeasure.

'Not exactly. She herself told someone that she had run into you on her way to the hotel yesterday afternoon.'

'Who could possibly have been interested?'

'Some mutual friends of yours, Mr and Mrs Richard Leyton. They ran into her in the foyer of the Black Swan last night. They were arriving for a function and she was on her way to the Nicholas Rain concert.'

'Ah, I see . . . I presume she also told them that I was going to the concert, too?'

'Yes, she did.'

'And, naturally, you want to know if I saw her during the evening?'

'As you say, naturally.'

'Well, the answer is yes, I did. . . . More tea, Inspector? Sergeant? No? Well now, let me see . . . I first saw her in the bar, during the interval. We chatted for a few minutes about the concert — you may or may not be aware that we both knew Nicholas Rain quite well, in our younger days — and I invited her to join me for a late supper, afterwards. I thought it would be interesting to hear what she'd been doing all these years . . . . But she said she was sorry, she couldn't, as she'd already arranged to see someone else.'

'Did she say who?'

'No. Later on, though, when I was in the foyer, I saw her talking to Rain. I didn't think anything of it at the time . . .'

'Did you assume it was Rain she'd arranged to meet?'

Bassett shook his head. 'No. After all, his fiancée, Melanie Knight, was there, she'd been playing in the concert with him. He and Alicia only talked for a few minutes, then he left her to join Miss Knight.'

'And Mrs Parnell?'

'I lost sight of her. There were a lot of people milling about, of course, and I didn't see her again, after they parted.'

'Were you close to them during their conversation?'

'No, some distance away. I just kept getting glimpses of them, as people in the crowd shifted.'

'What about Mr Rain? Did you see him again?'

'I saw him moving towards the door, with Miss Knight. People kept stopping them, to congratulate them, I imagine — they gave a really superb performance, by the way — so I assume they left together.'

'What time would this have been?'

'Let me see . . . the concert ended at a quarter to ten and I suppose it would have been about five past, when I saw Alicia talking to Rain. . . . It must have been about twenty past, when he and Miss Knight left.'

'So you have no idea what time Mrs Parnell left?'

'Sorry, no.'

'And you?'

'A few minutes after Rain.'

'And what did you do afterwards?'

'Came home, of course. No, wait a moment . . . I went for a

stroll by the river, first. It was a lovely night, and the concert hall had been rather stuffy. I thought I'd have a breath of fresh air before turning in.'

'You hadn't taken your car?'

'It wasn't worth it. The hall's only ten minutes walk from here, and as you've probably noticed, these houses have no garages. I rent one in Denholm Street, and by the time I'd got the car out I would have been half-way there. . . . Look, Inspector, I can quite appreciate that you need to build up a picture of Alicia's movements last night, but do you have to have quite so much information about mine?'

'Oh come, Mr Bassett. You're a man of the law, you know what a passion for detail we have . . .'

'And I'm your best bet so far,' said Bassett good-humouredly. 'Yes, I can see that. And as I'm pure as the driven snow I will demonstrate my innocence by providing you with cooperation par excellence. . . . What else would you like? Fingerprints? Shoe size? The clothes I was wearing last night?'

Thanet wasn't going to be distracted or deflected. He smiled. 'I don't think we need to go quite as far as that at present. We'd settle for your time of arrival home.'

'About ten to eleven, give or take a few minutes. I'm afraid there's no one to corroborate that, you'll just have to take my word for it.'

'Thank you,' said Thanet, rising. 'You've been most helpful.'

'Not at all. Though I can hardly call it a pleasure, in the circumstances. . . . I'll show you out.'

At the front door Thanet hesitated. 'Did Mrs Parnell tell you why she'd come to Sturrenden?'

'Not in so many words. I rather assumed, to go to the concert.'

Lineham waited until they were in the street and the door had closed behind them before commenting, 'Smooth, isn't he?'

'Oh, very. Do you think he was telling the whole truth and nothing but, Mike?'

'I think I'll reserve judgement on that one, for the moment . . . Do you think that was why she came to Sturrenden?'

36

'For the concert? Could be. Nicholas Rain was her boyfriend once. Perhaps she was curious about this girl he's just got engaged to?'

'Yes, I read about that in the local paper, not long ago. She's much younger than him, isn't she?'

'In her early twenties, I believe. I imagine he's been too busy buzzing all around the world on concert tours to have thought of settling down before. I understand they met about a year ago, when she stood in for someone who was due to play the Bach double violin concerto with him — the same piece that they performed last night, incidentally. . . . I saw them together in Sturrenden once, a couple of months ago,' Thanet added reflectively.

'And?' enquired Lineham, intrigued by his tone.

'They were leaning on the parapet of the bridge, looking down at the river.' Thanet was remembering the powerful waves of sensuality which had emanated from those entwined figures. They had reminded him of Joan and himself, on their honeymoon . . .'

'So?' Lineham sounded puzzled.

'They were very engrossed in each other, that's all.'

'Understandable in the circumstances, I should think . . . But to get back to Mrs Parnell, sir . . . it's a bit far-fetched, isn't it, to think she would have taken the trouble to come down here, spend the night in a hotel, just to take a look at the girlfriend of someone she hadn't seen in donkey's years?'

'What are you suggesting, Mike?'

'Well, don't you think it's a lot more likely that she and Mr Rain have kept in touch? Perhaps, if her husband is dead, she might even have been cherishing the hope that Rain might marry her. She was a very attractive woman . . .'

'And she came down hoping to put a spoke in the wheels, you mean? Possible, I suppose . . . Anyway, our next move's obvious.'

'Mr Rain?'

'Mr Rain,' repeated Thanet, nodding. 'He lives out at Barton.' He quickened his pace. 'Come on, we'll have to fetch the car.'

FOUR

The village of Barton is about three miles from Sturrenden and Thanet and Lineham wound their way along country lanes whose hedges were starred with dog-roses and festooned with the wild clematis. Through five-barred gates they caught glimpses of spreading acres of golden corn, ripe for harvesting, and once the monstrous bulk of a combine harvester loomed above a hedge on their left.

Thanet was not a countryman, but he loved the constant, unvarying rhythm of the seasons and the changing beauty of the Kent landscape with its orchards and arable land, sheep and cattle. This evening the sunlight lay upon the land like a benediction and it was with reluctance that he responded to Lineham.

'What did you say?'

'I said, I suppose you're now going to tell me you knew Rain at school, too.'

'Certainly. He was one of the same crowd. Though I don't suppose for a moment that he'll remember me.'

'How many more of them were there?'

Thanet frowned, thinking. 'Let me see. There was Alicia, of course, Paul Leyton — the one who committed suicide — Richard, his brother, Oliver Bassett, Nicholas Rain and Vivienne, the girl with red hair who's now Richard Leyton's wife. That's all, I think.'

'Six of them, then. Four boys and two girls. Bit uneven, wasn't it?'

'I suppose so, yes. But it didn't seem to matter. You'd never guess it from their behaviour now, but they were always together, during Alicia's last year at school. Wherever you went, there they were, the lot of them. You couldn't miss them because they went everywhere crammed into Oliver Bassett's car.' Thanet gave a reminiscent laugh. 'That car was the envy of the school. It wasn't like nowadays. In those days you were lucky to own a scooter, let alone a car, and a sports car at that. Bassett was an only child, his mother was a widow and it was said that she'd have gone up to the moon in a rocket if he'd wanted a piece for his supper.'

'It's all right for some,' said Lineham, with a hint of bitterness. His own mother had had a struggle to manage, after his father died. 'She couldn't have been short of a penny.'

'His father was the original Bassett in Wylie, Bassett and Protheroe. Then, later, Oliver went into the firm himself.'

'What about Mr Rain?'

'Ah, well he was something very different.'

Having known Nicholas Rain at school, Thanet had followed his career with an almost proprietorial interest. Rain's father had taught history at Sturrenden Grammar School for Boys, and being a devout Catholic he and his wife had produced a large family of four boys and a girl. Although it had quickly become obvious that Nicholas was musically gifted, his father had steadfastly refused to allow him to neglect his general education in order to concentrate on music; in his opinion it was both limiting and unwise to specialise too young. Nicholas had therefore taken his O and A levels like any other bright youngster and had then, at the age of eighteen, been allowed to devote himself exclusively to music. He had gone first to the Royal Academy in London and from there had won prize after prize, scholarship after scholarship until, at the age of twenty-three, he had at last considered himself ready to launch upon his career. After his first spectacularly successful concert in the Festival Hall his future was assured and it was confidently predicted that he would go down in musical history as one of the truly great violinists.

'When his father died seven or eight years ago,' Thanet finished, 'he bought his mother this house in Barton, and he uses it as a base whenever he's in England — which isn't very often.'

'She lives there alone, the rest of the time?'

'No, with his young sister, Penny. She's the baby of the family. She'd be, oh, about twenty now, I should think. His brothers are all married and living away.'

'Presumably he'll be looking for a house for himself, now.'

'Or a flat. His fiancée's a soloist too, remember, so I imagine she'd want something pretty easy to manage.'

'If he's that successful, he could afford permanent staff to run his home while he's away.'

'True.'

They had just come into Barton and the church bells were ringing for Evensong. They stopped to ask for directions and a few minutes later turned into the gravelled driveway of Three Chimneys. The house was beautiful, a black and white timbered yeoman's house set in a traditional cottage-style garden with mixed plantings of shrubs and perennials. A narrow brick path flanked by low bushes of purple lavender and the feathery greenish-gold flowers of Alchemilla Mollis, the Lady's Mantle, led up to the massive front door of bleached wood. Despite the warmth of the day all the windows were closed and there was no sign of occupation.

'Looks as though they're out,' said Lineham.

There was no answer to their knock.

'Let's take a look around the back, in case they're in the garden.'

But the place was deserted and they returned to the car frustrated.

'Back to the Swan, I think,' said Thanet. 'We'll try again later, but we'll ring first. I can't imagine why we didn't this time.'

'Probably because of what I said about finding most people in on Sundays.'

But luck was on their side after all. As Lineham turned cautiously out of the front gate into the narrow lane a young girl wheeling a bicycle emerged from a gateway a hundred yards further on.

'A neighbour?' said Thanet. 'We'll have a word with her. It's just possible she knows what time they'll be back.'

The girl was in her early teens, her long, fair hair tied back in a ponytail. She frowned at Thanet's question.

'I expect Mr Rain's at the hospital.'

'The hospital? Has there been an accident?'

'The day before yesterday.' The girl bit her lip and tears

40

filled her eyes. 'Penny was driving Mrs Rain back from Sturrenden and they collided with a lorry that was coming round a bend in the middle of the road. Mrs Rain's still unconscious and Penny's in a bad way, too.'

'I'm sorry to hear that,' said Thanet. 'You're obviously very fond of them.'

'They're lovely people.' The girl dashed her tears angrily away. 'Why should it happen to them?' she cried passionately. 'They never did anybody any harm . . .' And mounting her bicycle she pedalled furiously away down the road.

Lineham frowned after her. 'Let's hope she calms down. She doesn't look too safe, to me.'

They decided to go straight to the hospital. If Rain had been able to give a superb performance at the concert last night despite his mother's apparently critical condition, he was fit to be interviewed, Thanet thought. Little by little they were managing to build up a sketchy picture of Alicia's activites the previous evening, and although Bassett had said that Rain had left with his fiancée, not with Alicia, Thanet was anxious to find out what Rain and Alicia had talked about. If, as Bassett claimed, Alicia had been going to meet someone afterwards, she might even have mentioned this person's name to Rain.

Mrs Rain was still unconscious, and in intensive care, they were told. Her daughter had compound leg and arm fractures, broken ribs and mild concussion, but was in no danger and was making satisfactory progress. The Sister in charge of the intensive care unit told them that Mr Rain had been in to sit with his mother earlier, and had now gone to visit his sister. Thanet and Lineham duly tramped their way along seemingly endless antiseptic corridors to the women's orthopaedic ward, where a number of people carrying bunches of flowers, magazines or bulging paper bags of fruit were sitting or standing around in the corridor waiting to take their turn at the bedside of friends or relations. The two-visitors-to-a-bed rule was obviously strictly observed.

Up until the birth of their son, Lineham's wife Louise had been a Sister in Sturrenden General. The Sister in charge of this ward knew Lineham and readily agreed to take a message in to Rain, and to let them interview him in the privacy of her office.

'So long as it doesn't take too long, mind,' she said. 'Visiting time is usually fairly quiet, but I can't guarantee no interruptions.'

'Thank you, Sister,' said Thanet formally. 'It's very kind of you.'

Rain emerged from the double doors of the ward looking puzzled and slightly irritated.

Thanet stepped forward to meet him. 'Mr Rain?'

'Yes. What is it? What's happened?'

Everything about him was clearly defined — crisp, curly black hair, short, neat beard and piercing dark brown eyes. There were sharp creases in his navy-blue linen trousers and his pale blue open-necked shirt looked as though it had just emerged from its polythene wrapping.

Thanet introduced himself and ushered Rain into the office. 'I apologise for disturbing you at a time like this, but I'm afraid the matter is urgent. Won't you sit down?'

Rain shook his head impatiently. He was staring at Thanet with narrowed eyes. 'Thanet . . . haven't I . . .? Just a moment . . . weren't you at Sturrenden Grammar?'

Yes, I was. A couple of years below you.'

'And now an Inspector, no less, in the CID . . .' Rain was looking more genial, 'Well, well . . . so, Thanet, how can I help you?'

'It's to do with an old friend of yours, Alicia Parnell. You were talking to her after the concert last night.'

'Oh, Alicia Doyle, you mean. Parnell . . . I didn't know that was her married name.'

'She didn't mention it?'

'No. Just said she'd been married and was now a widow.'

'What else did you talk about?'

'Look, forgive me if I appear obtuse, but I really cannot see of what possible interest that conversation could be to you. Unless . . .'

'Unless?'

Rain shook his head. 'No, you tell me, Thanet. You said this is to do with Alicia. What about her?'

'I'm afraid I have some rather unpleasant news, Mr Rain. Mrs Parnell was found dead in her hotel bedroom this morning.'

'Dead?' Rain blinked, and there was a moment's silence. 'But I was talking to her only last night — well, you know that, of course — and she seemed perfectly all right then. Oh God, how awful. What was it? A heart attack?'

Thanet shook his head. 'I'm afraid she was murdered.'

'Murd . . .' Rain groped for the nearest chair and sat down, heavily. 'This is incredible. I don't believe it. How terrible. . . . How could such a thing happen here, in Sturrenden? How did it happen?'

'She was killed in her room at the Black Swan.'

'In her room . . . Was it . . .?'

Rain had been allowed to take the initiative long enough, Thanet decided. 'I'm sorry, Mr Rain, I can't tell you any more at present. The point is, we've been trying to trace her movements since she arrived in Sturrenden yesterday afternoon, and we've eventually arrived at five past ten last night, when she was seen talking to you after the concert.'

'Yes, I see . . . Well, anything I can do to help, of course . . . Though I don't really see how I can. It was a very brief conversation.'

'So we understand. Nevertheless, we'd be grateful if you could give us the gist of it.'

Rain frowned, thinking. 'Well now, let me see . . . It was in the foyer, after the concert. My fiancée had gone to look for her parents — they're staying here for a few days — and I was waiting for them. Alicia came up to me and said, "Hullo Nicky, remember me?" '

'And did you?'

'Yes, of course. It was astonishing, how little she'd changed. Anyway, she said how much she'd enjoyed the concert and congratulated me on my recent engagement, and then she enquired about my mother and sister — you're obviously aware that they were both involved in a serious accident on Friday morning.'

'You weren't with them at the time?'

'No. I didn't get back to this country until Friday afternoon — I've been on a ten-day tour of Canada. You can imagine how I felt, being greeted with news like that . . .'

'How did Mrs Parnell know about the accident?'

43

'She'd seen it in the newspaper, yesterday morning. Said she'd lit a candle for them both. . . . She knew my mother well at one time, our families were very friendly when the Doyles were living in Sturrenden. Anyway, that's about it. I don't think much else was said.'

'What about your end of the conversation?'

'Well, I asked her if she was married — that was when she mentioned my engagement. She told me that her husband died last year. She did most of the talking, actually, and in the end I caught sight of my fiancée and her parents coming towards us. I didn't want to get involved in introductions, explanations and any more polite chit-chat, so I said I was sorry I had to rush off, but I was anxious to get back to the hospital — which was true. I really was very concerned to find out if my mother had recovered consciousness.'

'I understand she's still in a critical condition. I'm sorry.'

'Yes. Well if that's all . . .'

'Not quite, I'm afraid. Just one or two small points . . . did Mrs Parnell say why she had come to Sturrenden?'

'No. And I didn't ask. As I said, it really was a very brief conversation.'

'Did she telephone you around four-thirty yesterday afternoon?'

'No, certainly not. Why on earth should she?'

'Or mention what she was going to do after leaving the Concert Hall?'

'Go back to the hotel, presumably.'

'She told you she was staying at the Swan?'

'No, I didn't know that until you told me, a few minutes ago.'

'So she didn't mention that she was meeting someone, afterwards?'

'No.'

'And you . . . what did you do, after you left her?'

'Put my fiancée and her parents into a taxi and came straight here. Originally we'd intended having supper together, but as I told you, I was anxious to find out if my mother had come round. They quite understood.'

'When was the last time you saw Mrs Parnell — before last night, I mean?'

Rain gave a derisory little laugh. 'Over twenty years ago. Not since she and her parents left Sturrenden, just after we'd both taken our A levels.'

'Do you happen to know if she'd been back to Sturrenden at all, during that period?'

'I don't think she had.'

'She didn't actually say so, then?'

'Not in so many words, no. But I certainly had that impression.'

'You were quite close at one time, I believe.'

'We did go around together for a while, yes. But that finished some months before she went away. Look here, Inspector, I don't want to seem unreasonable, but I really don't see the relevance of all this. And I would like to get back to my sister before visiting time ends.'

'Yes, of course.' Thanet stood up. 'Thank you for your time.'

'Well,' said Lineham as they watched him go, 'that didn't get us very far, did it?'

'She wasn't invisible, Mike. Someone must have seen her, after she and Rain parted.'

'They might have *seen* her, but would they have *noticed* her? The hotel was crawling with people that night, with the Ladies' Night going on. I enquired. The dinner finished at ten-fifteen and then the guests all drifted off to the cloakrooms while the Fletcher Hall was cleared for dancing. If Mrs Parnell did go straight back to the hotel she would have got there just about then, when everyone would have been milling around.'

'You'd have expected the Leytons to notice her, if they'd seen her. Sparks didn't seem too sure on that point, did he?'

'Are we going to see them next?'

'No. If possible I want to be armed with a little more information about Alicia, first.'

The Sister knocked on the door and put her head in. 'All finished?'

They thanked her and left.

'The trouble is,' said Thanet as they made their way back along the corridors, 'I can't help feeling that we're working in a vacuum at the moment. So far we know practically nothing about her — what she was like as a person, who her friends were — or her enemies, for that matter. . . . Before we see anyone else I want to talk to her partner, Miss Ross. We'll go up to London again in the morning. Meanwhile . . .'

'Don't tell me. Meanwhile, reports.'

'Reports,' said Thanet, grinning.

Thanet had a love/hate relationship with reports. He resented the demands they made on his time, but appreciated their value. Not only did they provide a detailed record of work in progress — a record which could prove increasingly useful as interviews proliferated and the mass of facts accumulated — but the act of writing them was an excellent discipline, forcing one to think back and assess and then to present one's findings succinctly. A sloppy report, he believed, reflected sloppy thinking, and by now his men had learned that if they didn't want to do the whole thing over again, they might as well spend time getting it right in the first place.

The trouble with setting standards, he reflected as he settled down at his desk, was that you had to make sure you upheld them yourself.

He said as much to Joan, when she commented sympathetically on his lateness. It was past eleven. She was in her dressing gown, having bathed and been on the point of going to bed when she heard his car.

'I've made you some sandwiches. They're in the fridge.'

He followed her into the kitchen and sat down at the scrubbed pine table, while she made him some tea. The sandwiches were good, crammed with succulent pink lamb from the Sunday joint he should have enjoyed at home. Slowly, he felt himself revive.

Joan was sitting across the table, sipping her tea slowly, to keep him company.

'Better?' she said, when he had finished.

'Much.' He yawned, stretched, winced as the aching muscles in the small of his back protested. Always, after a long day, the spectre of his old back injury raised its hoary head.

'What's the case?'

Thanet hesitated. He trusted Joan completely and had

46

always tried to share his working life with her, believing that this was the one way to prevent the barrier of resentment so often erected by policemen's wives against the impossible demands of their husbands' work. At one time, too, he had believed that the vicarious satisfaction she gained from such discussions was sufficient to compensate for the lack of variety and excitement in her own life as a housewife. He had learned otherwise when, a few years ago, she had announced that she wished to train as a probation officer. He still preferred not to think about the separation which they had been forced to endure during the last part of her training, when Joan had had to take a residential course.

'Luke?' Joan was puzzled by his reluctance. 'What's the matter? Don't you want to talk about it?'

'No, it's not that . . .'

'What, then?'

'It's just that . . . do you remember a girl at school called Alicia Doyle?'

'Alicia?' Joan grinned. 'Asking that question of any of the girls who were at Sturrenden Grammer the same time as her is rather like asking a Catholic priest if he's heard of the Pope. Why?'

'This new case . . . Alicia was the victim.'

'Oh, *no*.' The amusement died out of Joan's eyes and the muscles of her face slackened and re-shaped themselves into lines of shock.

Thanet was dismayed at the strength of her reaction. 'She wasn't a personal friend of yours, was she, darling?' He didn't think she could have been, or Joan would surely have mentioned her at some point.

'Oh, no. No, of course not. It's just that . . . to think that something like that should have happened to Alicia, of all people. . . . She was so full of life,' Joan said, in response to Thanet's questioning glance. 'So vivacious, so . . . To us third-formers all the upper sixth seemed to be impossibly beautiful, talented and glamorous, of course, but Alicia outshone them all. And she was so *nice*, too. Most of us had a crush on her at one time or another — I did myself. It was as if she were a candle, and other people the moths. She was always

47

surrounded by a crowd, the centre of attention. And of course we were all green with envy over her ability to attract the boys . . .' Joan gave a shame-faced little laugh. 'Sorry, darling, I don't suppose you want to hear all this.'

'Oh but I do. Do you realise, you're the first person I've talked to who's made her come alive for me.'

'Is that so surprising? I don't suppose you've seen many people, yet.'

'True.'

'Tell me about it, Luke.'

'You're sure you want to hear?'

'Yes, of course. More than ever, now I've got over the initial shock.'

She listened carefully to his account of the day's work.

'And nobody has any idea why she was in Sturrenden in the first place?'

'So they say. Unless she came down for the concert.'

'Possible, I suppose. If you once had a boyfriend who later became an international celebrity, sheer curiosity would make you want to go and hear him for yourself. But what about this person she was supposed to be meeting afterwards? Perhaps he — or she — was the real reason for coming to Sturrenden, and the concert was just to fill in time?'

'Odd time to be meeting someone anyway. Unless that person simply wasn't available until then.'

'You don't suppose it was Nicholas Rain she was meeting?'

Thanet shrugged. 'I've no idea. On the face of it, no. His fiancée and her parents were there, and if he hadn't had to go back to the hospital to see how his mother was, he'd presumably have gone ahead with the original arrangement, and had supper with them.'

'Don't you think it's strange that in the short time she was here, yesterday, she should have run into so many of her old crowd?'

'Oh, I don't know. Not really, if you think about it. It was a Saturday, after all, and people tend to be out and about. I don't suppose I could walk down the High Street on a Saturday without seeing someone I'd been at school with, could you?'

'I suppose not. And the meeting with Rain wasn't exactly by chance. She knew he'd be there, and probably sought him out. As I said, I expect she was curious, to see what he was like, now . . . It really is so sad, Luke, to think she should have died like that, so young, and alone in a hotel bedroom. And it doesn't sound as if she's had much of a life, does it, with her husband dying last year. And he was crippled, you think?'

'That's only a guess, at the moment. We'll know more when we've talked to her partner, tomorrow . . . Now, tell me about you. Did you have a good day?'

'Lazy. Sat in a deckchair in the garden, all afternoon . . . Luke, have you noticed how quiet Ben is, at the moment?'

'I had, yes. Why, do you think there's something wrong?'

Joan was frowning. 'I'm not sure. He says not, but I just have this uneasy feeling that he's hiding something.'

'What sort of thing?' Thanet was becoming concerned.

'I've no idea. As I say, it's just a feeling. He isn't his usual lively self, and he's off his food . . . And that's not Ben at all.'

'What did he do today?'

'Well, that's partly what made me wonder. Usually, over the weekend, he's off to see his friends, as you know, or they come here, but today — on a glorious day like this — he stayed up in his room most of the time, playing tapes. And when I looked in, he wasn't doing anything, just lying on his bed. I asked him why he wasn't out with the others and he snapped my head off. It's all so uncharacteristic . . .'

'Perhaps he's sickening for something.'

'He says he feels fine . . . Oh, I don't know, perhaps I'm fussing about nothing. But I can't seem to get anywhere with him and I was wondering if you might manage to have a word with him some time, see if you could find out what's the matter.'

'I'll do it tomorrow.' Without fail, Thanet promised himself.

FIVE

'There's a message from Manchester,' said Lineham. 'Mrs Parnell's father, Mr Doyle, is away on holiday, apparently, and can't be contacted.'

'When's he due back?'

'Some time on Saturday. Imagine coming home to news like that.'

'Have we managed to get in touch with either of the two couples who checked out of the Swan early on Sunday morning?'

'Not yet, no. Perhaps they're touring.'

'Keep trying.'

Thanet and Lineham were going quickly through the various odds and ends of information that had come in overnight before setting off for London to see Jessica Ross.

'Perhaps Miss Ross'll be able to tell us what was in the mysterious red folder,' said Thanet.

'Was Mrs Parnell carrying it when she met the Leytons in the foyer?'

'The receptionist didn't mention it. Just a minute.' Thanet shuffled through the stack of reports on his desk. 'Knowing Sparks I shouldn't be surprised if . . . Ah, yes, here we are, I thought so. He checked. . . . No, only her handbag, apparently. The receptionist says she's certain she would have remembered if Mrs Parnell had been carrying anything as conspicuous as a red folder. It would have looked very odd with what she was wearing, she says.'

'So if the murderer took it . . .'

'It could well be important.'

'You two look very grim.' Doc Mallard had come bustling into the room. 'Just popped in to tell you the PM's scheduled for tomorrow morning. How's it going?'

'We're off to London in a minute, to see Mrs Parnell's

partner. We hope to know more then. So far we've been kept busy trying to trace her movements on Saturday. She seems to have run into a number of her old friends in the short time she was here. She did go to the concert on Saturday night, by the way.'

'Alone?'

'Apparently. She had a chat with Nicholas Rain afterwards, in the entrance hall.'

'Really? You've talked to him?'

'Yes. At the hospital.'

'Of course. The accident. I heard about that yesterday afternoon. Terrible. Mrs Rain is still in a coma, I believe, and Penny was pretty badly hurt, too — though nothing that won't mend in time. She was driving the car, I understand, and if her mother doesn't recover, she'll never forgive herself. They're really devoted to each other, those two. I always think of them as the supreme example that adoption really can work.'

'So she's not really Rain's sister?' said Lineham.

'Not by blood, perhaps, but believe me, he cares about her just as much as if she were.'

Lineham was looking puzzled. 'But they already had several other children, didn't they?'

'Four. All boys. And that was the point.' Mallard perched on the edge of Thanet's desk. 'The Rains had always wanted a girl, you see. They weren't too worried when first Charles, then Nicholas appeared, but by the time John and Peter had arrived they were beginning to give up hope. They were practising Catholics, by the way, and half-expected more tiny feet to come pattering along, but they didn't. The four boys were all born within six or seven years and then — nothing. Until Peter, the youngest, was about thirteen, when lo and behold, Mrs Rain found she was pregnant again. And this time it was a girl.'

'But I thought you said . . .'

'Patience, sergeant.' Mallard flapped his hand at Lineham. 'As I said, it was a girl, and you can imagine how delighted they were, all of them. I think the boys had been a bit embarrassed at first when their mum started to bulge, but by the time the baby was born they were reconciled to her arrival and made a great fuss to her. And then, when she was three months old, she died. One of those fiendish cot deaths that strike out of the blue. Well, as you can imagine, they were shattered, all of them, but especially Mrs Rain. For a while she blamed herself for the child's death, as so many mothers — quite wrongly, of course — do, in those particular circumstances. She was pretty depressed for some time, especially as there had been complications after the birth and she'd been told she could never have any more children. Then, about a year later, I heard they'd decided to adopt. And, as I said, it was a resounding success. Penny's twenty now and they all adore her, and vice versa. So, as I say, if Mrs Rain doesn't recover, Penny's going to be desperately upset.'

'You sound very fond of them all,' said Thanet.

'They're a very nice family. And as I told you, Derek Rain was one of my closest friends. I don't see much of them now, but I still take an interest.' Mallard slid off the desk and strolled across to the window. 'That's when you really become aware of the passage of time, when your own friends start dying.'

It was unusual for Mallard to sound so serious or so sad, or to come so close to referring to the death of his wife. Neither Thanet nor Lineham, inhibited by the presence of the other, knew quite what to say. There were a few moments of uncomfortable silence and then Mallard gave a little snuffle of laughter and turned to peer over his spectacles at them. 'On which cheerful note I will leave you. No doubt we've all got better things to do at this hour on a Monday morning than sit around telling each other stories.'

'I've never seen him in that mood before,' said Lineham, when Mallard had gone.

'Don't be fooled by his usual manner, Mike. That's just a smokescreen. Underneath he's as soft as butter. We'll just arrange for Sparks to go to the hospital and check what time Rain arrived there on Saturday night after the concert, then we'll be on our way.'

As it was a weekday, traffic would be heavy and parking in London difficult, so they decided to go by train. They reached Jobline just before twelve. Two of the three desks in the main office were occupied, one by a young woman in her early twenties, who was on the telephone, and one by an older woman who, Thanet guessed, would be around the same age as Alicia. He approached her.

'Miss Ross?'

She looked up, warily. 'Yes?'

She was a large, plain woman with unnaturally blonde hair, pale blue eyes and a heavy jaw. She was heavily made-up and was wearing a tan linen dress which looked expensive. It was rare for Thanet to take an instinctive dislike to someone but he was aware of that little shock of emotional recoil which told him that this was what was happening now. On his guard against betraying his feelings, he introduced himself and Lineham. 'It's about Mrs Parnell.'

'Ah, yes.' Miss Ross closed her eyes and clamped large, yellowing front teeth over her lower lip, then took a deep breath and held it for a moment.

Genuine grief? Thanet wondered. Or a device to gain herself a few moments' breathing space? He glanced at the other woman, who had finished her call and was watching Miss Ross. She had been crying, he noticed, and he caught a cynical gleam in her eyes before she realised that he was looking at her. She flushed and began shuffling papers about on her desk.

Miss Ross stood up abruptly, steadying her chair as it almost overturned. 'We'd better go into my office. Lock the outer door when you go to lunch, will you, Faith?'

Her office, Thanet noted, not Alicia's. The room was clean, pleasant, functional. There was a small safe in the corner.

'I gather you've heard about Mrs Parnell's death.'

'I read about it in the paper this morning. It was a terrible shock.'

Her voice was accusing and Thanet was furious to find himself saying defensively, 'We tried to contact you yesterday, but you were out.'

'Oh? What time was that?'

'Around lunchtime.'

'I'd just gone out for a breath of air.'

'Really? Your neighbour had the impression you were away for the weekend.'

'That must have been because I wasn't moving around much. I wasn't feeling very well on Saturday — I get migraine and sometimes, if I catch it in time, I can stave it off to some extent. So when I got home at lunchtime I went straight to bed and stayed there.'

'The agency is open on Saturday mornings?'

'Yes.'

'And Mrs Parnell came to work as usual?'

'Yes, she did.' Jessica Ross shifted a little in her chair and frowned.

'You've just remembered something?'

'Well, I did notice that she seemed even more on edge than usual.'

'What do you mean?' Thanet glanced at Lineham, indicating that he should take over the questioning.

Miss Ross shrugged. 'She'd been looking terrible lately. She hasn't been sleeping well, she's lost weight . . .'

'Are you saying that she was ill?' said Lineham.

'I don't know. If she was, she never said so . . . But no, I don't think it was that. It all began soon after her husband died, six months ago.'

Alicia's marriage, it seemed, had been a happy one. She and her husband had been devoted to each other, despite the accident which had threatened to ruin their lives. Alicia and Kenneth Parnell had married in 1971, when she was twenty-four. He had been the personnel manager of a large company, she his secretary. On the way back from their honeymoon in Scotland they had been involved in a multiple pile-up on the M1 and Kenneth had been left paralysed from the waist down. His firm had kept his job open for him, but even when he had made as full a recovery as could be expected, the sheer physical difficulties involved in getting to work had made it an impracticable proposition. He and Alicia had therefore decided to use the insurance money they had received after the accident to start a small business. With his skills in personnel management and her secretarial training, an employment agency had seemed the obvious choice.

By 1977, when Jessica Ross had joined the firm, Jobline was thriving. Unfortunately, internal injuries sustained during the accident had left Parnell with health problems other than the paralysis, and increasingly he had had to withdraw from taking an active part in running the agency. Initially, Alicia had handled the administration, Kenneth the interviewing and job-matching, but as his health deteriorated they had switched roles and, more and more, Jessica Ross had been called in to take over Alicia's work. When he died it had seemed natural for her to run the business during Alicia's absence and eventually Alicia, depressed and distraught by her husband's long illness and death, had invited her to become a partner.

It took Lineham some time to elicit all this information and during the long, patient, question-and-answer session Jessica Ross revealed rather more about her relationship with her former employers than she realised. Thanet perceived that she had been fond of Kenneth Parnell and jealous not only of his good relationship with his wife, but of Alicia's warm personality, her ability to inspire loyalty and affection in her staff. Above all, he learnt that Jessica Ross was ambitious, that being offered a partnership in Jobline had probably been the most important thing that had ever happened to her.

'And then, of course, three months after Kenneth died, Alicia's mother died too, and that made things even worse.'

'How, exactly, Miss Ross?'

Lineham was doing well, Thanet thought. And he was clearly enjoying the challenge of coaxing all this information out of such an unpromising witness.

She shrugged. 'In the beginning, after Kenneth's death, Alicia was very, well, fragile, I suppose you'd call it. Not surprising, really. Kenneth had been ill for a long time, it must have been an awful strain. . . . And then, losing your husband and your mother in three months . . . it's a bit much for anyone to cope with, isn't it? But I did hope that as time went on she'd start to pull herself together. Instead, she became . . . withdrawn, positively . . .' Jessica Ross hesitated.

'Positively what, Miss Ross?'

The woman compressed her lips, cast an almost defiant glance at Thanet. 'I was going to say, irresponsible. I suppose you'll think I'm unfeeling, talking about her like this when she's . . . when she . . . But I'm just trying to tell you how it was.'

'And that is precisely what we're here to find out,' said Thanet. 'So please, do go on with what you were saying. How do you mean, irresponsible?'

She shook her head impatiently, made a helpless gesture with her hands — hands quite large and powerful enough to have squeezed the life out of Alicia's slender throat, Thanet noticed. 'Her mind just wasn't on the business, that's all. She'd be late for appointments with prospective employers — or worse, not turn up for them at all. She'd go off somewhere without telling me, forget to answer important letters, or file them away in the wrong places . . .'

'And you felt that this uncharacteristic behaviour wasn't simply due to distress over the death of first her husband, then her mother?'

'Well to begin with, yes, of course I did. But then I began to think . . .'

'Yes?'

'Well, that she was preoccupied with some other matter.'

'What, for example?'

'I don't know. I've thought and thought, of course, and tried to get her to confide in me, but it was no good. She simply said she didn't know what I was talking about. Though I did wonder . . .'

'What?'

'Well, I thought she might be trying to find somewhere else to live. It would have been understandable, wouldn't it? I mean, her flat was custom-built for her and Kenneth, she might have found it too depressing to go on living there. Though if it was that, I don't see why she wouldn't have wanted to let me know. Or it did cross my mind to wonder if she was trying to find someone else to take over her share in Jobline. She obviously just wasn't interested in the business any more.'

'But in that case she would have discussed it with you, surely?'

'You'd have thought so,' said Jessica Ross bitterly.

'Tell me a little more about her behaviour.'

'Well, it's difficult to describe, it was so variable. In the beginning she was very low, very depressed. She was just beginning to pull out of it a little when her mother died, and of course that set her back again. She went up to stay with her father for a week and when she came back she was different.'

'How, different?'

'She seemed brighter. Almost, well . . .'

'Almost what?'

Jessica Ross shrugged, lifted her hands in a gesture of frustration. 'I was going to say, almost excited about something.'

'But you have no idea what?'

'No idea at all. Anyway, it didn't last. A few days, a week or so, perhaps, and she went back to being depressed. Then she became very tense, jumpy, absent-minded. That was when she started going off, without so much as a by-your-leave. No matter how busy we were, she'd just take off, without warning. One minute she'd be here, the next she was gone.'

'How long did she usually stay away?'

'It varied. Three or four hours. Once it was a whole day.'

'And how did she seem when she got back?'

'Quiet. Withdrawn.'

'And this went on for how long?'

'A couple of months, I suppose. Then one morning, a couple of weeks ago, I came in to work and she looked really terrible. Pale, shaking, as if she'd seen a ghost. I asked her if she'd like me to call her doctor, but she said no, it wasn't necessary, she'd be fine in a little while. Anyway, I persuaded her to go and lie down for an hour and later on she came back into the office and carried on as usual. But ever since, she's been even more on edge. As if . . .'

'Yes?'

'Well, it was almost as if she was waiting for something to happen.' Jessica Ross shook her head. 'And now . . . You don't think . . . I mean, it couldn't have had anything to do with . . .'

'With her death? Who knows . . .? Do you think we could go back to Saturday morning? You say that she seemed even more tense than usual?'

'Yes. She looked awful, as though she hadn't slept all night — pale, bags under her eyes . . . As soon as I arrived she asked me if I'd mind if she took the morning off. Well, I suppose she felt she had to ask, we're always so busy on Saturdays. And I said . . .'

'Yes?'

'I . . . I said I did mind.' Jessica Ross tossed her head and added defensively, 'Well, one of the girls was away sick and I was just about fed up with Alicia not pulling her weight. I thought it was about time I came right out and told her so . . . Now, of course, I feel awful about it, after what's happened.' She put her hands up and began to massage her temples with her fingertips.

'Did she argue with you?'

'No, she just shrugged, said if that was how I felt, she'd stay. She was very quiet, all morning, and at lunchtime she went off without a word.'

'Did you know she was going away for the weekend?'

'Yes, she'd mentioned it earlier in the week. I'd suggested we go to the cinema, on Saturday night. I thought it might do her good to get out for an evening . . .'

'Did she tell you where she was going?'

'No. Just that she would be away.'

For the first time Thanet sensed that if Jessica Ross wasn't exactly lying, she was holding back on something. What could it be? He could tell, by the way her lips had folded in upon themselves, that it would be pointless to try and get it out of her. Up until now she had been remarkably forthcoming and he wondered if this had been intentional, designed to persuade him that she had nothing to conceal. He decided to let it go, for the moment. Patiently, he continued the questioning. Alicia, it seemed, had led a very quiet life. Her husband had taught himself to be as independent as possible but naturally his condition had made considerable demands upon her time. They had gone out very little, seeming content with each other's company, and Alicia had therefore made no close friends outside the office.

'I suppose I was her closest friend.' Jessica Ross gave what was obviously intended to be a modest smile. 'And of course, she relied on me, especially after her husband died.'

Thanet caught Lineham's eye. He could read the sergeant's mind. *With friends like that, who needs enemies?*

'And enemies? Do you know of anyone with a grudge against her?'

'Against Alicia? Good heavens, no. She just wasn't that sort of person.'

'No one amongst your clients, who might have thought he'd been unfairly treated?'

'Certainly not! We can't afford to offend people, it wouldn't do at all. A satisfied client will tell his friends about us, and that brings more business. And Alicia was very good with people.'

'Did she ever talk of her childhood?'

'I knew she'd been brought up in Kent, that's all. She may have mentioned things she'd done, or places she'd been to.'

'But never people?'

'No.'

'Just two more points, then, Miss Ross. You've been very patient. First, I wonder if you could tell me whether or not Mrs Parnell kept any personal papers in the office safe? There seem to be very few in her flat.'

'Yes, she did.' Jessica Ross rose, smoothing down her dress as she crossed the room. She opened the safe and took out an oblong, black metal box. 'It's locked, I'm afraid.' An ugly tide of colour flooded her face as she realised what she had said. She handed it to Thanet.

'Thank you.'

'And the other point?'

'Do you use folders in the office?'

'Yes. Why?'

'What colour are they?'

'Green, yellow, blue,' she said, promptly.

'Not red?'

'No.'

'Do you recall ever having seen a red folder in Mrs Parnell's possession?'

Her eyes narrowed. 'Now that you mention it, yes, I do.'

'Have you any idea what was in it?'

'I'm afraid not. I saw it on, let me see, only two occasions. Once when Alicia was looking for something in her briefcase, and had to take everything out, and once when I went into the flat with her, and it was lying on the dining table. I noticed it because it made such a splash of colour in that room — well, you've seen the place, you'll know what I mean.'

'Yes, I do. I see. Well, thank you, Miss Ross, you've been most helpful. Is there anything else you want to tell me?'

For a fraction of a second he could have sworn he saw a spark of fear in her eyes, then she said firmly, 'No, I don't think so. You seem to have covered just about everything, Inspector. But if there's anything else I can do . . .'

'I would like to look through Mrs Parnell's desk. It's in the outer office, I gather.'

'By all means. Yes, whoever does the administration has always worked in here, it's more convenient. Everything's to hand.' The defensive note was back.

'And also, I'd like a word with the young lady we saw in the outer office as we came in.'

'Faith, you mean. I'm sorry, that won't be possible.'

'Oh?' Thanet glanced at his watch. It was half past one. 'Is she still out at lunch?'

'No. I'm afraid she won't be back this afternoon. We have a new client, the manager of a factory out at St Albans, and Faith has gone to discuss his requirements with him. Alicia was going to do it, but now . . . Faith is very reliable, and I thought that in the circumstances it would be a good idea to give her more responsibility.'

'You mentioned another girl . . .'

'Yes, Carol.' Jessica Ross suddenly looked as though she were sucking a lemon. 'She's still off sick.'

He would be interested to meet Carol, Thanet thought. 'I see.' He stood up. 'Well in that case, if I could just take a look at that desk . . .'

But the desk yielded nothing of interest, so he and Lineham carried the metal box into Alicia's flat, where they could examine it at leisure. They had found the key on Alicia's key-ring. Its contents were disappointing, however: birth and marriage certificates, Parnell's death certificate, details of insurance policies and a modest list of shareholdings.

'No will,' said Lineham.'

'The next best thing, though.' Thanet picked up a single

sheet of paper at the bottom of the box. It was a letter from Alicia's solicitor, dated four months ago, informing her that her will was ready for signing and asking her to call. 'Made soon after her husband's death, by the look of it. We'll give this Mr Thrall a ring. He might manage to fit us in, while we're up here.'

But again they were out of luck. Thrall was tied up in court and wouldn't be able to see them until Wednesday morning.

'Pity,' said Thanet as he put the phone down. 'Never mind, we'll just be in time to catch the 2.36, if we hurry.'

SIX

At this hour of the afternoon the train was almost empty and they had a compartment to themselves. Thanet's back was beginning to ache again and he eased himself into a more comfortable position before lighting his pipe and flapping his hand to dispel the inevitable clouds of smoke.

Lineham unobtrusively edged away a little.

'Well, what did you think of Miss Ross, Mike?'

Lineham pulled a face. 'Can't imagine why Mrs Parnell offered her a partnership, that's for sure.'

'Gratitude, Mike. Gratitude and guilt.

'Guilt?'

'Alicia Parnell sounds the sort of person who'd be only too willing to do others a good turn, but would find it very difficult to be on the receiving end herself. I imagine that when she began to recover, after her husband's death, and realised that it was Jessica Ross who had really been keeping the agency going, she felt so grateful and so guilty that she offered her a partnership on impulse.'

'And no doubt repented at leisure.'

'Probably. In any case, I should think she found that she'd bitten off more than she could chew. It wouldn't surprise me if Jessica Ross changed considerably, once she was in a more powerful position. She strikes me as being just the sort of person to suck up to those in authority and then, when she acquires some power herself, to treat her subordinates in a way she wouldn't have tolerated being treated herself.'

'Also, that agency means a lot to her. She wouldn't have liked it one little bit when she saw it threatened. So when Mrs Parnell didn't manage to pull herself together, began to neglect the business and even damage it . . .'

'Quite. The question is, just how far would Jessica Ross have been prepared to go, to protect her interests?'

'You really think she might have been prepared to kill for them, sir?'

'I certainly think she would be capable of being ruthless, if necessary. We'll have to find out more about her and also check that non-existent alibi of hers pretty thoroughly. I'll put Sparks on to it, it's the sort of thing he enjoys. And I think we'll check all the overnight accomodation in Sturrenden, just in case she followed Alicia down on Saturday. There are no trains back to London after 10.15.'

'She could have come by car, sir.'

'If she's got one. We'll ask Sparks to find out. But one thing's certain. There's a good deal of strong feeling boiling away beneath that not very attractive exterior, wouldn't you agree, Mike?'

'Yes, I would. And I think she was jealous as hell of Mrs Parnell, don't you?'

'Trying hard not to show it, of course.'

'But failing.'

Thanet relit his pipe, which had gone out. 'I suppose it's not surprising, if you think about it. There would have been quite a bit to be jealous about. Alicia was a very good-looking woman and a very nice person, by the sound of it. Look at the way she stuck by her husband . . . I had the impression she was liked by the two girls in the agency, too. Faith had been crying, did you notice?'

'Yes, I did.'

'I'll ask Sparks to have a word with her, and with the other girl, Carol. I expect they could give us a pretty good idea of what's been going on. I imagine the atmosphere hasn't been too pleasant, lately. Jessica Ross doesn't strike me as being the sort of person to suffer a grievance in silence. And I'm quite intrigued to know what made her pull that face when Carol was mentioned.'

'Yes, I noticed that, too. . . . I have the impression Miss Ross felt the situation was getting out of hand, slipping away from her control. She presents herself as being very patient and forbearing, but I imagine the truth is, she tackled Mrs Parnell about it more than once, but didn't manage to get anywhere . . . I wonder where Mrs Parnell used to go during those unexplained absences?'

'Intriguing, isn't it? What do you think, Mike?'

'Well I certainly don't think she sounds the sort of person to sell her share of the agency without even discussing it with her partner. Anyway, that explanation doesn't really fit the pattern, does it? I think it may have been what Jessica Ross was afraid might happen, but that's a different matter.'

'I agree. Her other suggestion was marginally more likely, don't you think?'

'The house-hunting, you mean? I don't know. If so, I don't see why it would have been necessary for Mrs Parnell to be so secretive about it.'

'And what about that red folder, Mike?'

'Could have contained house agents' details, I suppose.' Lineham pulled a face. 'Scarcely a motive for murder, is it? Unless we're going to be really far-fetched and say she might have witnessed a crime while she was looking over an empty property and was killed because she could identify the criminal.' He grinned. 'How's that for a flight of fancy?'

Thanet laughed. 'We'll bear it in mind. Anyway, it certainly sounds as if she was preoccupied by some specific project.'

'Perhaps she decided to cultivate an interest, to take her mind off her unhappiness.'

'Such as?'

Lineham shrugged. 'Collecting something?'

'There's no sign of any kind of collection, in her flat.'

'But if she was only just getting started . . . She could have been going to auction sales, which would explain why the absences were irregular and for varying lengths of time. If she'd taken up French classes, or Pottery, she'd have been going at the same time each week.'

'And the mysterious folder?'

'Auction catalogues, lists of dealers, antique shops, adverts cut out of newspapers . . . No, it's pretty feeble, isn't it? Hell, sir, I'm only guessing. We've absolutely nothing to go on. Have you got any ideas?'

'Not really. I agree with you, it's pure speculation. Fascinating, but pointless, really. Maybe it's of no significance anyway. Maybe she just felt at times that she had to get out of the office, away from Miss Ross, and didn't see why she should have to give explanations.'

'Though that wouldn't explain away the red folder.'

'True. But we must remember that although it seems likely that there's a connection between the murder and the red folder, in view of the fact that it's missing, there's not necessarily any connection between the folder and those unexplained absences.'

'Yes, I see what you mean.'

Back in Sturrenden Sparks had been busy. He had spoken to the Night Sisters who had been on duty in both the intensive care unit and Penny Rain's ward on the night of the concert. Rain had arrived at the former at about ten to eleven, had spent a few minutes discussing his mother's condition with the Sister and had then gone up to enquire about Penny before leaving the hospital.

'Bending the rules a bit, weren't they, Sparks, allowing him in at that time of night?'

Sparks grinned. 'I gather he's a bit of a favourite, sir. And of course, he is a celebrity.'

'True. They're certain of these times?'

'The Sister in charge of intensive care was, because a patient died just after Mr Rain left, and the time of death is entered as eleven pm.'

'Right. Well now, I've got something else for you. A bit of digging in the Metropolis, tomorrow.' Thanet smiled as Sparks's eyes lit up. 'I thought you'd be pleased. There's a woman called Jessica Ross . . .'

Yes, he thought, as he watched Sparks depart after the briefing, the young constable wouldn't be with them long. Thanet had never yearned for the big city, but this boy would thrive on it. Not for him the parochial atmosphere of small-town crime. The faster pace, the excitement and challenge of an urban environment, would be more suited to his temperament and his ambition.

'Interesting,' said Lineham. 'If Rain put his fiancée and her parents into a taxi around twenty past ten, why should it have taken him half an hour to get to the hospital? It wouldn't have taken him more than a quarter of an hour even if he'd walked, and as he'd have had to come in from Barton I imagine he would have had his car with him.'

'I agree. We'll have to see him again. Give him a ring, this time. We don't want another wasted journey.'

Rain was at home and free to see them and they retraced the route they had taken the previous day. This time there were two cars parked in the drive, a silver Mercedes and a Renault 5 with the name of a Sturrenden car-hire firm printed on a notice stuck inside the back window.

'Visitors,' said Thanet.

'Very nice,' said Lineham, admiring the Mercedes. 'Oh, sorry, sir, yes. His fiancée's parents, perhaps?'

'Possibly.'

Rain himself opened the front door and led them through a wide passageway with walls of panelled wood into a spacious sitting room which extended right up to the exposed roof timbers.

It was a most attractive room. There were Persian rugs on the highly-polished floorboards, pieces of oak furniture gleaming with the unmistakable patina of the genuine antique and, predictably, a grand piano scattered with sheet music. Nearby was a music stand, and Rain's violin lay in its open case on a chair. The flower arrangements, Thanet noticed, were beginning to droop.

The three people seated before the huge ingle-nook fireplace looked up as they entered and Rain made the introductions: his fiancée, Melanie Knight, and her parents. They were having tea. A large silver tray stood on a low table near Mrs Knight's chair.

'May we offer you a cup, Inspector?'

'Thank you, no.' The sight of the dainty triangular sandwiches and mouth-watering cream sponge reminded Thanet that somehow he and Lineham seemed to have missed out on lunch today, and he hoped that his stomach would not begin to rumble. He wondered why Rain had not shown them into another room, where they could have talked in private. Because he had hoped that the presence of his fiancée and her parents might inhibit the police? If so, he was about to be disillusioned. Thanet had no intention of allowing himself to be manipulated into leaving without answers to his questions.

'It would be no trouble to get some more cups,' said Melanie, sliding forward to the edge of the settee, preparatory to rising.

This was the first time Thanet had had a good look at her. That glimpse in the street a couple of months ago hardly counted, as she had had her back to him. He saw at once that the newspaper photographs hadn't done her justice. She really was beautiful. Her hair was long, dark and shining, the soft, luscious waves tumbling in ordered disarray about her shoulders. Her face was a perfect oval, her features regular, her eyes large, dark and expressive, and the heart-shaped birthmark on her right cheek did not detract from her beauty but merely served in some mysterious way to underline it, in the manner of the beauty patches worn by the courtesans of old. She was wearing a pale yellow cotton shift dress which hinted at an excellent figure and revealed long, shapely legs. All this and talented too, Thanet thought. Rain was a lucky man.

'No, please don't bother. It's very kind of you, but this won't take long. And I don't want to intrude on your tea, so I'll have a word with Mr Rain in private, if I may.'

Everyone looked at Rain, who was standing in front of the enormous fireplace, hands clasped behind his back. Thanet glanced around. Melanie appeared apprehensive, her parents uncomfortable, and as he watched, Mrs Knight put her hand on her husband's arm. They were obviously a devoted couple, Thanet thought, one of those pairs who, with the passage of time, have grown to look so alike that they could almost be taken for brother and sister. They were both tall, like Melanie, with lean, angular bodies and neat, well-shaped heads. They were even alike in colouring, with short, well-cut light brown hair and clear blue eyes. They looked prosperous and well-groomed, perfectly at home in this affluent setting.

Rain laughed and rocked a little on his heels. 'That won't be necessary, Inspector. I can guess what you've come about. When I got home last night I was thinking back over our conversation yesterday and realised I'd unintentionally misled you. As I recall, I told you I went straight to the hospital after putting my fiancée and her parents into a taxi on Saturday night, but in fact I didn't. I imagine you've come to interrogate me about that rather sinister gap. Is that right?'

Thanet smiled. 'I think that perhaps "interrogate" is rather too strong a word, Mr Rain. But you're right, of course. Naturally, we have to check up on any discrepancy, however slight, in anything to do with any of the people to whom Mrs Parnell spoke on Saturday night, and during the course of our investigation it did emerge that there was, as far as you were concerned, a "sinister gap", as you put it, between twenty past ten and ten to eleven that night. I gather that there is a perfectly innocent explanation for it?'

'It's very simple, really.' Rain left the hearth and went to sit beside Melanie on the settee, his movements easy and relaxed. 'Do sit down, Inspector, Sergeant.'

He certainly didn't look like a man with an uneasy conscience, Thanet thought as he and Lineham complied.

'As you know, I've been desperately worried about my mother — still am, for that matter.' Rain's face was sombre now, and Melanie put out her hand to cover his. He didn't look at her, though, Thanet noticed, or respond to her gesture. He was too preoccupied with his anxiety, perhaps, to have been aware of it.

'I expect that was why I came to mislead you. I had rather too much on my mind. What actually happened on Saturday night was that after saying goodbye to Melanie and her parents, I suddenly realised that when I left home for the concert, earlier in the evening, I had forgotten to bring with me a small bag of stuff that my sister had earlier asked me to take in to her, the next time I visited the hospital. I'd already taken in a few essentials, in the morning, but by the afternoon she was feeling well enough to make a short list of things she thought she'd need. I could have left it until Sunday morning, of course, but I'd promised and . . . I don't know if you've ever been in a similar situation, Inspector, but one of the most difficult things to cope with is a feeling of complete helplessness, the knowledge that there's absolutely nothing useful you can do. I know this was only a very small matter, but it suddenly seemed very important that I should keep that promise. There was something almost, well, superstitious about it. You know . . . if I keep my word to the letter, the gods might smile on me and mother might recover . . .' He gave a sheepish little laugh. 'Stupid, really, but there you are . . . So what I did on Saturday night was to come back here, pick up the bag, which I'd already packed, and take it in to the hospital with me. Ask the Night Sister, she'll confirm this.'

While Rain had been talking the tension in the room had gradually seeped away, like air escaping from a balloon and now the Knights looked at Thanet, their faces bright with expectation, confident of his reception of Rain's disarming confession.

And of course, he had no choice but to accept it. There was one point, though . . . He opened his mouth, but again Rain forestalled him.

'There's no one to corroborate this, I'm afraid, Inspector. We have no permanent staff here and I don't recall seeing anyone I know, on the way.' He smiled. 'I'm afraid you'll just have to take my word for it.'

'I gather that you are not staying here with Mr Rain,' said Thanet, glancing at the Knights and their daughter.

'No. We were going to,' said Knight, 'but then, when Mrs Rain and Penny had that terrible accident, we felt it would be much simpler for Nicholas if he didn't have to bother about us. We couldn't get in at the Black Swan at such short notice, it was fully booked, so we went to the George — and I must say, in view of what happened, we were glad that that was the way it had worked out.'

'Poor woman,' said Mrs Knight. 'What a terrible business. When Nicholas told us he'd known her as a child, we lit a candle for her, this morning.'

So the Knights were Catholic too, Thanet thought. Nicholas and Melanie were indeed well-suited. Her parents must have been delighted at the match — except, perhaps, for the age-gap.

The main point, though, was that Rain had no alibi for half the crucial period on Saturday night. Lineham said as much, when they were in the car.

'We'll send someone to check up on the bag he claims to

69

have taken in for his sister,' said Thanet. 'Though even if he did take it in — and he would be very foolish to lie about something which can so easily be checked — it wouldn't prove he's telling the truth. He could easily have put it in the car earlier, when he left for the concert.'

'And decided to use it to cover up what he was really doing during that half an hour.'

'Meeting Mrs Parnell back at the hotel, you mean? I suppose it depends on whether they've kept in touch or not, as you suggested. I mean, you don't go up to a boyfriend you haven't seen for twenty years and after a few minutes' conversation invite him back to your hotel bedroom, especially when you know he's just got engaged and his fiancée's present.'

'No. But if, after her husband died, she had been hoping they might get together again. . . . She could have threatened to make a scene there and then, if he didn't agree to meet her later. . . . He might well have given in just to shut her up.'

Thanet's bleeper went.

'Wonder what that's about. Did you notice a telephone in the village, Mike?'

'Opposite the church.'

There was a message from Joan, apparently. Would Thanet ring home, at the first opportunity?'

Thanet frowned. 'She didn't say what it was about?'

'No, sir. Sorry.'

Thanet fished out some more change. What could be wrong? Joan never rang him at work unless it was really urgent.

SEVEN

In the few seconds it took to get through, Thanet visualised disaster after disaster. Obviously Joan herself was all right or she wouldn't have been able to ring, so it must be one of the children. Bridget or Ben, injured . . . maimed . . . dead, even . . .

'Hullo?'

'Joan? I got your message. What's the matter?'

'Oh darling, I'm sorry to bother you . . .'

'Never mind that. What's wrong?'

'It's Ben. Just a minute.'

Thanet could hear the television in the background. The noise was suddenly cut off. Joan must have gone to close the door. What had she meant, 'It's Ben.'? He ground his teeth with impatience.

'Hullo?'

'What's the matter with Ben? Is he hurt?'

'No, no. Sorry, darling. No, they're both all right, but . . . they brought a letter home from school, today.'

'A letter? But what . . .? Sorry, go on.'

'It's Andy. He's . . . he's dead.'

Andy was one of Ben's closest friends.

'Dead? Oh God, how awful. What happened?'

'That's the point, Luke. Glue-sniffing.'

'Oh, *no*.' Thanet was shocked and disbelieving. Until a year ago, Andy had been a cheerful, freckled extrovert. Then his parents' marriage had gone wrong and Thanet and Joan had watched helplessly while week by week he had become more withdrawn and unhappy. There had been talk of problems at school, truancy, even. Now, this . . .

Thanet was well aware that 'solvent inhalation', as it is officially called, is the most common drug abuse for children aged eight upwards, and that its danger lies in the risk of convulsions, brain damage or death by suffocation. He knew too that parents are often first alerted to the problem by a change in their child's behaviour, and fear twisted his stomach as his mind flashed back to the weekend.

'Ben's desperately upset,' Joan was saying. 'I think he's been bottling it up all day. The whole school was told about it at assembly this morning, Bridget says, and warned again of the serious risks involved in glue-sniffing. And, as I said, they all brought a letter home to their parents. I didn't know any of this when I picked them up from Marion's of course, and there wasn't time for her to tell me, because I didn't go in, just tooted, and the children came running out. I noticed Ben was very pale and quiet, but he wouldn't tell me what was wrong — looking back, I honestly think that by then he was literally incapable of speaking — and it was Bridget who told me what had happened. By the time we got home Ben was shaking and when we got indoors I bent to put my arms around him, but he just shoved me aside, burst into tears and raced up the stairs to his room. I left him for a little while, then went up. He'd stopped crying by then, but he's lying face down on the bed and he just won't talk to me.'

'You don't think . . .?'

'I don't *know*. Oh Luke, I am sorry to bother you like this, in the middle of an important case, but I don't want to do the wrong thing.'

Thanet could never remember Joan being at a loss like this before. Always, in the past, she could be relied upon to handle any and every crisis with the maximum skill and delicacy.

'I'll come home right away.' *And please, God, don't let Ben be involved in glue-sniffing.* He ran back to the car. 'Drive me home, will you, Mike?'

'Sure. What's wrong, sir?'

Thanet opened his mouth to tell him, then hesitated. He was so used to thinking aloud with Lineham present that it seemed unnatural to hold back when the words were waiting to tumble out in an anxious flood. But this was private, personal. It wasn't that he didn't trust Lineham to keep his mouth shut, just that to express his fear aloud would have seemed like a betrayal of his son.

'A problem to do with one of the children, that's all.' *All.*

'Nothing serious, I hope?'

'I hope not, too.' *Why didn't I notice that there was something wrong? Look at the way he was behaving over the weekend.*

Lineham knew better than to press the matter. 'Is there anything you want me to do, at the office?'

Thanet forced himself to concentrate. One of the next items on the agenda was a visit to the Leytons, but that wasn't urgent and would now have to wait until tomorrow. Meanwhile . . . 'One thing I'd intended to do was to look out the inquest report on Paul Leyton.'

'Paul Leyton? Oh, the boy who committed suicide, you mean?'

'Yes. It may be quite irrelevant, but let's face it, if Jessica Ross turns out to be innocent, there's nobody else we know about in Alicia's present life who could possibly have a reason for wanting to kill her. In which case, we might have to look to the past — especially as her former friends keep cropping up. And we can't get away from the fact that it was very strange that having been away from Sturrenden all these years, she was killed almost immediately after setting foot in it again.' *He was off his food for one thing. And quiet. Shut himself away in his room. It was staring me in the face. Why didn't I see?*

'You'd like me to glance through it, sir?'

'Through it? Oh, the inquest report. Yes. I'll take a look myself, tomorrow morning. And get someone to drop my car back for me some time this evening, will you, Mike?'

They had arrived. Thanet said a hasty goodbye and hurried up the path to the front door. Joan was waiting for him and they went into the kitchen, where she had been preparing supper. Even in a crisis, routine must go on.

'How is he?'

'I haven't been up since. There didn't seem to be much point.'

'What do you think?' said Thanet grimly. 'Has he been involved, in the glue-sniffing?'

'I don't know. He hasn't been showing any of the symptoms

— no smell of glue on him, no signs of drunkenness, no sores around nose or mouth . . .'

'And no hallucinations either, thank God. But he has been very quiet lately.'

'He stayed in on Sunday, remember,' said Joan optimistically. 'We thought it odd at the time. But if he has been involved it could mean he's decided to keep well out of it.'

'Oh God, I hope so. I do hope so. . . . You think I ought to have a word with him now?'

'I don't know. What do you think?'

Each saw his own anxiety mirrored in the eyes of the other while they considered what to do for the best.

'We can't just leave it,' said Thanet at last. 'We'll have to tackle him some time.'

'But when would be the best moment, that's the point. He must be desperately upset about Andy.'

'And just think how Matt and Angela must be feeling.'

Andy's parents were not amongst Thanet and Joan's closest friends, but they knew them quite well and shared a moment of mourning now on their behalf.

'Restricting the sale of glue just isn't enough,' said Joan angrily. 'They'll always get hold of it, if they really want to — like any other drug.'

'I know . . . But Ben . . . you're right. If we question him too soon, he might clam up on us.'

'On the other hand, now might be the best time, while he's still shaken . . .'

'I think I'll pop up and see him anyway,' said Thanet. He needed to see Ben, to touch him, to reassure himself that Ben was all right. And if all the boy needed at the moment was comfort, well, that was fine by him. Bracing himself for a difficult few minutes, Thanet went upstairs and let himself quietly into Ben's room.

Ben was lying face down on the bed, his head turned towards the wall.

'Ben?'

No response. Thanet sat down on the edge of the bed and laid a hand on the boy's shoulder. He felt him stiffen.

'Are you all right?'

74

No reply.

'We're both very, very sorry, about Andy.'

Ben said nothing, but made an inarticulate little sound somewhere between a gasp and a sob.

Thanet began to stroke his son's hair. 'We do understand how upset you are.'

Still no reply.

'We know how fond you were of him.'

In a sudden flurry of activity Ben scrambled on to his knees and hurled himself at his father, bursting into noisy floods of tears. Thanet put his arms tightly around the small body and hugged it close, rocking to and fro and murmuring softly in Ben's ear, taking the boy's pain into himself and absorbing it.

Slowly, Ben's tears abated and eventually Thanet was able to release him. With sinking heart he noted that Ben was still not able to meet his gaze. Should he question him now or not? He agonised over the decision. It was so important to get the timing right. He made up his mind. No, despite his own desperate need to know, it would be better to do it when the boy was calmer.

'Come on,' he said. 'Let's get you undressed. Then Mummy'll bring you some ice cream. Would you like that?'

Ben nodded and submitted to being fussed over. By the time Thanet left him he was looking much more settled.

'I'll come and read you a story later, if you like.'

Deliberately, he waited for an answer, determined to get Ben to say at least a few words before he left him. 'Would you like that?' he persisted.

'Yes please, Daddy.'

Satisfied, Thanet went downstairs and gave Joan an account of what had happened.

'Do you think I ought to call the doctor?'

Thanet shook his head. 'We don't want to make too much of a thing of it. He'll be all right now, I think.'

'What about school, in the morning?'

'Let's wait and see. Children are pretty resilient. He may be feeling much better by then.'

And he was. Ben appeared at breakfast looking pale and subdued but otherwise normal. Far better for him to go to school, Thanet thought, than to sit about at home feeling miserable. Besides, they weren't sure how their usual baby-sitter would cope with this rather delicate situation. They would have a further talk with Ben that evening, they decided.

It was Thanet's turn to take the children to school and he gave them both an extra hard hug before dropping them off. Watching them run towards the school gates he hoped that in their concern for Ben he and Joan hadn't completely neglected Sprig's reaction to the news. But she had seemed fine, he reassured himself. He allowed himself at last to start thinking once more about work.

Had Alicia been the sort of person to resort to emotional blackmail? he wondered, as he remembered yesterday's conversation with Lineham about Rain. He wouldn't have thought so, but then he still knew very little about her, as yet. Jessica Ross had been too self-absorbed to give him any dependable idea of what her partner had been like. Alicia had been loyal, that was clear, and must have had considerable reserves of inner strength to have stuck to her husband and helped him to rebuild his life after the accident. She must have been under severe strain for years, and it wasn't surprising that after his death she had apparently gone to pieces.

Nevertheless, she had survived. She had continued to take an interest in her appearance, had run her home efficiently and had continued to work, albeit with less enthusiasm than before. And she appeared to have found some new interest in life, a preoccupation which had been sufficiently important to her for her to ignore or shrug off Jessica Ross's displeasure at her neglect of the business.

Could that interest have been Nicholas Rain? Unconsciously, Thanet shook his head. If Alicia had been slipping out to meet a lover, she would surely have looked at least a little more cheerful upon her return, and Jessica Ross had said that she invariably seemed depressed. It really was pointless to speculate. Enlightenment could come only through finding out more about Alicia's life, her character, and as she appeared to have no close friends and her father, her only relative, was still away on holiday, there seemed to be only one possible avenue of exploration. He would have to talk to her former friends here in Sturrenden. Alicia at seventeen must of course have been very different from the mature woman of thirty-eight, but the seeds of her future development would surely already have been sown and for all he knew those links with former friends may never have been broken. She might well have kept in touch with the only other girl in the group, Vivienne Leyton, for instance.

Yes, a visit to the Leytons was long overdue, but he still thought it might be profitable to study first the report of the event which had caused that group to disintegrate, Paul Leyton's suicide.

Lineham was already at his desk.

'Anything interesting come in, Mike?'

'Oh, morning, sir. Nothing much. We've got the forensic report now, but there's nothing of any use to us. The room was plastered with different fingerprints, as you would imagine, in a hotel bedroom. Let me see. what else . . .? Ah, yes. The hospital confirms that Mr Rain did bring in a bag of stuff for his sister late on Saturday night, but as you said, that doesn't really get us any further. And that's about it. Everything all right at home, now?'

'Yes, crisis over.' If only he could be sure that were true, Thanet thought. He wasn't looking forward to this evening.

Lineham's enquiry had put him in a slightly awkward position. The sergeant had been very helpful yesterday and Thanet really owed him some sort of explanation, but he didn't want to give one yet. Not until he was sure that Ben was in the clear.

He would just have to appear ungrateful. 'Did you manage to read the inquest report on Paul Leyton?'

'Yes. I was just making some notes on it when you arrived. Here it is.'

'Thanks. What are your impressions?'

Lineham leaned back in his chair. 'Well, it seems there's no doubt that it was suicide. He took an overdose and left a note for his parents.'

'What did it say?'

' "Sorry, I just can't go on." That's all. As you told me, the precipitating factor was the split with Alicia Parnell — Alicia

77

Doyle, as she was then — earlier in the evening. But there was more to it than that, apparently.'

'I'd better read it through myself.'

Paul Leyton had killed himself on the night of June 4th 1964. His body had been found next morning by his mother, when he had failed to come down for breakfast and she had gone up to call him. He had apparently been withdrawn and moody for some time before that. He had been a brilliant boy and everybody had hoped that he would win a scholarship to Oxford when he sat the Oxbridge examination the following November, but for the month previous to his death his work had fallen off badly and the day he died his Latin master had taken him to task over a very poor essay he had handed in.

The master, a man called Hollister (whom Thanet remembered from his own time at the school as being an exacting but excellent teacher) had been called at the inquest and had said that he had told Paul that if he didn't very quickly pull himself together and start concentrating on his work again he could not only say goodbye to Oxford but to getting respectable grades in his A levels as well. Hollister had said that he now deeply regretted having been so forceful. He had known of Paul's association with Alicia Doyle and had assumed that the boy's preoccupation with her was affecting his work, but he hadn't mentioned the girl, had simply said that the next few months would be crucial as far as Paul's future was concerned and that he must try to let other interests sink into abeyance for the moment.

Alicia had then told the court about two conversations with Paul later that day. For some time she had felt that his feelings for her were becoming too intense. She knew that in the autumn they would both be going away to university and she hadn't wanted to become too involved with any one boy. So, when she met Paul in the coffee bar where they often used to congregate with their other friends after school, she asked him to walk home with her and told him that she had decided that it would be best if they didn't go out together again. She hoped that they would still remain friends, she told him, but she would prefer him not to think of her as his girlfriend any more.

Paul had argued with her, pleaded, and was still very upset when he left her. Later in the day, after supper, he had returned, begging her at least to say that she would reconsider her decision, but she had felt that if she conceded at this point, she would never find the determination to go through all this again, and she had held firm. She was terribly upset by what had happened, she said, and wished now that she had behaved differently. Perhaps it would have been better just to let the relationship peter out when they both went away. That way, Paul would gradually have become used to living without her and would have found the final break easier when it came.

Oliver Bassett had then been called. He had been on his way home at about nine o'clock that night, he said, when he had passed Paul in the street. He had pulled up and offered him a lift home. Paul had seemed very depressed, and when they arrived at the Leyton house Oliver had accepted Paul's rather half-hearted offer of a cup of coffee, thinking that perhaps Paul might find it helpful to talk. But Paul had remained sunk in gloom and after a while Bassett had left, thinking that there was nothing more he could do. He bitterly regretted not having stayed on longer, at least until one of the family arrived home.

The next witness to be called was Richard Leyton, Paul's younger brother. He told the court that he had also been out that evening and had got home at about ten-thirty. His parents had not yet returned from their bridge evening and as he was tired and there was no one about, he had gone straight up to bed. Paul's bedroom door was closed and there was no light showing beneath, so Richard, knowing that Paul had gone to see Alicia after supper, had assumed that his brother was still out. It was not until the following day, when he heard that Paul must have taken the overdose at about ten-fifteen pm, that he realised that if he had indeed looked in on Paul that night, he might well have been able to save his life. He would always regret not having done so.

Verdict: suicide while the balance of the mind was disturbed.

'Nothing too unusual there,' said Thanet, when he had finished reading. 'Sadly, it's a situation which arises all too often.

You get an adolescent under stress because of impending exams, he has an unhappy love affair and it's all just too much for him to cope with.'

'Amazing, isn't it, how after a suicide everyone feels guilty, thinks he could have prevented it if only he'd behaved differently.'

'Understandable, though.'

'You really think all this stuff might be relevant, sir?'

'Who knows? I certainly think it might be useful to talk to these people. We still don't know nearly enough about Alicia.' And Thanet expained what he had been thinking, on the way to work, in the car.

'With respect, sir, I can't see that it'll be much use talking to people who haven't seen her for twenty years.'

'But how do we know they haven't seen her for twenty years, Mike? Even if she lost touch with them during the time her husband was alive, after his death she might well have begun to wish she hadn't. And from there it's only a step to deciding to contact them again.'

'It's possible, I suppose.' But Lineham didn't sound in the least convinced.

'The point is,' said Thanet, becoming exasperated, 'we've got to explore every possibility. Now Sparks is digging away in London, so we'll do some digging here. Where shall we start? With the Leytons? It's about time we had a talk with them.'

'How about going to see that schoolmaster. What was his name . . .?'

'Hollister, you mean? Why?'

'It could be useful to have an impartial opinion of them all, sir.'

'I'm not sure how forthcoming he would be.' Thanet was intrigued with his own reluctance to take up Lineham's suggestion. Was it possible that he was still intimidated by Hollister, after all these years? The mere possibility was enough to clinch the matter. 'Still, you're right. It could be useful. See if you can find his address in the phone book, will you? I know he retired some years ago, but as he's a bachelor he might well have stayed put.'

While he waited Thanet glanced through the forensic

report. Lineham was right. There wasn't anything of any use to them there. He sighed. They certainly weren't getting much material help. He hated casting around in the dark, like this.

'Here we are, sir. J.C. Hollister. That's him, isn't it?'

'Yes. Where does he live?'

'41 Benenden Road.'

'Give him a ring. No, on second thoughts, don't bother. It's not far, so we won't be wasting much time. If he's out, we can go on to see someone else . . . Is the PM scheduled yet?'

'This afternoon, sir.'

'Good. Then let's go.'

EIGHT

The houses in Benenden Road were of nineteen-thirties vintage: neat, detached and solidly built, with bay windows upstairs and down. Most of them showed signs of the recent boom in home improvement in the way of double glazing or replacement windows, freshly-painted woodwork and even, here and there, the odd burglar alarm. Over the years the Englishman's home has become more his castle than ever, thought Thanet. He wouldn't mind betting that most of these modest houses also boasted central heating, insulated lofts and kitchens which would have made the original owners swoon with delight.

Number 41 stood out like a sore thumb. The tiny front garden was knee-high in nettles and long grass, there were dingy net curtains at the grimy windows and the paintwork hadn't seen a brush in years. An ancient Morris Oxford stood in the drive.

'Can't think how it passed its MOT,' said Lineham, peering at the licence on the windscreen and wrinkling his nose at the rusting metalwork.

Thanet was already on the front doorstep. 'Mike, we're not in traffic division. Come *on*.' He banged the rusty knocker on the peeling wood.

'And I bet the neighbours love that.' Lineham nodded at the overgrown garden.

'He obviously doesn't give a damn.' Thanet couldn't help having a sneaking admiration for someone who so completely disregarded the conventions. He often felt that he himself was boringly conformist. He was beginning to look forward to this interview. He enjoyed eccentrics.

'Who is it?' A muffled voice from within.

'Police, sir. CID.'

There was a moment's silence and then the sound of bolts

being drawn. The door opened a few inches.

'Mr Hollister?'

'What do you want?'

Thanet introduced himself and offered his identification.

'Thanet . . . Weren't you at the Grammar?'

'Yes, sir.' With difficulty Thanet prevented himself from standing to attention under the old man's scrutiny.

'In the police now, eh?' The door opened a little wider.

'Yes, sir. And we were wondering if you could help us.'

'Me? How?'

'We wanted to talk to you about Paul Leyton . . . If we could come into the house, perhaps? It might be a little less public . . .'

'Paul Leyton . . .'

There was a pause, a long one. Then, just as Thanet was beginning to think that he would have to conduct the interview on the doorstep, the door opened wider and he saw Hollister properly for the first time. Confronted with the reality, his mental image of the man abruptly disintegrated. He remembered the classics master as a tall, commanding figure, a man who had been respected if not liked, notorious for the impossibly long homework he set and feared for his rages if his standards were not met. He expected and got the most excellent results and in his time had nurtured several fine classical scholars.

It was difficult to believe that this neglected scarecrow was the same man. He seemed to have shrunk during the intervening years and he was gaunt, stooping, unshaven. He was wearing stained, wrinkled trousers, a creased open-necked shirt and a shabby fawn knitted cardigan. His eyes, however, were as keen as ever, the cold, penetrating grey that Thanet remembered so well.

'I suppose you'd better,' he said grudgingly, and stood back to allow them to enter. As he turned to close the front door behind them Thanet and Lineham could not prevent themselves from exchanging a look of pure amazement. At first glance it seemed that the house was constructed of books rather than of bricks and mortar, wood and plasterboard. Every available wall surface was stacked with books, right up

83

to the ceiling. They even marched up the stairs, piled shoulder high on every riser, up and up into the dimness of the landing above.

'We'd better go into the kitchen.'

They passed two open doors on the way and in both rooms books prevailed, to the degree that there seemed to be little floor space left, just a narrow corridor between encroaching walls of volumes, leading to a single armchair with a standard lamp beside it. How on earth, Thanet wondered, did Hollister ever manage to get at a book in one of the stacks at the back? For that matter, how could he hope to have even a vague idea of where he had put the one he wanted, let alone find it?

The air was fusty, musty, the smell of a second-hand bookshop magnified a thousand times over by dust and neglect. Hollister had evidently become a recluse of the first order, living in a world of his own bounded by the printed page. And the original owner of this house would certainly have recognised this kitchen, Thanet thought. There was the old china sink, the built-in dresser with cupboards below, the white enamel table, chipped and stained with rust, the walk-in larder beside the back door. It was possible, of course, that Hollister himself had bought the house newly-built and, supremely indifferent to his surroundings, had simply never bothered to make any changes.

This appeared to be the one room relatively free of books. A few were piled on the dresser, with little pieces of paper sticking out of them, but that was all. On the table was a sheaf of papers and an open, typed catalogue. A pencil lay nearby. Hollister had evidently been engaged in the pleasurable task of selecting new acquisitions. Where on earth would he put them? Were the bedrooms, too, book depositories? Despite the warmth of the day the back door was firmly shut and the window closed, and there was a smell of drains and stale food.

Any idea that Hollister was in his dotage was quickly dispelled. He sat down on the only chair, gave Thanet a piercing glance and said, 'Now, perhaps you would enlighten me as to your interest in this matter. It is twenty years since Paul Leyton's death and I fail to see how anything I could tell you could be of any possible interest to you.'

Thanet wouldn't have expected to find anything as incongruous as a television set here, but a quick glance around had shown him that there did not appear to be a radio, either. Nor, so far as he could see, were there any newspapers.

'Do you remember a girl called Alicia Doyle, Mr Hollister?'

'Of course I do,' snapped Hollister. 'I am far from senile yet, Thanet. She was that little trollop Leyton was running about with. If it hadn't been for her, he would never have killed himself.'

His venom startled Thanet and he wondered, could he by chance have stumbled across Alicia's murderer? That Hollister should speak with such passion after all these years astonished him.

'You may not have heard, sir, but Alicia Parnell — Alicia Doyle, as you knew her — was found dead in the Black Swan on Sunday morning. She had been strangled.'

Hollister didn't even blink. 'Doesn't surprise me. A fitting end, I should think.'

'It would evidently be putting it mildly, to say that you didn't like her.'

'It would. Girls like that should be locked up. The degree of havoc they wreak amongst unsuspecting adolescent males is incalculable.'

'You speak in the plural, sir.'

'I do. Boys may think that their masters are blind, but I can assure you that they're not. Earlier in the year Miss Doyle,' — and he almost spat the name — 'had had her claws into Nicholas Rain. His work, too, was deplorable for a while after she tossed him aside, but it didn't matter so much for him. It had been evident to everyone for a very long time that he was destined for a brilliant musical career. As it transpired, he recovered sufficiently to gain a respectable grade at A level. But Leyton was a different matter. When his work began to deteriorate I didn't realise why, at first. And when I did find out, there seemed to be nothing I could do. He was deaf to reason. It was a tragedy.' Hollister banged the enamel table with a clenched fist, making the two policemen jump. 'I really fail to understand why someone as intelligent as he should . . . That boy had the finest brain I ever taught. And it was addled

—that's the only word for it, addled—by that little chit of a girl.' Hollister shook his head. 'I couldn't believe he'd been so foolish as to succumb to her "charms". I'd thought he had enough sense to realise that at that stage in his life there was no room, no room at all for dalliance. I'd seen the other one mooning around after him and it obviously hadn't affected him in the least, so . . .'

'The other one?'

'The one with red hair. Forever following him around like a love-sick cow.'

Thanet caught Lineham, who was standing behind Hollister, smothering a grin. It was rapidly becoming obvious why Hollister had never married. His view of the fair sex was, to put it mildly, somewhat jaundiced.

'That was Leyton's tragedy,' Hollister went on. 'He was too well-liked, too popular. If he'd been less sought-after, he'd be alive today and the Regius professor of Greek, no doubt.'

'You felt that his friends were a distraction?'

'Distraction? Hah, you have a talent for understatement, Thanet. They distracted him, they distracted each other and, believe me, they distracted me. If they'd given only a fraction of the attention to their work that they gave to their social activities, it would have been a very different story.'

'I don't know about Richard Leyton, Paul's brother, but the other two men did well enough though, sir, didn't they? Rain has a fine career and Bassett . . .'

'Bassett was only a hanger-on. It was that sports car of his that was the attraction.' Hollister snorted. 'Absolutely ridiculous, giving a sports car to a boy of that age. Asking for trouble. Parents should have more sense. Over-indulgence and too much laxity, they're the ills of the modern age.'

It was obvious that Hollister's prejudices were too strong for him to be of any help to them, and Thanet left as soon as he decently could.

'So much for an impartial opinion,' said Lineham, when they were outside. 'Sorry, sir.'

'Don't worry about it.' Thanet grinned. 'To be honest, Mike, I only decided to interview him because the prospect made me nervous. After all these years! I just couldn't resist going to see what he was like.'

'He must have been a real tartar, at school. I'm thankful he never taught me, that's for sure. Classics was never my strong point.'

'Nor mine, alas,' said Thanet. 'And he obviously hasn't forgiven me for it.'

'Pretty weird set-up he's got there. Do you think he spends all day, every day, reading?'

'Looks like it.'

'What a life! I'd go round the bend.'

'Presumably it's by choice, so I shouldn't feel too sorry for him.'

'Where now, then?'

'Oliver Bassett first, I think, as we're so close to his office.'

'He may not be free to see us.'

'Then we'll make an appointment.'

But Bassett would see them in fifteen minutes, they were told, if they cared to wait.

They were shown into a neat, impersonal waiting room.

'Nice little practice he's got here,' said Lineham, shuffling through the magazines on a low table. '*Country Life, Ideal Home, Practical Photographer, The Field, What Micro* . . . all pretty upmarket, and current issues, at that. Perhaps I should have gone into the law.'

'You *are* in the law, Mike.'

'Yes, but . . .'

'Mr Bassett will see you now.'

Bassett's office was on the second floor, overlooking the High Street. Here, too, were the carefully chosen antiques, the air of solid prosperity which had pervaded his home.

They all sat down and Bassett steepled his fingers in what was clearly an habitual gesture. 'What can I do for you?'

'We've come to ask for your help.'

Bassett waved a hand. 'I told you last time, Thanet, any-thing . . . You have only to ask.'

'I'll be frank with you, sir. We are still not sure why Mrs Parnell came to Sturrenden. It's possible that you are right, that she did indeed come simply to attend the concert. But I think you will agree with me that it is very odd that after living away from Sturrenden for twenty years or so, she is murdered just a few hours after she sets foot in it again.'

'True, but possibly coincidental.'

'Also, possibly not. And you must see that while that possibility exists, that she was killed *because* she came back, for whatever reason, it is clearly our duty to take a close look at her former friends and acquaintances.'

'Including me.'

'Including you, naturally. But in fact, we haven't come here this morning to question you further about your own movements . . .'

'About what, then?'

'You were one of Mrs Parnell's closest friends, and . . .'

'Oh, hardly that, I'd say, Inspector.'

Back to formality now, Thanet noted. 'At any rate, one of the group of young people she went around with during the last summer she was here.'

'But we don't know whether that necessarily was when she was last here. During the past twenty years she could well have made other friends who live in this area.'

'Perhaps. And if so, no doubt we'll find out in due course. But frankly, I doubt it. She was very much tied to her home. Her husband was very dependent on her. He was badly crippled in an accident, on the way back from their honeymoon, and confined to a wheelchair for the rest of their married life. He died about six months ago.'

Bassett's prim little mouth had pursed in concern, 'Poor Alicia. I'm sorry to hear that. She didn't have much of a life, did she?'

'Nor death,' said Thanet grimly. 'So anything you could tell me . . .?'

'About what, then, precisely?'

'I would like to know about the relationships within that group of young people, about their attitudes to each other and to Mrs Parnell. Or anything else you think it might be helpful for me to know, of course.'

Bassett didn't like it. He hooked his thumbs into the armholes of his waistcoat and gave Thanet a long, speculative look. 'Strange,' he said, 'but do you know, even after all this time I experience an uncomfortable frisson of disloyalty when you make a suggestion like that.'

'You did promise us your full cooperation.'

'Yes. Rash of me, wasn't it? These people were my friends, Inspector.'

'And Mrs Parnell was one of them.'

'Death alters the boundaries of what is considered acceptable behaviour, you mean?'

'Wouldn't you agree with that proposition?'

'Perhaps. I suppose so. I have to hand it to you, Thanet. You're no mean tactician. . . . Well, I suppose I shall have to put aside my scruples and do as you ask. . . . Where would you like me to start?'

'Wherever you wish.'

NINE

Bassett drummed his fingers thoughtfully on his desk.

'Since you came to my house on Sunday, Thanet, I've been thinking — well, I suppose it's inevitable that when this kind of tragedy occurs, memories of the past are resurrected. And do you know what seems to me the most ironic thing of all?'

Thanet raised his eyebrows interrogatively.

'That of the six members of our group, the two who were most full of life are now dead.'

'And that both died unnaturally.'

Bassett bowed his head.

In acknowledgement or mourning? Thanet wondered. 'You're talking about Paul Leyton, of course.'

'Yes. He and Alicia . . . the rest of us just revolved around them. They were always the leaders, the ones who suggested what we should do, influenced our thinking, our attitudes . . . Not consciously, mind. It just came naturally to them. And they made it such . . . fun.' Bassett sighed. 'That doesn't seem to be a word one hears much these days, amongst the young. Not that I know many young people, but my impression is that they are looking for stronger meat — thrills, excitement. But in those days . . . well, you'll know yourself, it was different.'

'When did you begin to cohere, as a group?'

'At the beginning of my second year in the sixth. We knew each other before then, of course, in ones and twos, and then, in the November of that year, let me see, it would have been . . .'

'1963, I believe.'

'That's right. 1963. A week or two before Paul's birthday he approached me and said he'd like to get up a theatre outing, but it would be too expensive if they all went up by train. Was there any chance that I would be prepared to drive them up to London, as one of the party? I'd been given this car, you see, when I passed my test in the summer of that year. Of course, I agreed. I don't mind admitting that I was flattered to be included. So, on Paul's birthday, off we all went. It was a marvellous evening and on the way home someone suggested another outing the following Saturday — ice-skating, I believe. And it went on from there.'

'It was a very unbalanced group, as far as the sexes were concerned. Four boys and two girls.'

'True. But it didn't seem to matter, to begin with, anyway.'

'How did it come about?'

Bassett shrugged. 'I think it was the natural outcome of our friendships at the time of that first trip. Richard was Paul's brother, and as it was a birthday celebration I suppose he felt he had to ask him along . . . and Richard was keen on Vivienne, even then, so that's why she was asked. Later on he married her. But I suppose you knew that.'

'I had heard, yes.'

'They've got two children now, in their teens. Anyway, that's why Richard and Vivienne came. Nicky — Nicholas Rain — came because he was Paul's closest friend. And Alicia was Nicky's girlfriend. Then there was me.'

Asked because you were able to provide a mode of transport, thought Thanet. 'So both Alicia and Vivienne started out as girlfriends of boys in the group?'

'Yes . . . well, not exactly, perhaps. Vivienne wasn't as keen on Richard as he was on her, at the time. That came later.'

'Much later, I gather.'

Bassett frowned. 'What do you mean?'

'I understood that Vivienne was attracted to Paul.'

'Ah, yes. You're right, she was. In fact, that was half the trouble. Paul was too attractive — to women, I mean.' Bassett shifted a little in his chair and cleared his throat.

Thanet did not betray his sudden interest. Had that last rider been added a shade too hastily? Because if so . . . he glanced at Lineham and their eyes met. So Mike had spotted it too.

'What do you mean, "half the trouble"?'

'Well, to begin with, there was no problem. We knew where we were. Richard was keen on Vivienne, we all knew that, and we also knew that she wasn't as keen on him. Alicia and Nicky were pretty close, and if they wanted to be alone together, they used to go off by themselves. Then it became obvious that Vivienne had fallen for Paul. And Richard wasn't very happy about that, as you can imagine.'

'Paul reciprocated?'

'Oh no. But that didn't seem to put Vivienne off. Quite the reverse, in fact. She didn't seem to have eyes for anyone else. And then, to complicate matters, we noticed that Alicia was falling for Paul too.'

'When was this?'

'Let me see . . . some time in the Easter holidays, I should say. Nicky was still just as keen on her as he had been all along, but it was obvious to us that Alicia had lost interest. It was all very awkward. Nicky was Paul's best friend, after all, and to begin with, Paul didn't respond. Finally, around the end of April, Alicia broke off with Nicky and I suppose Paul felt that there was then no reason why he shouldn't go out with Alicia if he wanted to. She was a very attractive girl and he really went overboard for her. He'd had lots of dates, but he'd never had a steady girlfriend before and the whole thing was a disaster. The timing was all wrong for him, with his A levels coming up, and his work went to pieces. He couldn't seem to think of anything but Alicia. He was . . . obsessed by her.'

Bassett had betrayed himself. The tone of the last few words had been unmistakeable. Like Hollister, Bassett had bitterly resented Alicia's hold over Paul Leyton, if for a different reason.

Now, he caught Thanet's eye, gave a shame-faced little grin and shrugged, lifting his hands in a disarming gesture of surrender. 'We were all furious with Alicia, for what she did to him. Paul was really brilliant, you know. His death was such a waste . . . and so unnecessary. If only Alicia had waited just a few more weeks, until his exams were over, before breaking off with him, he would have been able to cope better. But to tell him then, with his first A level only a few days away . . . it was unforgiveable.'

'You saw him the evening he died, didn't you?'

'You've been doing your homework I see, Inspector. Yes, I did.'

92

Thanet noticed Bassett's hands begin to curl up on the surface of the desk before the solicitor casually folded them together and put them in his lap out of Thanet's sight.

'You gave him a lift home.'

'Inspector, I've gone along with you so far, but I see absolutely no point whatsover in relating to you an experience which is still painful to me. Everything I had to say on the subject I said at the inquest and is available to you in black and white. So if you don't mind . . .'

'Of course, sir. I didn't mean to distress you.'

'I'm sure you'd feel the same, if one of your closest friends had killed himself and you were the last person to see him alive.'

'I'm sure I should,' said Thanet with sincerity.

Despite his plea to drop the subject, Bassett now couldn't leave it alone.

'You're bound to be left wondering what you said to help push him into it, or what you didn't say that could have prevented it . . .'

'I believe many people felt the same, in the case of Paul Leyton.'

'Yes, that's true. I wasn't the only one.'

'In fact, he seems to have aroused very strong feelings in everyone who knew him.'

Bassett was staring at Thanet but not seeing him.

'So what happened afterwards, as far as the group was concerned?'

'Sorry? Oh, we were all badly shaken, of course. And we just drifted apart. Nicky, Alicia and I had our A levels, so we didn't have much time for social activities in any case. Richard and Vivienne were a year below us, but I had the impression they didn't see much of each other either. And then, soon after the end of term, Alicia and her family moved away.'

'This was a sudden decision, to leave the area?'

Bassett shrugged. 'I've no idea. All I know is that shortly after the inquest the Doyles' house went up for sale. Perhaps her father moved because of his work, perhaps they thought it would be best for Alicia if she could put the tragedy behind her . . .'

'She'd intended going to university, I believe.'

'Yes. She had a place at Bristol. She was pretty bright. But she didn't do nearly as well in her A levels as she'd hoped — failed one of them, I believe — so I suppose they wouldn't take her. She was badly shaken by Paul's death.'

Thanet felt that he'd learned as much as he could at this particular juncture, and he thanked Bassett and left.

'All very interesting, I'm sure,' said Lineham as they went down the stairs. 'But where does it get us, that's what I'd like to know.'

'Patience, Mike. I thought one or two interesting things emerged, didn't you?'

'You mean, the way Bassett felt about Paul Leyton, for example.'

'I thought you'd spotted that. Yes. It seems that Bassett was the outsider in more ways than one.'

'You think the others knew?'

'Quite likely, I imagine. No doubt they were prepared to tolerate him because he was useful to them. Also, I find the whole dynamics of the group interesting. Leyton seems to have been the focal point of it all. The two girls were attracted to him, and if we're right, so was Bassett, and the other two boys were jealous of him. I imagine he must have been under considerable emotional pressure — in fact, it wouldn't surprise me if it was a contributory factor in what happened later.'

'His suicide, you mean?'

'Yes. And it's interesting that when Paul killed himself, the group split up. You might have expected them to stick together for moral support, but they didn't. Perhaps they just couldn't face each other. Perhaps they found it possible to cope with their individual feelings of guilt, but their collective guilt was too much for them. In any case they seem to have cast Alicia in the role of scapegoat, and what I'm wondering is . . .'

'What?' Lineham had unlocked the car and was about to open the door. Now he stopped, facing Thanet across the roof.

'Let's get in.'

Thanet waited until they were settled. 'Well, suppose

someone in the group felt very strongly — passionately, even, about Paul. And suppose that someone blamed Alicia for his death . . .'

'You're suggesting he might have killed her for revenge?'

'Why not? It's as good a motive as any.'

'But with respect, sir . . .'

'Mike, will you stop saying that, every time you're about to disagree with me? It drives me mad. If you've a point to make, make it.'

'I was only going to say it's bit unlikely, isn't it, after twenty years when he'd done nothing about it?'

'I'm not so sure. Consider the matter, Mike. Soon after the tragedy Alicia moves away, out of this person's reach. He hopes he'll get over it in time and he does, to the extent that he goes on living a normal life. But underneath the desire for revenge is still there, biding its time. And then, finally, one day that time comes. Quite by chance he sees Alicia again. He knows that she is only here on a brief visit, and that if he is going to act, he must act swiftly . . .'

'By "he", I presume you also mean "she".'

'You're thinking of Vivienne Leyton?'

'Well if she was in love with Paul Leyton, as Bassett claims, she'd certainly qualify, wouldn't you agree?'

'Mike, you've the soul of a romantic after all! You're suggesting that this apparently happily married woman has for twenty years been yearning for her long-lost love!'

Lineham was not amused. His jaw tightened and he glanced reproachfully at Thanet before saying, 'You know perfectly well what I mean, sir.'

'Oh come on, Mike. Don't take everything so seriously. Of course I know what you mean. And I agree with you. Vivienne Leyton should definitely be considered a suspect.'

Lineham gave him a penetrating glance, as if he suspected that Thanet were still teasing him, and then said, 'Except that strangling is not usually a woman's crime, sir.'

'Beware of generalisations, Mike. The case you're dealing with may always prove to be the exception.'

'Then there's Bassett.'

'Yes.' Thanet absent-mindedly started patting his pockets.

Lineham wound down the window.

'Yes,' repeated Thanet, his fingers closing over the stem of his pipe, 'Now Bassett is quite a promising prospect, I should think.'

Lineham watched with resignation as Thanet began to feed tobacco into the bowl.

Thanet waited until it was drawing well before he said, 'If we're right, and he has got homosexual leanings, and he was deeply attached to Paul, has never found anyone to replace him . . . Yes, I could well imagine a desire for revenge burning away in him like a slow fuse, all these years. . . . He's too conventional, too embedded in respectability, actively to have tried to seek her out, but when he bumps into her, by chance . . .'

'He knew where she was staying, sir.'

'And that she was going to the concert, that night.'

'And we've only got his word for it that she refused his invitation to have supper with him, afterwards.'

'We must put someone on to checking that useless alibi of his, Mike, that walk he claims to have taken by the river in the moonlight.'

'There is one snag though, sir. Surely, even if Mrs Parnell did accept an invitation to meet him after the concert, and they went back to her hotel to pick up a coat or something, she wouldn't have asked him up to her room? He'd have waited downstairs, in the foyer.'

'True.'

'But,' said Lineham, on a sudden note of excitement, 'how about this? That red folder. Suppose it was really Bassett she had come to Sturrenden to see, that if she hadn't run into him by chance, she'd have engineered a meeting somehow. Suppose she *had* to ask him up to her room because she wanted to show him what was in the folder.'

'What are you suggesting was in it?'

'Compromising photographs of him and Paul Leyton? It could fit, sir. Maybe this could explain why she broke off with Leyton so suddenly — because she'd discovered he and Bassett were carrying on together . . .'

Thanet was shaking his head. 'It's no good, Mike. I can't

96

really see the Alicia we've been hearing about setting out cold-bloodedly to blackmail someone over something that happened all that time ago.'

'I suppose you're right.' Lineham shrugged. 'Ah well, it was a nice theory . . .'

'Still thinking along the lines of a revenge motive, though, Mike, there's Richard Leyton.'

'Paul's brother? I should think he'd have been more likely to be grateful to Mrs Parnell.'

'For causing his brother's suicide!'

'No, for leaving the way clear for him to get the girl he wanted. From what Bassett was saying, Richard didn't have much of a look in with Vivienne, while Paul was still alive.'

'True. Or there's Hollister. He obviously hated Alicia for destroying his great white hope.'

'Unlikely, sir, surely, that he should have bumped into her by chance. I had the impression that he didn't emerge from his book-burrow from one year's end to the next. And I really can't visualise those two meeting by arrangement. The mind boggles.'

'I admit we're scraping the barrel a bit.'

'So, where next?'

'I think it's about time we met the Leytons, don't you?' Thanet glanced at his watch. 'It's ten to twelve, and Leyton's a farmer. With any luck we might catch him at home for lunch.'

TEN

Kent is a county of infinite variety. Between the rolling majesty of the Downs in the north and the flat expanse of Romney Marsh in the south lies some of the richest agricultural land in England. In the flattish area in the middle, known as the Weald, grow the hops for which the county is famous and tourists frequently make a point of visiting the celebrated Whitbread Oast houses near Paddock Wood, where there is an interesting museum of Country Crafts and bygones.

But many feel that the most beautiful area of all is the broad swathe of land encircling the Weald, with its little wooded hills and sheltered valleys, its spreading acres of golden corn and the annual miracle of blossom-time in the spring. In this part of Kent, in summer, little notices sprout everywhere, advertising anything and everything which grows. Everyone, it seems, has green fingers and wishes to profit by his talent. Beginning with tomato plants and brassica seedlings, one may trace the progress of the seasons by the produce set out on little tables by garden gates on the roadside: boxes of bedding plants, punnets of luscious strawberries glistening ruby-red in the sunshine, plump cabbages and fresh greenhouse tomatoes with that distinctive, once-tasted-never-forgotten smell and flavour, bunches of stately gladioli and jaunty dahlias and bags of that crisp, juicy king of apples, the Cox's Orange Pippin.

This is the setting for Bickenden, which lies midway between Sturrenden and Ashford, a tiny village of scattered black and white timbered houses and pretty little red-brick Georgian cottages grouped around a traditional village green with duckpond, church and pub.

Pulling up at the latter to enquire the way of an old man sitting on a bench in the sun with pipe and pint, Thanet gathered that Apple Tree Farm still belonged to Richard's father.

The Leytons senior lived in the main farmhouse, Richard and his family in a 'new' bungalow built for them at the time of their marriage. They found it without difficulty, an impressive, one-storey building set in a large garden surrounded by orchards.

'Very nice,' said Lineham, as they turned into the gravelled driveway. 'They can't be short of a penny.'

'We're not here to assess their income, Mike.'

'Still . . .'

Thanet recognised the woman who opened the door at once by her hair, which haloed her small, pointed face in an elaborately frizzed burning bush. If it hadn't been for this, her most striking feature, he would have passed her in the street without a second glance. There was nothing distinctive about her pale, rather close-set eyes and sharp little nose.

'Mrs Leyton? I'm sorry to trouble you.' He introduced himself and Lineham. 'We're investigating the murder of Mrs Alicia Parnell.'

'Oh.' The frown which had already made permanent lines on her forehead deepened. 'But we've already made a statement. Someone called the other day.'

'Yes, I know. And I do apologise for disturbing you again. But there are one or two points I'd like to go over with you and your husband, if you don't mind.'

She still hesitated. 'It's not very convenient. We're having lunch, and my husband doesn't take a very long break. He's up to his ears with the raspberries, at the moment.'

'Who is it, Viv?'

Vivienne Leyton half-turned, opening the door a little wider, and a man came out of a room at the far end of the hall. Briefly, Thanet experienced a moment of confusion. What was Nicholas Rain doing here, sounding so proprietorial? Then the man came closer and he saw that he had been mistaken. Leyton was slightly taller and slimmer, his hair and beard lighter in colour. Thanet would scarcely have recognised him — but then, nothing alters a man's appearance so much as a luxuriant growth of hair on the face, he told himself.

Once again Thanet said his piece.

Leyton shrugged. 'If we must, I suppose. But I really can't think that we'll have anything to add.'

He led them into a room to the right of the hall, a spacious L-shaped sitting room which ran the depth of the house. The patio doors were wide open and beyond them a green and white striped awning shaded a terrace furnished with swing seat and loungers cushioned in the same fabric. It all looked very civilised and inviting.

Not so the atmosphere in the room. Almost at once Thanet became aware of Mrs Leyton's antagonism towards her husband. She had immediately flopped down into one of the deep chairs and folded her arms across her chest, one swinging foot betraying her irritation. Perhaps she was angry because Leyton had not backed her up and had invited them in, or because the food she had cooked was spoiling. Though she didn't look the domestic type, Thanet thought. Her crisp, well-cut white trousers and yellow and white top wouldn't take kindly to housework.

'If you'd like to finish your lunch, we'd be quite happy to wait,' he said, testing his impression.

'No, no. We'd just about finished, hadn't we, darling?' said Leyton.

In contrast to his wife, he was wearing stained jeans and an open-necked shirt with sweat-marks under the arms.

She didn't bother to reply or even to look at him.

'If we could just get on with it, Inspector.' She spoke in a slow, maddening drawl.

Out of the corner of his eye Thanet saw Lineham tense. The sergeant was less phlegmatic than Thanet, less able to control his reactions. It would be good experience for him to conduct what was obviously going to be a tricky interview. Thanet could always bale him out, if necessary.

'My sergeant has some questions he would like to put to you.' Thanet grinned inwardly at Lineham's quickly suppressed surprise.

'Yes, well . . .' Lineham leafed through his notebook, clearly giving himself a moment or two to collect his thoughts.

Vivienne Leyton gave an exaggerated sigh and rolled her eyes.

'Perhaps we could begin by running quickly through your account of your meeting with Mrs Parnell.'

'Oh, really! But we've been through all that once. What's the point in going over it again?'

'We often find that the second time round, people remember things they didn't the first time, Mrs Leyton.'

'But we were only with the woman a matter of minutes!'

'Nevertheless . . .'

'Come on, Viv,' said Leyton. 'Why waste time prevaricating? The police have their job to do and it won't take long . . . It's all very simple, Sergeant. My wife and I arrived at the Swan at about six-thirty on Saturday evening, for a Rotary Club Ladies' Night. Guests were not due to arrive until seven, but we were early because I had helped to organise the affair, and I had one or two things to see to. Just before seven o'clock we were standing in the foyer when Alicia — Mrs Parnell — came out of the lift, put her key on the reception desk and started to walk towards the door. We'd known her well at one time, before she moved away from Sturrenden, and I recognised her at once — it was astonishing how little she had changed. I pointed her out to my wife and we moved to meet her as she came towards us. We all said hullo, how surprising to see you after all these years, how are you, what are you doing here and so on . . .'

'What did she say, when you asked her that?'

'Said she had some business to attend to.'

'Did she say what it was?'

'No, and I didn't enquire. Then we asked how long she was staying, and she said, just for the night. She told us she was going to the concert. Nicholas Rain was playing in Sturrenden that night and he was a mutual friend. We'd probably have been going ourselves, if it hadn't been for the Ladies' Night, and I said so. Then we said how nice it had been to run into each other, and that was it.'

'Didn't she say something about Mr Bassett?'

'Oh sorry, yes. She said how amazing it was that she'd only been in Sturrenden a few hours and she'd already seen three people she knew. Then she told us she'd run into Bassett in the High Street, earlier on, on her way from the station. And that he was going to the concert too. And that really was it.'

'How did she seem?'

'What do you mean?'

'What sort of a mood was she in? Depressed? Excited? Nervous?'

Leyton frowned and began to stroke his beard. 'I don't know. I hadn't thought about it. She seemed perfectly normal to me. Except that, well, perhaps I'd say she was more subdued than she used to be. But that didn't strike me as surprising. She was much older, after all. What do you think, Viv?'

Mrs Leyton shrugged, the picture of indifference. 'I didn't take much notice, I must confess. She looked older, of course, and her hair was different, she always used to wear it long.'

'Did you happen to notice what she was wearing, Mrs Leyton?'

Vivienne Leyton raised one well-plucked eyebrow. 'Naturally. Black dress, cream jacket, high-heeled black patent sandals.'

'You're very observant. Was she . . .'

'Women always notice clothes, Sergeant. If they take an interest in them themselves, of course.' And she glanced down complacently at her own, brushed an imaginary speck from one white-trousered leg.

'Did you happen to notice if she was carrying anything?'

'A black patent clutch handbag.'

'Nothing else?'

'No.'

'You're certain?'

'Sergeant, if I say she wasn't carrying anything else, she wasn't.'

This was confirmation of what the receptionist had said. So, no red folder, thought Thanet.

'If she had been, I'd certainly have noticed. Why? Should she have been?' For the first time there was a spark of curiosity in Vivienne Leyton's eyes.

Lineham was non-committal. 'We just wanted to check, that's all. You're sure there's nothing you'd like to add to what your husband has said . . .? In that case, perhaps we could move on, to later.'

'What do you mean, later?'

Had there been a hint of wariness in her voice, just then?

Alerted, Thanet studied her closely. She was, he observed, giving Lineham her full attention for the first time, behind a mask of pretended indifference. She ran a hand casually through her mop of hair, stretched out her legs and studied her scarlet toenails — but glanced covertly at her husband, apparently to gauge his reaction to Lineham's question.

'We understand that the dinner ended at ten-fifteen, and that most of the guests then left the Fletcher Hall to . . . er . . . powder their noses and so on, while the room was cleared for dancing.'

He'd have to speak to Lineham about that ridiculous euphemism, thought Thanet.

'So?'

'Is this what you did?'

'Certainly. But I really don't see . . .'

'And you, sir?'

'Yes, certainly.'

'So you split up.'

Vivienne Leyton gave a sarcastic smile. 'Brilliant deduction, Sergeant. Of course, you've noticed that the Swan does not have unisex lavatories.'

'Viv, please. There's no need . . .'

But his wife ignored him. Swinging herself up out of her chair she glared at Thanet. 'Really, Inspector, I simply cannot see the point of sitting here wasting time answering pointless questions. Besides, my husband has to get back to work and I have an appointment in Ashford at one-fifteen, so if you don't mind . . .'

What was she afraid of? Thanet wondered. 'Do sit down again, Mrs Leyton,' he said patiently. 'We realise how very irritating this must be for you, but you must understand that this is a serious business. Mrs Parnell, a former friend of yours, has been *murdered*. Now I'm quite sure that if you had been murdered, your husband would expect us to explore every possible avenue . . .'

'Aha. I see. So that's it, is it? It's her husband who's pushing you . . .'

'No one is pushing me,' said Thanet. His voice had become ominously quiet and Lineham gave him an apprehensive

103

glance. Thanet invariably treated witnesses with courtesy and his patience was legion, but press him too far and he became formidable.

'So you *say*.'

'*Viv*!'

But she was not to be deterred. 'She was wearing a wedding ring, I noticed. And a flashy engagement ring . . .'

'Mrs Leyton! Mrs Parnell's husband is dead. He was a cripple. They were in a serious accident on the way back from their honeymoon and Mrs Parnell spent the rest of her married life nursing him. Apart from an elderly father who is away on holiday and still doesn't know of his daughter's death, there is no one, no one at all, to take an interest in whether we solve this case or not. Sergeant Lineham and I are, believe it or not, merely trying to do our job, and it is our experience that most members of the public are prepared to be cooperative in making that job as easy as possible for us. So we'd be grateful if *you* would stop wasting *our* time and answer our few remaining questions as succinctly as possible.'

There was a dead silence, then Vivienne Leyton tossed her head. 'My word, what have we here? A dedicated policeman, no less . . .'

'Viv, for heaven's sake!'

'Oh, very well. I can see that you're not going to go away until you're satisfied, so let's get on with it, shall we?' And she plumped down in her chair again, her face settling into familiar lines of sulkiness and frustration.

Thanet allowed himself a moment or two to regain his composure.

'You were with a party of friends, at the dinner?'

'Aquaintances, Inspector, not friends. But yes, we were.'

'Their names and addresses, please.'

'Oh, really . . .'

'I'll write them down for you,' said Leyton, rising. He took a sheet of paper from a writing desk in the corner and began to scribble.

'And after the dinner was over, the ladies and gentlemen parted company?'

'To powder our noses, as your sergeant so delicately put it.

Yes. At least, the ladies did, I'm not sure about the men. Make-up isn't much in their line.'

Leyton shot a furious glance at his wife. 'We went to the men's room, yes, Inspector.'

'And did you both stay with the other members of your party throughout the interval?'

'I didn't,' said Leyton. 'I had to go and check on the arrangements for the raffle.'

'And that would have been at what time?'

'Around ten-twenty-five, I should think. Dancing began at ten-forty-five.'

So Leyton had been free to wander around the hotel at will, at the very time when Alicia must have arrived back from the concert. Had they run into each other a second time?

'Did you see Mrs Parnell at any point, during the interval?'

'No.'

'Did you, Mrs Leyton?'

'Absolutely not. And if you want to know what I was doing during that vital half an hour, I really can't remember.'

Her mocking, dismissive tone infuriated Thanet, but he didn't show it. He'd already once given her the satisfaction of knowing just how much her deliberate needling was annoying him, and he had no intention of allowing it to happen again.

'Try.'

She gave him a defiant look. 'I have. And I told you, I really can't remember.' She lifted one languid hand and made a vague gesture which was clearly intended to convey the haziness of her recollection. 'We'd had rather a lot to drink, at dinner. I expect I drifted around chatting to people I knew. That's what one usually does on such occasions.'

'Here you are, Inspector.' Leyton handed Thanet the sheet of paper.

There were six names on it, three married couples, by the look of it.

'Thank you . . . Well, I think that's all, for the moment.'

Vivienne Leyton sat up. 'What do you mean, "for the moment"? We've told you all we know, every last, trivial detail . . .'

Thanet was folding the paper and putting it in his wallet.

'It hasn't struck you as strange, that after being away from Sturrenden for twenty years, Alicia Parnell returns and almost at once is murdered?'

'Strange? What do you mean, strange?'

'Too much of a coincidence, perhaps?'

'What are you implying?'

She was afraid. He knew it. Behind that implacably hostile façade, she was afraid. But, of what, exactly? Was she his quarry? 'I should think, Mrs Leyton, that the implication is obvious. Someone in Sturrenden had some kind of grudge against her.'

Vivienne Leyton gave a harsh laugh. 'A grudge that's lasted twenty years? What a ridiculous idea!'

'In any case,' said her husband, 'what conceivable grudge could anyone have had against Alicia?'

'That's what I'm hoping someone will tell me. Has either of you any suggestions?'

Leyton shook his head and his wife muttered, 'Preposterous idea . . .'

'Is it, Mrs Leyton?' Thanet looked at her husband. 'I understand a lot of people blamed her for your brother's suicide.'

Leyton didn't flinch, but the edges of his eyelids twitched, almost imperceptibly. 'My brother has been dead for *twenty years*, Inspector. That's all long past, long forgotten.'

'Is it? People have long memories, you'd be surprised.'

'Who've you been talking to?' said Vivienne Leyton sharply. 'Nicky? No, he wouldn't stoop so low. Oliver, then. It must be Oliver, Oliver Bassett. Am I right?'

Thanet said nothing.

'You see, Richard,' she said, with a triumphant glance at her husband. 'He can't deny it — either that, or he hasn't got the guts to admit it, it comes to the same thing. Well, Inspector, I must say I certainly don't envy you your job, going around digging up dirt that's twenty years old.'

'Every job has its unpleasant aspects, Mrs Leyton.'

'And some more unpleasant than others, eh? Well, dig all you like, you won't find anything that rebounds on us, will he, Richard?'

'Is it really necessary, to . . . to go into all that again,

Inspector?' The skin around Leyton's eyes had gone very pale, in contrast to his deep tan.

'To be honest with you, Mr Leyton, I don't know. But you can be sure that I mean to find out. Thank you for your help. We can see ourselves out.'

Outside, Lineham said, 'My God, what a woman! Imagine . . .'

Thanet laid a hand on his arm. 'Shh . . . Listen, they're not watching, so walk across to the car, making as much noise as you can on the gravel, get in and drive off, tooting your horn at the gate, to make sure they think you've gone. Go a hundred yards or so down the lane, then find a convenient place to park. I'll be with you as soon as I can.'

'What are you going to do?'

Thanet shook his head impatiently. 'Tell you later. Just do as I say, will you?'

ELEVEN

While Lineham crunched across the drive Thanet moved quietly along the paved path which ran along the front of the house, conscious of the pungent scent of rosemary as his legs brushed the low bushes on his right. At the corner he waited while the sergeant got into the car, then used the crackle of tyres on gravel to cover the sound of his movement along the side of the house as far as the open patio doors.

As he had guessed, Richard and Vivienne Leyton were in the middle of a full-scale row. He didn't like what he was doing, disapproved of eavesdropping, and would consciously have gone out of his way to make his presence felt if he had found himself in this sort of situation in his private life. But this was murder, the most heinous crime in the book, and he was certain that Vivienne Leyton had been covering something up. This way, he might find out what it was. He prayed that no one would spot him, and quickly thought up a specious question to ask, if he were discovered.

'. . . don't care what you say, if you hadn't insisted on going to talk to the bloody woman in the first place, none of this would be happening.'

'Oh come on, Viv, be reasonable. I just thought it would be nice to say hullo to her. I didn't think . . .'

'Oh God, you're so naive . . . No, you never do think, do you, that's half your trouble. Jump in first and regret it afterwards, that's you all over. I told you at the time I'd rather not have anything to do with her, but oh no, you have to have your own way . . .'

'You didn't protest that much, as I remember.'

'Well of course I bloody didn't! What d'you expect me to do, make a scene in the middle of the foyer? But I told you I didn't want to talk to her, and that should have been enough.'

'Oh it should, should it? And don't I get any say in the

matter? What about what I want? I admit that as it's turned out, it would have been better if we hadn't spoken to her, but how was I to know that she would get herself murdered later on the same night?'

'Oh, so you do admit that you might just have been wrong?'

'For wanting to say hullo to an old friend? No, why should I?'

'Despite the fact that she just happened to be the "friend" who drove your own brother to his death?'

'Ah, now we're getting to the heart of it, aren't we? That's the point, isn't it? You've never forgiven her for what she did to your precious Paul.'

'My precious Paul! Well, I like that! He was your brother, too, remember. I shouldn't have thought you'd exactly be eager to get down on your knees and thank her . . . Or perhaps that's it. Perhaps you *were* grateful to her, have been grateful to her all these years. Yes, I'd never thought of it quite like that before, but I see, now . . . You'd never be where you are today, would you, if Paul had still been alive? After all, he was the eldest son . . . You wouldn't now be expecting to inherit your father's farm, would you, if Paul were still with us, he'd either have got the lot or you'd have been forced to sell up to give him his share . . .'

'For God's sake, Viv, Paul wasn't interested in farming, and you know it. All he cared about was his work . . .'

'Your parents wouldn't have been able to afford to build this house for us, either, would they, if they'd had to see Paul through Oxford. . . . And one thing's for sure, you wouldn't have got me, either.'

Leyton murmured something inaudible.

'What did you say? Go on, say it aloud, like a man.'

'I said, perhaps you weren't much of a bargain, after all.'

'Oh, so the worm's turning at last, is he? Well, let me tell you this, you're not half the man your brother was, you never have been and you never will be. You don't measure up to him in any way, in brains, in looks . . .'

'And in bed?'

Leyton's voice was very quiet and Thanet had to strain to hear him. Was this a scene which had been enacted many times before between these two, over the years? What a soul-destroying way to live, he thought.

'Unfortunately I never had that pleasure, as well you know. Alicia,' and she spat the name out, 'got there first.'

'Are you sure of that?'

'What do you mean?'

'Do you *know*, are you absolutely certain, that Alicia went to bed with Paul?'

'Not *know*.' For the first time Vivienne Leyton sounded unsure of herself. 'I just assumed . . .'

'Ah, I thought so.'

'What's that supposed to mean?'

Silence.

'What do you mean, "I thought so"?'

Still no response from her husband.

'Richard, you can't just stop there. You can't drop mysterious hints and then just back off, refuse to speak. What did you mean? What were you implying?'

'It doesn't matter.' Leyton's voice was scarcely more than a murmur.

Vivienne Leyton gave a little moan of exasperation. ' "It doesn't matter", he says. You make me mad!' she went on in a low, furious voice. 'You make me so mad I feel as though I'm going to explode with sheer frustration. You're always doing this, winding me up and then pulling out . . . I suppose you just haven't got the guts to see it through. You're pathetic, do you know that, pathetic . . .'

Her voice had been rising and now Leyton had to shout to make himself heard. 'All right! I'll tell you!'

There was a sudden silence in which Leyton's last words seemed to echo, and it was only now that Thanet became aware of their complex tone. There was desperation in them, mingled with despair and yes, too, a hint of satisfaction. Whatever else had been said during this conversation, this, at least, was going to be news to Vivienne Leyton. And she wasn't going to like it one little bit.

'You blame Alicia for Paul's death, don't you, Viv? You always have.'

'Yes. Well, everybody did. The inquest . . .'

Leyton laughed, an unpleasant sound. 'The inquest. Ah, yes. But you see, my dear Vivienne, the fact of the matter is that the whole truth did not come out at the inquest.'

'What do you mean?' She was beginning to sound alarmed. 'And how do you know?'

'I know because I was the one who withheld the information.'

She was silenced at last.

'Shall I tell you what that information was, my darling? Very well, I will. Yes, I can see you want to hear. You do, don't you? *Don't you?*'

'Yes! Yes, of course I do.'

'Of course she does!' mocked Leyton.

He was certainly enjoying the prospect of this revenge, whatever it was, thought Thanet. And by now he had an inkling of what was coming.

'Very well, I'll tell you . . . my dear brother Paul didn't kill himself because Alicia had broken off with him. He killed himself because that very night he had discovered that it was *men* he was attracted to.'

Dead silence.

Then Vivienne Leyton made a little choking sound. 'I don't believe you.' The words were almost a whisper. 'You . . . you're making it up.'

'I am not.'

'Yes you *are*!' She had found her voice again and almost shrieked her distress and disbelief. 'You're lying. You're just trying to . . . to besmirch Paul's memory, that's all. You've always resented the fact that he was cleverer than you, more popular than you . . . and that I loved him, I've always loved him.'

'Maybe that's true. Maybe I have always resented those things, as you say. But, my dear wife, I am not lying about this. I actually saw them in bed together, him and Oliver Bassett.'

'No!'

'Yes. Come on, take your hands away from your ears. All these years I've had to listen to you telling me how inferior I am to Paul, now you listen to me for a change . . .'

'No . . . it's not true . . . I don't believe you. . . . Let go of my hands, let *go* . . . you're hurting me!'

Thanet braced himself. He didn't want to intervene, had no real right, even, to interfere in a row between man and wife in their own home. But he couldn't just stand by while violence was done only a few feet away . . .

'Sit down,' shouted Leyton. 'Go on, sit *down*. . . . Right, now whether you like it or not, you're just going to sit there and listen until I've finished what I've got to say. And it's in your own interests to hear it. After all, if you don't, you'll never know whether I was telling the truth or not, will you? You can judge for yourself. That's better . . .'

Thanet relaxed a little. It sounded as though the threatened flash-point had been averted, for the moment at least.

'Well now, if you remember, after leaving Alicia that night, Paul ran into Oliver, and Oliver gave him a lift home. Now, according to what Oliver said at the inquest, when they arrived at our house, Paul asked him in for a cup of coffee. Do you remember all this?'

Vivienne Leyton must have nodded.

'Then you probably also remember that I said I'd got home about ten-fifteen that night, that my parents were out and I went straight up to bed. The light was out in Paul's room, I said, the door was closed and I thought he must still be out with Alicia. So I never looked in. Agreed?'

Again, he must have waited for her nod.

'Well, now I'll tell you what really happened. . . . It was nearer a quarter to ten than a quarter past when I got home. I'd seen Oliver's car outside, of course, so I knew he was there, but when I got in there was no sign of either him or Paul. But I could hear music, upstairs, and I thought they must be playing records in Paul's bedroom. So I went up. Paul's door was shut, but the light was on, so I looked in. And I saw them . . . No, just listen. You *will* listen. I *saw* them, I tell you, with my own eyes. On the bed. And there was no mistaking what they were doing . . .'

'No!' shrieked Vivienne Leyton. 'I don't believe you. You're making it all up. You're jealous of Paul, you've always been jealous . . .'

'Maybe I have,' shouted Leyton, 'but this is the *truth* I'm telling you. Every word is the truth, I swear it. And Paul saw me. I . . . I didn't wait, I just backed out, quickly, and shut the door behind me. I couldn't believe it. I was shocked, disgusted, upset . . .'

'Upset!'

'Yes, upset! Of course I was bloody upset! I was only seventeen and he was my *brother* . . . I went into my room and locked the door. A little while later I heard Oliver leave. My parents still weren't home, and a few minutes later Paul came and knocked at my door. I didn't answer. He had to talk to me, he said. What I'd seen . . . it had never happened before and it wouldn't happen again . . . I just couldn't bring myself to let him in, face him. I couldn't get that picture of him and Oliver on the bed out of my mind . . . I buried my head in the pillow and in the end he gave up, went away.'

'So it was your fault! Your fault, that he killed himself! I expect he thought you'd go sneaking to your parents in the morning . . .'

'Rubbish. I'd never have done that, and he knew it.'

'He thought he wouldn't be able to face you, then . . .'

'You didn't really know Paul very well, did you, Viv? If you had, you'd know that that wouldn't be what was worrying him. It was himself he couldn't face.'

'Anyway, I don't believe a word of all this. It's nonsense, it's rubbish, you're making it all up, out of spite . . .'

'You can believe it or not, as you like. But it's the truth. And what's more, inside, I bet you know it. You know me. Faults I may have, like anyone else, but spiteful I am not. And what possible other reason could I have, for making up a story like this?'

'Perhaps you thought that if you managed to destroy Paul in my eyes, I might forget about him, and turn to you . . .'

'Oh, Viv,' and there was a profound sadness in Leyton's voice, 'do you think I could ever really hope for that? You've made it pretty obvious, over the years, what you think of me . . .'

'All right, then, just tell me this. If all this is true — and I'm only saying "if", mind — why haven't you come out with it before? Why wait till now?'

113

'What was the point of telling you? I certainly had no intention of letting it out at the inquest. The row with Alicia was evidence enough for them . . . I had to think of my parents, too. Imagine how upset they would have been, if it had been made public. And then, later . . . well, as I say, there didn't seem to be any point. I felt a loyalty to Paul . . . Oh, there's no need to look at me like that, I did, I tell you. And he wasn't here, to defend himself . . . I don't suppose I would ever have told you, if it hadn't been for this Alicia business, resurrecting it all. Viv, don't look at me like that. . . . Don't cry. Don't. I'm sorry. I suppose I shouldn't have told you, even now. It's just that I was sick and tired of you holding him up as some sort of model of perfection . . . Viv, please . . .'

'Leave me alone.' She was crying openly now, noisy, tearing sobs. 'Get away from me, don't touch me . . .'

There was a flurry of movement, a door slammed, and then silence.

Thanet moved quietly away from the patio doors, ran across the lawn to the front gate and hurried down the lane to the car, where Lineham was waiting.

Lineham opened the door for him, from inside. 'What was all that about?'

'I could tell a row was brewing, and I knew Mrs Leyton was holding something back. I thought I might find out what it was.'

'And did you?'

'No. She was deflected.' And Thanet told Lineham what he had heard.

Lineham pursed his lips. 'So we were right about Bassett.'

'So it seems.'

'If Leyton was telling the truth. D'you think he was?'

'Yes. It all hangs together, makes sense. And if you could have heard him . . . Oh yes, he was telling the truth, all right. Twenty years ago homosexuality was a very different matter from nowadays. Shrouded in shame and secrecy.'

'I don't know that things have changed all that much, actually. I often think that despite all the noise the "gay" groups make, ordinary people still feel pretty much the same about it.'

'In a small town like this, anyway, yes, I tend to agree. It certainly wouldn't have done Bassett any good, if the truth had come out.'

'Anyhow, it seems that Mrs Parnell didn't come down just to go to the concert. What do you think she meant, by "business to attend to", sir?'

'Your guess is as good as mine. It's a deliberately vague expression, isn't it? One thing's certain, though. There was a good deal of pretty strong emotion floating about in that group of youngsters, and a lot of it is still about today. We should never underestimate the power of the past, Mike. If you'd heard those two going at each other, you'd never have believed they were talking about something that happened all those years ago.'

'But they're different from the others, sir, in that they're married. They'll have had twenty years of other arguments — pretty unhappy years, by the sound of it — to fuel a row like the one you just heard.'

'True. Nevertheless I wouldn't mind betting that this particular issue — Vivienne Leyton's idolisation of Paul — is the one that has underlain all those other disagreements over the years.'

'Well, if she still feels as strongly as that, we certainly shouldn't rule her out as a suspect, strangling or no strangling.'

'I agree.'

'Though if what Richard Leyton says about the night of Paul's suicide is true. I'm not sure it doesn't rule Bassett out.'

'I don't follow you, Mike.'

'Well surely, in the circumstances he'd be blaming himself, more than Alicia Parnell . . .'

'I don't see why. Richard Leyton didn't say that Bassett had seen him, when he put his head into Paul's bedroom, that night. Bassett may well have known nothing about it. He may still simply think that his attempt at "consolation" failed.'

Lineham's bleeper sounded. 'Wonder what that's about.'

They drove back to the village and Thanet waited in the car while Lineham phoned. The sergeant made two calls, and was frowning when he emerged from the phone box. He had left the receiver off the hook, Thanet noticed.

'What is it, Mike?'

'It's Louise. Apparently she saw a house she really fell in love with, this morning. It's just what we're looking for, she said, and I must say it sounds almost too good to be true — right type, right size, good position, fair price . . .'

'The one in Frittenden Road you were telling me about on Sunday?'

'No. That was hopeless. We only got the details of this one this morning.'

'So what's the problem?'

'Someone else was shown over it before Louise and they're coming back this afternoon — it's not an agent's ploy, she actually saw the woman and heard her say she'd like her husband to see it. She's afraid they might get in first, with an offer.'

'So she wants you to take a look at it?'

Lineham nodded sheepishly. 'I'm sorry, sir, I told her I didn't think I could get off, but she insisted I ask you . . .'

'Where is it?'

'In Market Cut.'

'That little cul-de-sac off Market Street?'

'That's right.'

'Very nice, too. Well, there's no difficulty there. We haven't had anything to eat yet, so if you want to go hungry and spend your lunch hour looking at houses . . . Tell her you'll be there in ten minutes.'

'Thank you, sir.' Lineham ran back to the phone box and returned beaming.

'If you like the place as much as she does, you can get it all sorted out on the spot. I'll drive, then I can drop you off and you can walk back to the office afterwards.'

The Market Square in Sturrenden lies at the lower end of the town, just before the river bridge, a broad, cobbled area which is really an extension of the High Street. Market Street leads off it at right angles, following the curve of the river and eventually leading out into open country. The houses here are very old, many of them falling into disrepair, and it has been rumoured that one day in the not too distant future they will all be pulled down to make way for a new leisure complex. Thanet hoped that that day would never come. He loved the picturesque juxtaposition of lathe and plaster, ancient beams, mellow stone and rosy brick, the irregular peaks and slopes of the roofs of old red Kentish peg tiles, the encapsulated history of Sturrenden which these houses still preserve for the seeing eye to read.

Market Cut was once, as its name implies, a link between two streets, but when the inevitable one-way system was introduced into Sturrenden some years ago, one end was blocked off with bollards to prevent traffic siphoning off into the chaos that is Market Street on market days, and it is now a pleasant little cul-de-sac of a dozen Victorian semi-detached houses facing each other demurely across wide pavements planted with cherry trees which are a froth of pink blossom in the spring. The situation is ideal, within walking distance of the High Street and the river, yet tranquil, undisturbed by the noise of passing traffic.

Thanet said so.

'Handy for work, too,' said Lineham with a grin.

The For Sale notice was half-way along on the left-hand side and Louise was waiting outside with the estate agent, her sturdy figure in its bright cotton sundress a splash of vivid colour in the shade cast by one of the cherry trees. She ran to the car as they pulled up, and spoke through the open window. 'Oh, Mike, I'm so glad you could come. You'll love it, I know you will. It's exactly what we've been looking for.'

Her cheeks were flushed with excitement, her eyes shining.

Thanet was surprised that she should betray her enthusiasm to the man waiting at the gate. Louise was normally cautious, sensible, restrained. But then, if there really were other prospective purchasers in the offing, she and Mike would probably have to offer the full price anyway. And it was good to see her so animated. She was smiling at Thanet, now.

'It's kind of you to spare him.'

Thanet smiled back. 'It's his lunch hour. I told him, if he wants to starve, that's his affair. See you back at the office, then, Mike.'

'Right, sir.'

Bentley pounced on Thanet the moment he stepped through the door.

'There's a girl waiting to see you, sir. Been here for an hour or so. A Miss Carol Marsh.'

Carol . . . The girl from Jobline? The one Jessica Ross didn't approve of? 'What's it about, do you know?'

'She wouldn't say. She works in Mrs Parnell's employment agency.'

She must have come down from London especially to see him. Excitement flared. She wouldn't have bothered, if it hadn't been important.

'Where is she?'

'In interview room three, sir.'

'Tell her I'll be with her in a quarter of an hour. I just want to see what's on my desk. Offer her something to eat, and a cup of tea. Oh, and see if you can get Doc Mallard on the phone for me, will you? The PM should be finished by now.' Not that he expected anything very startling there, but you never knew.

He took the stairs two at a time. The phone was ringing in his office. He snatched it up.

'Luke? Mallard here.'

'That was quick.'

'Don't know what you mean. It took the usual length of time.'

'Not the PM. Finding you.'

'Finding me? What are you talking about?'

'I asked . . . Oh, never mind. Anything interesting?'

'You could say that.'

'Oh?'

'Cause of death was asphyxia, of course, as we thought. Manual strangulation. The hyoid was broken.'

'And?'

'This is the interesting bit.'

Thanet listened intently and when he had put the phone down, sat for a few moments staring into space.

He wondered what Lineham would make of this.

TWELVE

Perched on one of the metal chairs in the grey anonymity of the interview room, heels hooked over the lower rung and shoulders hunched, Carol Marsh looked like a dejected budgerigar. The spikes of her orange-dyed hair were limp at the tips as if fierce emotion had melted the wax with which she had stiffened them, and copious tears had streaked her cheeks with mascara. Her skimpy mini-dress, boldly striped in green and yellow, emphasised her skinny body, sharp elbows and stick-like legs. She looked up as Thanet entered and slowly her red-veined eyes focused on his face.

He smiled at her. 'Miss Marsh?'

She gave an almost imperceptible nod.

'I believe you wanted to see me. Detective-Inspector Thanet.'

'You're in charge of the . . . you're investigating the . . .' But she couldn't bring herself to say it. More tears welled up, spilled over and began to roll down her cheeks. She dabbed at them with a sodden, balled-up handkerchief, shook her head hopelessly and said, 'I'm sorry, I just can't seem to stop.'

'That's all right. Don't worry about it. I quite understand.'

Thanet turned to the Woman Police Constable standing patiently near the door and said in an undertone, 'Fetch a box of tissues, will you?'

He waited in silence until she returned. Carol Marsh took the box with an attempt at a smile. 'Ta.' She pushed her wet handkerchief into her white plastic shoulder bag.

When she had mopped at her eyes and blown her nose Thanet said, 'I'm in charge of the enquiries into the death of Mrs Parnell, if that's what you wanted to know.'

'Yes,' she said gratefully. She was looking a little more composed now. 'Sorry to be so stupid.'

'I told you. Don't worry.'

'I've been off sick, so I didn't hear about it till this morning.' She shook her head. 'I just couldn't believe it.' The tears threatened again and she straightened her shoulders, drew a deep breath.

'You were obviously very fond of Mrs Parnell.'

'She was . . .' Carol took another deep breath, tried again. 'Yes, I was. She was very good to me.'

'In what way?'

The thin shoulders lifted, fell. 'All sorts of ways. This was the first job I ever really wanted to make a go of, you see, and I was scared stiff of making a mess of it.'

'How long have you worked at the agency?'

'Just over a year, now.' She was beginning to relax and she gave an incredulous little laugh. 'Can you believe it? A year! Who'd ever have thought I'd have stuck at any job that long! Not me, that's for sure. Do you know, before I went there, I'd had twenty different jobs in six months?'

'You're saying that it was because of Mrs Parnell that you stayed?'

She scowled. 'Well it certainly wasn't because of Miss High-and-Mighty Ross, that's for sure. But Mrs Parnell . . . Right from the very first day she was really good to me. Started off by saying not to worry if I made mistakes at first, it was pefectly natural in a new job, everyone did, and she was sure I'd soon get the hang of things . . . Catch Miss Ross saying something like that! I won't be staying on there now, that's for sure. I don't think I could stand it.'

'Why not?'

'She's always breathing down our necks, checking up on what we're doing. And it makes me nervous, so I keep making mistakes. And if I do . . . oh boy, the fuss she makes . . . I should think they could hear her at the other end of the Fulham Road. But Mrs Parnell . . . Oh God, here we go again,' she said, as the tears suddenly spilled over once more. She shook her head hopelessly. 'I just can't seem to stop,' she said again.

It occurred to Thanet that this strange little waif-like creature was the first person he had met who could truly be said to mourn Alicia's death. He waited until she had calmed down, then said, 'Do you feel able, now, to tell me why you've come?'

She nodded. 'When I heard about Mrs Parnell . . . and saw *her* lording it over everything . . . I felt I just had to tell someone.' She blew her nose and sat up straighter in her chair. 'About the rows, I mean.' There was defiance in her voice, as if Jessica Ross were present and still exercising authority over her.

'Between Mrs Parnell and Miss Ross?'

'Yes. Old cow,' she muttered. 'She's got no . . . no . . .' She sought for the word and found it, triumphantly. 'No *humanity*, that's what. She knew how Mrs Parnell had felt about Mr Parnell. He was terrific. You knew he was in a wheelchair, had been for years?'

She waited for Thanet's nod before continuing. 'Not that you'd ever hear him complain, mind. Mrs Parnell did everything for him, you know. It was really lovely to see them together, you could tell just by looking at them how fond of each other they were.'

Her eyes were dreamy now and Thanet could see how deeply she had been touched by the Parnells' devotion. He found himself wondering what kind of background this girl had come from. A tough one, probably, possibly a broken home or at any rate one where love and tenderness were totally lacking. Which was perhaps why she needed to shout her identity with that hideous hair-style, those shrieking colours . . . He refocused his attention on what she was saying.

'. . . so upset, when he died.'

'This was about six months ago, wasn't it?'

'In February, yes. I'd seen the difference in him myself, since I first started at Jobline. He was ill more and more often and then, towards the end of January, he got this chest infection he just couldn't shake off. In the end it turned to pneumonia and he had to go into hospital. He died two days later. Mrs Parnell was that upset . . . She more or less lived at the hospital, while he was in, and then afterwards she just shut herself away in her flat, didn't want to see anyone. I put a note through the door, saying if she wanted me to do anything, anything at all, she only had to ask — shopping, cleaning, anything, but she just wrote me a few lines back saying she preferred to be by herself for the moment, she had to get used to living alone and she might as well start now. And that Miss Ross . . . well, you could see she enjoyed being in charge, bossing us around and throwing her weight about. . . . Of course, when Mrs Parnell came back to work Miss Ross didn't dare carry on like that, and it used to make me mad, it really did, to see how different she was with her, all smarmy and helpful, when behind her back . . . I really can't think why Mrs Parnell made her a partner. I should think it was the worst thing she ever did.'

'Maybe she was grateful to Miss Ross for taking the weight of the business off her shoulders, while she was unable to cope.'

Carol shrugged. 'I dunno. It's beyond me. Anyway, Faith and me weren't suprised when, once Miss Ross had got what she wanted, got that partnership, she started acting different towards us in front of Mrs Parnell — oh, only in little ways at first. But Mrs Parnell noticed. Sometimes I'd see her look at Miss Ross in a funny way, as if she didn't quite recognise her. And then, of course, Mrs Parnell started slipping up herself — only in small things, mind, and anyway it wasn't surprising, was it, after what she'd been through?'

'It takes a long time to get over the death of someone you love, especially if you've been as close as Mr and Mrs Parnell obviously were.'

'Just what I said to Faith! But do you think Miss Ross understood that? You bet she didn't! I don't suppose that woman has ever loved anyone but herself in her whole life. I mean, you couldn't really expect Mrs Parnell to be able to concentrate on her work as if nothing had happened, could you? But Miss Ross did. And of course, it made her mad when Mrs Parnell made mistakes and even more mad because she didn't dare show it. She used to take it out on us instead. But things weren't too bad until Mrs Parnell began leaving the office without telling Miss Ross. And then . . . Well, you can imagine, can't you? Talk about thunderstorms! Miss Ross used to carry on like crazy, banging about the office and muttering to herself about irresponsibility and so on. Faith and me hardly dared breathe, let alone open our mouths. As I said to Faith, who could blame Mrs Parnell for wanting to get out of the place from time to time? And if she didn't choose to give explanations, why should she? She was the boss, after all.'

'Do you happen to know where Mrs Parnell went, on those occasions?'

Carol shook her head. 'No idea. It wasn't my business and as far as I was concerned she could go off as much as she liked. If it meant extra work for the rest of us, that was just too bad. And Faith felt the same . . . Anyway, as I say, the atmosphere got worse and worse. And then, for no reason that we could see, Miss Ross suddenly started being all sweetness and light again.'

'When was this?'

'About a month ago. Faith and me couldn't believe it. Before then, if Mrs Parnell had gone out without telling her, Miss Ross would have been giving her black looks for the rest of the day, and you could have cut the atmosphere with a knife. And then, as I say, suddenly, no complaints, nothing was too much trouble . . . We wondered what she was up to, I can tell you.'

'You thought she had an ulterior motive?'

'That woman wouldn't be nice to her own grandmother unless she was hoping to get something out of her. And then, last week, I found out what was behind it all.'

Carol sat forward on her chair, lowered her voice, as if Jessica Ross were listening outside the door. 'It was on Wednesday, late in the afternoon. Faith and me had both finished work for the day, and left. I'd only gone a few yards down the road when I realised I'd left behind the book I'd bought in my lunch hour. I'd put it in the drawer of my desk. Well I'd been looking forward to starting it that evening — it was the new Danielle Steel, she's my favourite author — so I went back for it. The office wasn't locked up yet, so I just walked in, and I heard them arguing straight away — well, I heard Miss Ross, that is. The door of the inner office was ajar and the outer office is carpeted, so they didn't hear me.'

She paused dramatically and then said, 'They were arguing about the will.'

'Mrs Parnell's will?'

Carol nodded solemnly. Her eyes, Thanet noticed, were beautiful, a clear green flecked with gold.

'Don't you *see*?' she said impatiently.

Thanet saw several things. He saw the implication of what she was saying, but he also saw that Carol was deeply distressed by Alicia's death and anxious to see her murderer brought to justice. He saw too that she was very anti-Ross and that her feelings might have caused her to jump to a conclusion which had little foundation in fact.

'I think I'd like to hear more, first, before I can say that I "see" anything.'

She shrugged. 'Fair enough.'

She leaned back in her chair, hooking one bony knee over the other and smoothing the cheap cotton material over her thighs. Now that she had overcome her initial distress her natural ebullience was reasserting itself, and despite the gaudy colours Thanet thought that if he had met her now he would have likened her to a pert little Cockney sparrow rather than a budgerigar. There was something very engaging about her, something which aroused both his sympathy and his admiration and at the same time made him feel curiously protective towards her. He could understand why she had quickened Alicia's maternal instinct.

'Well, as I said, they were talking about Mrs Parnell's will. Miss Ross was saying that she thought they ought to . . . how did she put it? Now let me get this right . . . She thought they ought to regularise the position, that's it. By which she meant, make a will in each other's favour.'

'She actually said so?'

'Yes.'

'You're certain of this?'

'Course I am. Oh, I see. I know what you're thinking. You think I'm making it all up, because I can't stand Miss Ross.'

'I didn't say that . . .'

'You didn't have to, did you? Well you're wrong, see. I'll tell you exactly what they said, and you can make up your own mind. Like I said, Miss Ross was talking. And what she said, *her very words*, was, "I think the only satisfactory thing to do would be for both of us to leave our share to the other. Then we'd both be secure." '

Carol had caught the imperious, overbearing tones of Jessica Ross's voice exactly, and Thanet had to suppress a smile.

'And what did Mrs Parnell have to say to that?'

'She said — and I'd never heard her sound so cross before — "I would remind you, Jessica, that Kenneth and I spent many years building this business up. You and I are not equal partners and I'm really beginning to wonder if I've made a serious mistake, in offering you any kind of partnership at all." Then Miss Ross tried to say something and Mrs Parnell said, "No, Jessica, *you* listen to *me*. I shall make my will when I'm ready to do so, and not before. But I can assure you of this. When I do, you will not be a beneficiary. I have my own family to think of." And Miss Ross burst out, "But your father's *old*. He's in his seventies. What if he . . ." And Mrs Parnell said, "I'm not referring to my father. And now, if you don't mind, I've had just about enough of this . . ." Well, I didn't wait to hear any more. I just grabbed my book and left.'

'Yes. Yes, I see.'

'Well, what d'you think? You see what I mean?'

'I do, of course. And I'm grateful to you for taking the trouble to come all the way down here and tell me about it.'

'Yeah, well, it was the least I could do, wasn't it? For her, I mean.' Carol stood up and put the box of tissues on the table.

'There's just one other thing . . .'

'What?' Carol tilted her head and looked at him expectantly.

'Mrs Parnell. Did she have any friends that you know of, outside the agency?'

The orange spikes swung from side to side as she shook her head vigorously. 'Didn't have time to make any, did she? Looking after Mr Parnell was a full-time job.' Without warning the tears brimmed over again. 'She didn't *deserve* to die like that.'

THIRTEEN

Lineham was just coming in as Thanet left the interview room.

'Well, how was the house?'

'Terrific! Exactly what we've been looking for. I can't believe we've actually found it. I was beginning to believe it didn't exist.'

'You've made an offer?'

'Yes, a written one. We're taking no chances. Subject to survey and contract, of course.'

'Good. Excellent.'

Lineham enthused over the house as they walked upstairs. 'Anything interesting been happening here?'

Thanet grinned. 'You could say that. I had a visitor. From London.' And he told Lineham Carol Marsh's story.

'You think she was telling the truth, sir?'

'Yes, I do.' Thanet gave a reminiscent smile. 'She was an excellent mimic.'

The office smelt stale, stuffy with stored-up heat. 'Open the window, will you, Mike?'

Lineham struggled with the sash window, eventually managing to lower the upper section two or three inches. 'That's the best I can do, I'm afraid, sir.'

'One of these days they'll come in here and find we've collapsed for lack of oxygen . . . Open the door for a while, instead.'

'What d'you think Mrs Parnell meant by "I have my own family to think of"? And, "I'm not referring to my father"? Who else was there for her to leave it to?'

'Ah, now this is where things get interesting, Mike. I had a word with Doc Mallard just before I saw Carol Marsh.'

'About the PM?'

'Yes.'

'And?'

Thanet said nothing, simply raised his eyebrows and waited for Lineham to make the connection.

'Mrs Parnell had had a child!' said Lineham.

'Full marks, Mike. She had.'

'So that's who she was referring to.'

'Seems highly likely, don't you think?'

'It couldn't have been her husband's or we'd have come across some reference to it before now, so she must have had it before they were married, and had it adopted. So it must be — what? — at least thirteen by now, possibly much older.'

'Quite. So we now have to find the answers to three questions — when did she have the baby, who was the father and what is the child's new identity?' Thanet sat down at his desk, took out his pipe and started to fill it. 'I was thinking, Mike, everyone has always assumed that Alicia and her family moved away from Sturrenden because of Paul Leyton's suicide. But suppose that's not true.' He lit up, waited until he was satisfied that the pipe was drawing well. 'Suppose they really moved because she had discovered she was pregnant. Now, according to Bassett, Alicia was still going around with Nicholas Rain until the end of April of that year. And on June 4th she broke off with Paul Leyton. I was thinking . . . suppose that the real reason for her breaking off with him then was because she had just discovered she was pregnant?'

'Could be. That would explain why her timing was so bad. I mean, everyone said they couldn't understand why she didn't wait until after his exams were over. Maybe she felt she just couldn't continue to go out with him if she was already pregnant by someone else.'

'And she would have been worried stiff, of course.'

'Quite. There couldn't have been any question of a legal abortion, the new act didn't come in until 1967.'

'Not only that. You're forgetting something, Mike. She was a Catholic.'

'Of course . . . abortion would have been out of the question anyway. And you're suggesting Rain was the father?'

'It's certainly a possibility, wouldn't you agree?'

'But only one. After all, we're simply speculating about the

Doyles' reason for leaving Sturrenden. It could genuinely have been because they couldn't face all the talk after Paul Leyton's death, or because Mr Doyle had got another job. In which case she might have become pregnant long after she left Sturrenden — it was another seven years before she got married.'

'True. Or she might not have known she was pregnant when they moved, and Paul Leyton was the father, despite what his brother says about him being a homosexual. Though . . .' Thanet abruptly stopped talking and his eyes glazed.

Lineham had seen that look before. 'Sir?' he said, on a note of excitement.

'It's just ocurred to me, Mike. If — and I know it's only "if" — the pregnancy was confirmed at the beginning of June 1964, and if we assume that Alicia was then around eight weeks pregnant, then the baby would have been born the following January, January 1965, and would now, by my calculations, be twenty years old.'

'So?'

'Think, Mike, think.'

'I *am* think . . .' Lineham broke off as he suddenly realised what Thanet was getting at. There was a moment's stunned silence and then, 'Penny Rain . . .' he breathed.

Thanet nodded slowly. 'Penny Rain.'

The two men stared at each other, considering the implications.

'She's the right age,' said Lineham at last. 'I distinctly remember Doc Mallard saying she's twenty.'

'So do I. I wonder if he knows exactly when she was adopted.' Thanet was already reaching for the telephone. 'Get Doc Mallard for me, will you?' He replaced the receiver. 'The baby wouldn't have been put out for adoption until it was at least six weeks old, so if it was born in January the chances are that it would first have gone to the adoptive parents some time in late February or early March.'

'Do you think it would have been arranged privately, or done through conventional channels, via an adoption agency?'

Thanet shook his head. 'Not through an agency. They rate anonymity very highly and I should think they'd consider this kind of arrangement to be fraught with future complications. No, if the Rains did adopt Alicia's baby, I would think it much more likely that the whole thing was quietly set up by the two families.'

'But surely people like the Rains wouldn't have entered into an illegal arrangement like that?'

'You know as well as I do that when people are desperate they don't act rationally. And there would have been a lot of desperation involved here.'

The phone rang.

'Mallard here. You wanted a word?'

'Yes. You know you told me Alicia Parnell had had a child at some point? Well we've just come up with a rather interesting idea.' Briefly, Thanet explained.

When he had finished there was dead silence at the other end of the line. 'Are you still there, Doc?'

'Yes, of course I'm here,' snapped Mallard. 'I'm just trying to make up my mind if there could possibly be any truth in what you're saying.'

Thanet took the hint and waited.

Eventually, 'My immediate reaction is to say "Stuff and nonsense".'

'But?'

'I told you. I'm thinking about it. You do want a *considered* opinion, I suppose?'

Mallard had known the Rain family well and Thanet was interested to know what he thought. 'Of course.'

There was another, longer silence.

'Well,' said Mallard reluctantly, at last, 'I suppose it's *possible,* all things considered. But it would have had to be a private arrangement, you realise that. No adoption agency would have touched it.'

'Yes, I know.'

'Anyway, I don't flatter myself that you just wanted my opinion . . . . What else did you want to ask me?'

'Well, in view of the fact that Alicia was not obviously pregnant when the Doyles moved away in the summer, we worked out that if Nicholas Rain was the father, the baby would probably have been conceived towards the end of her association with him, say between the middle and end of April 1964. In which case it would probably have been born some time in January 1965 and would have been ready for adoption around the end of February or early March. We were wondering if you can remember exactly when Penny arrived in the Rain household.'

'I can do better than that. I can tell you when Penny's birthday is — not the precise date, but within a few days. And I must admit it supports your theory. I only know because I ran into her and her mother on the train back from London one day. I'd been up to a meeting and they'd been shopping for a coat for Penny's birthday, in the January sales. She was joking about it, saying that she hated having a birthday only three weeks after Christmas, that the only advantage she'd ever discovered was that she could often find a really nice advance birthday present in the sales, something her mother would not normally be able to afford.'

'So, mid-January, then.' The excitement which Thanet had deliberately been holding in check now pricked at his scalp, raised gooseflesh on his arms. *Careful,* he told himself. *Don't get carried away.*

'And you did say she was twenty, didn't you?'

'I did . . . . I suppose if you're right about all this, it would explain a lot.'

'Such as?'

'Well, I was saying to you the other day how well Penny fits into the family. There's a really close bond . . . she even looks like her adoptive mother — same build, same colouring . . . . But if Mrs Rain is really her grandmother . . . I always thought the resemblance was just a happy accident.'

'Which it might well still be, of course. At the moment this is all pure speculation.'

'Still . . . Let me know how you get on, would you?'

'Of course.'

Thanet thanked him and rang off. Then he told Lineham what Mallard had said.

'So Penny Rain really could be Nicholas Rain's daughter, not his sister.'

'*Could* be, Mike, remember that.'

'But if she was . . . . You could just see how it might have come about, couldn't you, sir? If you think about it, it would be the natural outcome of the whole situation. Alicia would be free to start a new life unencumbered by an illegitimate child, and both she and the Doyles would know that the baby would be brought up in a secure, happy home by people who were actually blood relations and would have her welfare at heart.'

'Also, of course, the Rains were Catholics, like the Doyles. I imagine that would have been an important point in their favour.'

'And from the Rains' point of view, it must have seemed the perfect answer. Mrs Rain couldn't have any more children, but this way she'd get a granddaughter instead of the daughter she'd always longed for, and no one any the wiser.'

'True.'

'*And,*' said Lineham, becoming really excited now, 'if Mrs Parnell was Penny Rain's mother, it would explain something that's puzzled us all along — why she came to Sturrenden on Saturday.'

'Because of the accident, you mean? But you're forgetting, Mike. The manager of the Swan told us she made the booking for Saturday night a fortnight before.'

Lineham's enthusiasm received only a temporary check. 'But the accident could be the reason why Mrs Parnell seemed upset on Saturday morning, sir, and why she wanted to get off early.'

'Possibly.' Thanet's pipe had gone out in all the excitement and he took time now to relight it. 'I wonder why she booked ahead for that one particular night.'

'Sir! It could have been because she knew Rain would be in Sturrenden on Saturday. I know the concert was mentioned in the papers when his engagement was announced, because I saw it myself. Perhaps, since Mrs Parnell's husband died, she'd been thinking more and more about getting in touch with Penny. She mightn't have felt she could, before. If she didn't tell him about the baby before they were married she probably wouldn't have felt she could, afterwards, because he couldn't give her any children himself and she wouldn't have wanted to hurt him. But after his death, when

131

she was alone, with a lot of time to think, I suppose it would have been natural for her to start thinking about the baby and wondering what she was like, how she'd grown up. And from there it's only a step to deciding to try to find out. Then she'd have had to work out the best way to go about it, and she must have thought she'd begin by getting in touch with Rain. The problem is that he must be very difficult to pin down. His career takes him all over the world. Then, with all the publicity over his engagement, she learns that he will be giving this concert in Sturrenden last Saturday. So she books a room at the Swan, buys a ticket for the concert and then, when she gets here, decides it's too important to leave the meeting to chance. So she rings him up — that could be the local call she made, soon after she arrived.'

Lineham paused, grinned. 'How'm I doing, sir?'

'Magnificently, Mike. Carry on.'

'Well, Rain is very tied up because he's spending so much time at the hospital and the only time he can suggest is after the concert. They meet in the foyer and she tells him she must talk to him urgently, in private, about Penny. She doesn't say so, of course, but the news of Penny's accident has made her even more determined to re-establish contact with her daughter. Anyway, he agrees, reluctantly no doubt, and he fobs off his fiancée and her parents by telling them he wants to go straight back to the hospital, then he and Mrs Parnell go back to the Swan. Or they could have gone separately, arranged to meet there.

'Once they're in her room she tells him she's decided she wants to make herself known to Penny. The idea really horrifies him. He knows that if Penny finds out that her adoptive mother is really her grandmother and her adoptive brother is really her father, and realises that they've been deceiving her about this all her life, she might never trust them again. It could ruin what until now has been an exceptionally close and happy family. Somehow he's got to persuade Alicia to change her mind. He begins to argue with her, but she won't listen. The trouble is, Rain is already in a pretty fragile state. He's worried sick about Penny and his mother, especially his mother, and he's just been through the tension of a concert performance. The argument becomes a quarrel, the quarrel escalates, Rain loses his temper and . . .' Lineham waved a hand. 'That's it.'

Thanet had never heard Lineham so eloquent. He had worked out much the same scenario himself, but had no intention of saying so. Instead he clapped. 'Bravo, Mike. Convincing. Very convincing, in fact. And the red folder?'

'Rain had to take it away with him because it contained proof of Penny's true identity — birth certificate, letters, perhaps . . . He just couldn't risk leaving it there for us to find.'

'And proof, of course, is precisely what we now need, for this theory to stand up.'

'Of Penny's true identity, you mean.'

'Not exactly. Proof, rather, that she is in fact Alicia's daughter.'

'I see what you mean. If they're one and the same, fine. If not, our case falls apart, right?'

'Right. The question is, how to go about finding out? We daren't risk asking Rain, of course. If he is guilty, that would simply alert him to the fact that we were on to him. And the only other people who would know are Mrs Rain, who's in a coma, and Alicia's father, who's still away on holiday.'

'Old Mr Doyle is the only possibility, really, isn't he?' Lineham frowned. 'Looks as though we'll have to wait until Saturday.'

'Yes. Just a minute, though. Alicia's solicitor might know. We've got an appointment with him tomorrow. Looks as though that might be quite an interesting interview, in view of what Carol Marsh told me.'

'That certainly puts Miss Ross in the running too, don't you think?' Lineham clapped a hand to his forehead. 'Hell.'

'What's the matter?'

'I've just realised. You asked me to put someone on to checking overnight accomodation in Sturrenden, in case she followed Mrs Parnell down and stayed here on Saturday night, and I forgot. Sorry, sir. I'll get Bentley on to it first thing in the morning. Did you remember to ask Sparks to check if she's got a car, or can drive?'

'Yes. I wonder how he's getting on.'

Lineham grinned. 'Having the time of his life, I should think . . . . To get back to Miss Ross, though. Reluctant as I am to admit it, on second thoughts I can't see that what Carol Marsh told you strengthens the case against her that much.'

'Why not?'

'Well even if Miss Ross and Mrs Parnell did quarrel about the terms of the will, I can't really see that Miss Ross had much to gain by preventing Mrs Parnell from making a new one. Presumably the terms of the original will now stand, and as her husband is dead, her share in the business will go to her father.'

'Precisely. And he's an old man. Jessica Ross might well think it would be easier to get a better deal from him than from a legatee who is an unknown quantity.' Thanet glanced at his watch. A quarter past five already, and he had promised Joan that he'd try to be home early so that they could have that talk with Ben . . . 'Anyway, there's not much point in discussing it further at the moment. We might know more tomorrow, after seeing the solicitor. I'm going to write up my reports now, then go home.'

'Anything else you want me to do, sir?'

'Yes. Come on, Mike, don't look so crestfallen.' Thanet grinned. 'It'll make up for you actually having the nerve to take your lunch hour off. The thing is, I'm not too happy about Vivienne Leyton. She obviously hated Alicia and was bitterly jealous of her. And I'm still convinced she's holding back on something. I want you to talk to the party of friends the Leytons were with on Saturday night, see if they can tell us anything helpful. Oh, and make sure you get a description of the dress Mrs Leyton was wearing.'

'Right, sir.'

Two hours later Thanet sat back with a sigh, flexed his aching spine. The reports had taken longer than he had hoped, but he would still be home early enough to carry out his promise. He wasn't looking forward to the coming confrontation one little bit, but it was obviously vital to find out the truth of what had been going on. Thanet prayed that Ben had never actually been drawn in to experimenting with glue-sniffing. But what if he had? What if he had more than experimented, was on the way to becoming an addict?

Don't be stupid, Thanet told himself as he drove home through the familiar streets. *If he had, Joan or I would surely have noticed the symptoms.* But how evident were they in the early stages of the addiction?

He began to rehearse what he was going to say to his son.

FOURTEEN

Joan came to meet him in the hall and he kissed her, put his arms around her. Their shared anxiety gave this ritual embrace a deeper significance tonight and they stood motionless for a few moments, each drawing strength from the other's closeness.

Then Thanet pulled back a little, looked into her troubled grey eyes.

'How is he?'

She gave a little shrug. 'All right, I suppose. Quiet.'

'Has he mentioned Andy at all?'

'No.'

'And what about Sprig? How's she?'

'Seems fine.'

'Where are they?'

'Ben's just got into bed, Sprig's in the bath.'

'Good.' Perfect, in fact. Much as he loved his daughter, Thanet would prefer not have this talk with Ben interrupted. 'Shall we go up, then?'

To his surprise, Joan hesitated. 'Luke, I was wondering . . . do you think it would be better if you saw him by yourself?'

For a moment he was annoyed that she should be deserting him, leaving him to deal with this delicate situation alone, then commonsense reasserted itself. If Joan made a suggestion like this, she had good reason for it.

She must have glimpsed his fleeting anger and before he could speak she flared up in response. 'I'm not just chickening out, you know.'

He put out his hands and held her lightly by the shoulders. 'I do know. I was just being stupid.' He kissed her on the tip of the nose. 'Come on, darling, calm down. We're both on edge.'

He felt the tension leave her body and she gave a rueful smile. 'You're right. I'm sorry. . . . It's just that Ben and I don't seem to be getting on too well together at the moment and I thought he might be more prepared to open up if you saw him alone. Also, I thought he might find it a bit over-whelming, if we both tackled him about it.'

'You're right. He probably would. I don't in the least mind seeing him by myself.'

Thanet wished that this were true. As he climbed the stairs he wondered which was worse: to have this terrible sinking feeling in the pit of his stomach at the thought of the next half an hour, or to be stuck in the kitchen downstairs, knowing that whatever happened you were not going to have any con-trol over it. Ben's door was ajar and Thanet popped his head around it. 'Boo!'

Ben did not shriek with laughter, jump out of bed to run and throw his arms around his father, or even smile. He just looked up and said listlessly, 'Hullo, Dad. I didn't hear you get home.'

'What are you doing?' Thanet approached the bed and sat down. It was painfully obvious that Ben was not doing any-thing. A discarded electronic game lay on the bedspread.

Thanet picked it up. 'Playing with this?'

Ben shook his head. 'Didn't feel like it.'

He looked so small and lost, it was all Thanet could do not to gather him up and hold him fiercely, protectively, reassure him that everything was all right, Daddy was here. But that would achieve nothing. Not yet, at any rate. Did all parents feel like this, he wondered? Obviously not. Child-battering was on the increase and every day stories of child abuse and neglect found their way into the newspapers. And yet, he believed, the majority of parents did care for their children. How could it be otherwise? They were, after all, extensions of their parents' bodies, their physical characteristics and their genes only one link in the endless chain of creation and procreation which joins a man indissolubly to his ancestors and to all those future generations as yet unborn. How painful it must be, he thought, to lose a child. Small wonder, then, that the most harrowing battles in the divorce courts were fought over custody of the children, or that someone like Alicia, who had lost her child at birth, might in later life seek to re-establish that most fundamental of relationships. *Your pain is my pain, Ben,* Thanet said silently, *your sorrow my sorrow. If I could only bear it for you. . . . But I can't. My job is to teach you to bear it yourself.* But, how to go about it, that was the problem.

'Ben,' he said, tentatively.

'Yes, Dad?'

'We have to talk.' *Gentle but firm, that was it. But above all don't make him clam up before we get to the important bit.*

Ben said nothing, but his eyes clouded and he looked away.

'About Andy.'

Ben frowned and bit his lip.

Thanet took his son's hand and held it, gently. 'I'm sorry, I know it hurts you even to think of him — how upset you must be feeling. . . But it is important to talk about it, just the same. You see, Andy died because, well, because he didn't realise just how dangerous glue-sniffing is . . .'

He'd lost him. He could tell by Ben's eyes that the boy had blanked him out. He didn't want to hear, was too frightened to listen, perhaps. He would have to back off, change tack.

He stood up, walked across to the window, hoping that the movement would attract Ben's attention, tug him back again.

Outside, flowers and shrubs, trees and grass basked peacefully in the evening sunshine. The white Iceberg roses beneath the weeping pear which Joan had planted at the far end of the garden were luminous in their patch of shade, their great clusters of blooms nodding gently in a little breeze that had sprung up.

'Ben, what would you say if I gave you a gun to play with? A real gun, with bullets in it?'

He had Ben's attention now, all right. 'What if I gave you this gun and said, "There you are Ben, it's yours, now run away and play with it"?'

Ben didn't know how to reply. 'But you wouldn't,' he said at last.

'Why not?'

'Because it might go off by accident.'

'And you'd hurt yourself.'

The boy nodded, still puzzled. 'Anyway, it would be illegal, wouldn't it?'

'You're quite right. It would. Perhaps it was a bad example.' Thanet returned to his perch on the edge of the bed. 'Take a bottle of paracetamol, then.'

'What do you mean?'

'Well, as you know, Mum and I have always told you that you are never to take any kind of medicine or tablets that have not been given to you by us.'

'Everyone knows that.' Ben was scornful. 'It's written all over the labels.'

'Exactly. But what if, before you could read, Mum and I hadn't bothered to warn you how dangerous these things are, and then we'd left a bottle of paracetamol somewhere where you and Sprig could easily get at it . . .'

'You wouldn't have!'

'No, but if we had . . .'

'You never would.'

'Right. Because we do try, very hard, to make sure that you are aware of such dangers. We'd be very bad parents if we didn't. But I'm very much afraid, Ben, that we *have* been bad parents.'

'No, you haven't!' Ben was sitting bolt upright now, looking fierce.

'In one respect we have. We have not taken care to make sure that you and Sprig were fully aware of the dangers of glue-sniffing.'

Ben's eyes dropped and he shrank down a little on to his pillows. 'The trouble is, you see, Ben, that glue seems such ordinary stuff. You find it in every household and for years and years we've taken it for granted. It's difficult to take seriously the idea that it might be dangerous. Parents wouldn't dream of giving their children loaded guns to play with or leaving bottles of dangerous drugs around for them to take by accident, but they leave glue openly in the kitchen drawers or cupboards and don't think twice about it. And I think that's why many children simply don't realise how dangerous it is. The problem is, also, that it's addictive. Do you know what that means?'

Ben shook his head.

'It means that once you start doing it, it becomes harder and harder to stop.'

139

The fear that flared in Ben's eyes made Thanet's throat go dry and his stomach clench. 'I don't mean to say that if you've just done it once or twice, and then you realise how dangerous it is and decided to stop, that you won't be able to stop, just that the more often you do it, the harder it becomes to stop and in the end you can't and that's when you get the kind of terrible accident that happened to Andy.'

Why wasn't Ben saying anything?

'So you see, Ben, that's why I'm saying that in this respect, Mum and I have been bad parents. We should have warned you, properly. And because we didn't, I don't feel we could blame you if you'd had a sniff yourself, once or twice . . . Have you?'

Thanet had put the crucial question in as casual a manner as possible and now he held his breath. His heart was pounding in his ears like the beat of a distant drum. *Please God, let him say no.*

The silence stretched on and on. Ben was staring down at the bedspread, either thinking over what Thanet had said or plucking up the courage to reply. Eventually he shifted uncomfortably and, without looking up, muttered, 'Well, once or twice.'

Thanet forced himself to sound calm, matter-of-fact. 'More than that, perhaps?'

'Three times, actually.'

'So why didn't you go on?'

'I didn't like it!' Ben burst out. 'I didn't like what it made the others do. They looked stupid, all falling about, as if they were drunk. And one of them spewed up all over the place. *Yuk!*'

Relief exploded in Thanet's brain, the shockwaves spreading out and down in tingling waves through torso, arms and legs. For a moment he felt light-headed. Then he took a deep breath. 'Congratulations,' he said, and ran his hand caressingly over Ben's hair.

'What for?'

'It's the hardest thing in the world to say 'No', when a group of friends is urging you on. I want you to know that I'm really proud of you, Ben.' *And relieved. Oh, so relieved.*

Ben had flushed with pleasure and now he muttered, 'They were a load of wallies anyway. Except for . . .'

'I know. Except for Andy.'

'So why did he do it, Dad? Go on sniffing glue? *Why?*'

'The thing is, Ben, when people are unhappy it makes them do silly things, things they wouldn't normally do. And I think this is what happened to Andy.'

Ben was listening intently, his eyes huge and solemn.

'Remember when you asked me, a few months back, why Andy's parents were getting divorced, and we had a long talk about it? Well, I think that was why Andy was unhappy. And I think that was why he started getting into trouble at school and so on . . . The glue-sniffing was only one aspect of it.'

Ben began to cry. 'I told him!' he sobbed. 'I told him it was stupid. I tried to make him stop. But he told me to leave him alone, he couldn't care less what I thought . . .'

Thanet put an arm around Ben's shoulders and pulled him close. 'I'm sure that wasn't true, Ben. As I said, Andy was very unhappy and that would have made him say things he didn't really mean . . .'

The conversation went on and on, round and round, with Thanet reassuring and Ben at last able to talk his hurt, anger, distress and bewilderment out of his system. By the end of it Thanet was exhausted and Ben's eyelids drooping where he sat. Enough was enough, Thanet decided. Ben would be all right now.

'Come on,' he said firmly. 'Time you settled down, and went to sleep. Would you like a story?'

'Yes, please.'

'Daddy!' Bridget flew into the room and flung her arms around his neck. Her skin was still damp from the bath and she smelt like sunshine and flowers.

'I was beginning to think you must have been washed down the plug-hole,' said Thanet teasingly.

'I was reading . . .' She stood up, tugging at his hand. 'Come and see my photos of Princess Diana. Mummy got them done Express. They're terrific!'

'In a minute,' said Thanet, smiling up at her. 'I'm just going to read Ben a story.'

'I'll listen too.' She flopped on to the bed on her stomach, propping her chin on cupped hands.

'Right. What shall we have? You choose, Ben.'

The story over and the photographs duly admired, Thanet returned downstairs.

Joan was tossing salad in a big green pottery bowl. She stopped, turned, her face apprehensive. 'How did it go?'

'Not too badly.'

'Really?'

'Really,' said Thanet, smiling at her and holding out his arms. She came into them and laid her head against his shoulder. 'What a relief! And did you find out . . . ?' She pulled away. 'No, come on. Let's carry these things through and you can tell me all about it over supper. Hope you don't mind having salad again.'

'It's what I prefer in this hot weather, you know that.'

'I've got some really good roast beef . . .'

While they ate he related to her his conversation with Ben, in detail.

'So you really think he's in no danger?'

'I'm pretty certain he was telling the truth. In fact, I *am* certain.'

'What a relief!' she said again. 'I was so afraid . . .'

'I know. So was I.'

They continued their meal in a companionable silence for a while and then began to talk about the day's work. The mother of Tracey, the pregnant fourteen-year-old, was still refusing to have anything to do with her and the girl was still determined to have the baby and bring it up herself. After endless phone calls Joan had at last managed to find a mother and baby home willing to take her.

'Interestingly enough,' said Thanet, 'it's beginning to look as though the Parnell case might revolve around a similar sort of situation.' And he explained the elaborate theory which he and Lineham had worked out about Alicia and Penny Rain.

'I suppose the adoption could have happened that way,' said Joan. 'That kind of arrangement is not unprecedented. I'd no idea Penny Rain was adopted, though.'

'There's no doubt about that, according to Doc Mallard. I

didn't know you knew her. What's she like?'

'A very nice girl. I don't know her well, mind. It's just that she helps out occasionally at the Youth Counselling Centre.'

'As a counsellor?'

'Oh no. She serves refreshments, plays table-tennis with the kids, that sort of thing. She looks so like her mother I'd never have . . . Oh, of course, how stupid of me. If what you say is true, Mrs Rain is really her grandmother.'

'Yes. If.'

'You really don't sound too certain about it.'

'I can't be, yet. We might know more after we've seen Alicia's solicitor tomorrow. The whole case seems so complicated.' And he told her about Carol Marsh's visit, about Vivienne and Richard Leyton and about Oliver Bassett and Paul Leyton.

'I see what you mean. Of course, even if Penny Rain is Alicia's daughter and Alicia did come down to Sturrenden with the intention of telling Nicholas Rain that she was thinking of making herself known to Penny, that still doesn't necessarily mean that Mr Rain killed Alicia, does it? It doesn't sound as though anyone saw them together after that brief conversation at the concert hall, and for all you know they might just have been arranging to meet the following morning. That would have been much more likely, surely. After all, you don't just go up to a boyfriend you haven't seen for twenty years and invite him back for an urgent meeting in your hotel bedroom, especially if he has a fiancée and prospective parents-in-law in tow.'

'We're not just talking about any boyfriend, Joan. If we're right, this was the father of her child. Surely that would give her a strong claim on him.'

'True. But I still can't see why the matter should have been sufficiently urgent for her to press him to go back with her then and there. Where's the hurry? Alicia hadn't seen Penny in twenty years, why should she worry about a few more hours?'

Thanet sighed. 'I suppose you're right. Anyway, as I said, it's all pure speculation at the moment. All we really know is that Alicia had a child. We don't know when, or where, or by whom, or even if the child is alive or dead. Besides . . .'

'What?'

Thanet shook his head. 'Nothing.' Which wasn't strictly true. There was something, some tiny piece of information that was nagging at him, eluding him, stubbornly remaining just beyond the reach of his conscious memory. Was it something someone had said, or something that he had noticed? He shook his head again.

Joan was watching him. 'Trying to remember something?'

'It won't come.'

'Think of something else, then.'

'It's infuriating . . . Right. Is there anything interesting on television? Or shall we have some music?'

'Music, I think. But I'd like to clear away, first.'

They did the washing up together and went back into the sitting room. Thanet put Vivaldi's Four Seasons on and then went and lay on the settee, his head in Joan's lap, easing himself into a more comfortable position as the taut muscles of his back relaxed. He closed his eyes and the intricate, ordered music flowed around him, soothing and restoring him.

But that elusive memory continued to remain tantalisingly out of reach, destroying his peace of mind.

FIFTEEN

DC Spark's report on his activities in London the previous day was waiting on Thanet's desk when he arrived in the office next morning. It was, predictably, everything a report should be: thorough, succinct and immaculately typed, without a single error of grammar, spelling or punctuation.

Thanet accorded it the respect which it deserved. He read it through quickly, first, then again, slowly. After that he checked once more on certain points which had caught his interest. Then he sat back and thought about Jessica Ross.

Sparks had managed to talk to most of the other tenants of her block of flats, returning in the evening to question those who had been out at work earlier in the day. The consensus of opinion was unanimous: Jessica Ross had been away on Saturday night.

As well as the old woman to whom Thanet had spoken on Sunday, one other neighbour had seen Miss Ross depart for work at eight-fifteen on Saturday morning. After that the flat had been silent until late on Sunday afternoon — no plumbing noises, no radio or television and, despite the heat of the day, no window open. One neighbour had noticed Miss Ross's daily pint of milk still standing outside at midday on Sunday and as it was such a warm day had taken it in to put it into her own refrigerator. Jessica Ross had knocked on her door at five o'clock to enquire if this was what had happened, and had explained that she had been in bed all day with a migraine. The neighbour had been surprised to hear this. She had never heard Miss Ross complain of a migraine before and in any case had been convinced that Miss Ross had been away for the weekend, even though this would have been unusual — unprecedented, in fact. Miss Ross hardly ever went out, or had friends in, and this was why the neighbour had been convinced of her absence. She was used to noises from next door and could more or less chart Miss Ross's routine from them. This was why they had been so conspicuous by their absence. The woman herself had been in all weekend except for an hour and a half on Sunday, when she had gone to lunch with a friend — which was presumably why Thanet himself had missed her.

From other neighbours Sparks had learnt that Jessica Ross 'kept herself to herself' and was generally regarded as having no interests in life apart from her work. No one had ever seen her have a visitor and it was generally believed that she had no family.

But this was apparently not so. Sparks had managed to manoeuvre a long conversation during the lunch hour with Faith Bevan, the other girl who worked in Jobline — Carol Marsh, of course, had been in Sturrenden talking to Thanet. According to Faith, Jessica Ross had come from a large family of seven children. Faith assumed that it was a working-class background because Jessica's father had insisted that she leave school at sixteen to start work, and she had had to go to night classes to earn her secretarial qualifications. It had been a long, slow process, but she had been determined to see it through, and to achieve the kind of standards which would be attractive to prospective employers. Faith accorded her a grudging admiration for this perseverence, but was tired of having it 'rammed down my throat' and, like Carol, was resentful of Jessica Ross's highly critical attitude not only towards the two girls but also, behind her back, towards Mrs Parnell. Miss Ross, she said, was two-faced and also very jealous of Mrs Parnell's looks and pleasant personality. Faith had no idea where the rest of the Ross family lived, so Sparks had been unable to find out more about them.

There was one other interesting piece of information: Jessica Ross had never learned to drive.

Lineham came in looking like a thundercloud.

'Just been finishing this report on Mr and Mrs Leyton's party of friends on Saturday night, sir.' He handed it to Thanet.

'Thanks. What's the matter, Mike? You look as though you've just had an unpleasant conversation with your bank manager.'

'Not with my bank manager, with my estate agent. We've been gazumped.'

'Oh, no.'

'Oh yes. By five hundred.'

'It really is time something was done about this. It's iniquitous. In my opinion, if you've made a written offer for the full asking price, that should be it.'

'Yes, well there we are. Iniquitous or not, it hadn't been accepted in writing by the vendor and these other people got in fast. She seemed so nice, too, the woman who was selling. She's a widow, so I suppose you can't blame her for wanting to make as much as she can get, but we're going to be out on the street at this rate, if we're not careful.'

'So what are you going to do?'

'I don't know. I only just heard, a few minutes ago. I haven't even told Louise yet.'

'Can you afford to raise your offer?'

'I'm not sure. We'd have to bid at least five hundred more than these other people, which means a thousand more than we'd bargained for.'

'You'd better give Louise a ring, see what she thinks. Perhaps while we're in London she could get on to the building society, see exactly what it would mean in terms of mortgage repayments.'

'Would you mind, sir . . .?'

'I told you, go ahead. I'll glance at this, while I'm waiting.'

Lineham's report made interesting reading. According to the other members of their party, Vivienne Leyton had sniped at Richard throughout dinner in a way which had created a very uncomfortable atmosphere and spoiled everyone else's enjoyment. The impression was that the couple had had a row earlier in the evening and Vivienne wasn't going to let Richard forget it.

After the dinner was over the men and women had split up to go to their respective cloakrooms and then, between around twenty-five past ten and twenty to eleven, both Richard and Vivienne had disappeared. When the party had reassembled for the dancing at ten-forty-five, the Leytons had returned together, and everyone had assumed that they had gone off somewhere during the interval to sort out their disagreement, because for the remainder of the evening the sniping had stopped. Vivienne had been much more subdued and Richard, although somewhat wary of her, more convivial.

'Louise seems to think it's worth going into,' said Lineham, putting the phone down.

'She's going to see what she can do?'

'Yes. I hope she doesn't get too carried away. She really has set her heart on that house.'

'I think we can safely leave it in her hands. Louise is a very capable woman.' Thanet tapped Lineham's report with one finger. 'This is interesting.'

'Yes. isn't it? I wonder what those two were really up to.'

'Paying a little visit to Alicia, perhaps? I wonder if we were wrong, Mike, and it was Richard Leyton who was the father of Alicia's child.'

'But no one has ever suggested that he had even the slightest interest in her.'

'No, but if he had, there are all sorts of interesting implications, aren't there? Let's just suppose for a moment that he took up with Alicia, however briefly, in between the time she broke off with Rain and started going out with Paul . . . . Perhaps he was fed up with mooning around after Vivienne, even thought she might sit up and take notice of him if he went out with another girl, especially one as attractive as Alicia . . . Anyway, at the time I don't suppose it would have mattered much to Vivienne. She had eyes for no one but Paul. But then Alicia starts taking an interest in Paul and, worse, Paul reciprocates — goes overboard for her in fact, and our faithful Vivienne is left high and dry. She is furiously jealous of Alicia. Then comes Paul's suicide and in Vivienne's eyes Alicia and Alicia alone is responsible for Paul's death . . . Richard meanwhile has reverted to the role of adoring lover and later, much later, perhaps, Vivienne at last gives in and marries him. But it infuriates her to think that even Richard, whom she had regarded as her own exclusive property, had at one time succumbed to Alicia's charms. Over the years she never forgets Alicia, and those feelings of jealousy and hatred fester away at the back of her mind, poisoning her marriage. And then, one day . . .'

'One day,' said Lineham eagerly, 'Alicia contacts Richard and says she has to see him. They arrange to meet some time over the weekend, but she doesn't realise that he's going to be at the Swan on Saturday evening for the Rotary Club Ladies' Night, and they bump into each other in the foyer . . . No, this won't work, sir. In that case, Leyton would surely not have insisted on going to talk to her. He would have pretended not to notice her . . .'

'Not necessarily. You're not allowing for human nature, Mike. It's obvious that Leyton's wife treats him like dirt most of the time. He might have insisted on dragging her across to see Alicia through sheer perversity or from a desire to punish Vivienne, or stir her up . . .'

'He certainly succeeds in doing that, anyway. She's a real bitch all through dinner . . .'

'So much so that he thinks, what the hell . . . And decides to slip up to Alicia's room during the interval, if he can manage to get away. He knows the concert will be over by then . . .'

'They could originally have arranged to meet then, for that matter.'

'Unlikely, I should think, Mike, but possible . . . Anyway, up he goes. And Vivienne, who's been keeping an eye on him, sneaks up after him.'

'Or it could possibly have been the other way around. Perhaps it was Vivienne who decided to go and pay a little visit to Alicia during the interval, and her husband who followed her . . .'

'True. But in any case there they are, one or the other or both. And then . . . well, then the situation is open to all sorts of permutations . . . Not much point in going into them all now, not until we have some kind of verification. . . . We'll have to question the hotel staff and guests again. That dress she was wearing . . .'

' "The colour of a copper beech leaf, with lurex in it," ' quoted Lineham. 'That's that glittery stuff, isn't it?'

'Yes. That's what I mean. It was pretty striking, by the sound of it.'

'Long and slinky. And with that hair of hers . . . She wouldn't have been exactly unobtrusive.'

'We'll get Sparks on to it. He made a good job of that report on Jessica Ross. Have you seen it?'

'Just glanced at it before I went downstairs, yes.'

'Get him in.'

Spark's thin eager face flushed with pleasure when Thanet complimented him on his day's work and the excellent report.

'I've got another job for you today, while Lineham and I are in London. We're going to see Mrs Parnell's solicitor.' Thanet explained what he wanted Sparks to do. 'Take your time. It could be very important. Fortunately Mrs Leyton has a pretty distinctive appearance, but Leyton is more difficult. The place was crawling with men in dinner jackets.'

'His beard might help, sir. Anything else?'

'Just one point. Two couples checked out of the Swan early on Sunday morning, before Mrs Parnell's body was found, and one of them had a room two doors away from Mrs Parnell. We still haven't managed to contact them — we think they must be touring — and obviously their evidence could be important. Have another go at getting hold of them, will you? Here's their address.'

'Right, sir.'

'That's all then.'

But Sparks was hesitating.

'What is it, Sparks?'

'When you sent for me, sir . . . I was just on my way up. To show you this.'

'This' was an excellent photograph of Jessica Ross.

'Where did you get it?'

'I printed it myself, sir. Last night, when I got back.' Sparks shifted his feet a little, uncomfortably, as if he were afraid that he had exceeded his brief. 'I took my camera with me yesterday.'

Thanet had difficulty in hiding his amusement. 'Hmm . . . Yes, well as it happens, it'll come in very handy. I was going to send someone around the hotels and boarding houses this morning, to check if she stayed in Sturrenden on Saturday night.'

'That's what I thought, sir . . .'

'I'll put Bentley on to it. Send him in, will you, on your way out.'

'Yes, sir.'

When he had gone Thanet and Lineham grinned at each other.

'Keen as mustard, isn't he, sir?'

'Enterprising, too. And versatile. He even printed it himself! If we're not careful we're going to be outclassed.'

'Worry you, sir, does it?'

'No need to be impudent, Mike. No, I'm afraid I never was very ambitious. I like things just the way they are.' Thanet glanced at his watch. 'If we're going to catch the ten-ten we'd better get a move on. As soon as we've seen Bentley, we'll be off.'

The offices of Thrall, Hardy and Blythe were a complete contrast to the Georgian elegance of Wylie, Bassett and Protheroe. They were housed in a brand new high-rise office block near Paddington station, some floors of which were still untenanted.

Thanet and Lineham were whisked up to the sixth floor in a lift and found themselves in a spacious, air-conditioned foyer artfully divided into separate areas by exuberant potted plants and plate-glass screens. The receptionist matched the decor. She was sleek and well-groomed, her manner a well-tutored blend of politeness, warmth and efficiency.

'Someone's been watching too much "Dallas",' whispered Lineham.

Thrall came out to meet them hand extended. Unerringly, he picked Thanet as the senior.

'Inspector Thanet?'

He was in his thirties, plump and smiling, dressed in a sleek pale grey dacron suit, pale pink shirt and deeper pink tie. 'And this is. . .?'

'Detective-Sergeant Lineham.'

Thrall shook Lineham's hand too, then led the way into his office. 'I apologise for being unable to see you before now. I've been very tied up, this week. Do sit down.'

He ignored the enormous desk with its padded executive-style swivel armchair and led them to the other end of the room, where there was a small seating area furnished with a comfortable leather bench-settee and matching armchairs.

'It was a terrible shock, to hear about Mrs Parnell. Ah, thank you, Marcia.'

The receptionist had entered with a tray. Not just cups of coffee, Thanet noted, but a glass jug and attractive pottery cups and saucers. Thrall and partners obviously believed in attention to detail. A delicious aroma of freshly ground coffee filled the air as Marcia poured and handed cups around.

'A tragic business,' said Thrall when the girl had gone. He helped himself liberally to brown sugar.

'You knew Mrs Parnell well?'

'Not well, exactly. One doesn't really see clients often enough to know them well. But we have dealt with Mr and Mrs Parnell's business for some years — perhaps I should explain that before our lease expired our premises were also in the Fulham Road. One does rather feel that Mrs Parnell had a raw deal in life. First Mr Parnell's accident — you know about that, of course? — then his death, then her mother's death, and now this . . . She was a charming woman, you know.' Thrall shook his head mournfully and sipped his coffee. 'But of course,' sip, 'you haven't come here to hear all this,' sip, 'you've come, I presume, to find out about her will?'

'If there was one.'

Thrall finished his coffee. 'More coffee, Inspector? Sergeant? No?' He poured some for himself and sat back, nursing his cup. 'Yes, there is one.'

'But not the one she'd intended leaving, I believe?'

Thrall gave Thanet a sharp, asessing glance. 'That's true, yes. She was on the point of making a new one.'

'In favour of the child which she had given away for adoption, at birth.'

Again that shrewd look. 'I see you've been busy, Inspector.' Abruptly Thrall leaned forward and set his cup down on the table. 'I'll be frank with you, Inspector. I was dead against it. I don't believe in stirring these things up. It causes nothing but trouble. When a child has been settled for years in one family . . . If she is unaware that she is adopted, such a legacy could be a considerable shock.'

Thanet noted the 'she' with satisfaction.

'So you tried to persuade Mrs Parnell not to change her will in favour of her daughter.'

'I did. But she wouldn't listen.' He lifted his hands helplessly. 'What could I do? One can only advise . . . If a client then chooses to ignore that advice, one has no option but to follow his instructions. It was understandable, I suppose, that she should wish to dispose of her property in this way. She had no one else to leave it to. There's her father, of course, but in the normal way of things, one would have expected Mr Doyle to die first.'

'When did she first mention this matter to you?'

'Soon after her mother died — about three months ago, I suppose. Mrs Parnell came to see me. She wanted me to advise her. She told me that she had had this child when she herself was still in her teens, way back in January 1965. She had never told her husband about it. . . . She was very devoted to Mr Parnell, and I think she felt that he would have been deeply hurt to know that she had had a baby by another man, especially in view of the fact that he himself had never been able to give her one. So until now she had never thought of trying to trace the child, and indeed . . .'

Thanet and Lineham exchanged glances.

'Just a moment. Sorry to interrupt, but did you say, "trace the child"?' Thanet could see their carefully constructed theory tumbling about their ears.

'Yes. Why?'

'You're saying that Mrs Parnell had the baby adopted through conventional channels and had no idea of its new identity?'

'Naturally. Do I gather you thought otherwise?'

Thanet waved a hand. 'Just an idea we had, Mr Thrall. It doesn't matter. Do go on.'

But it did matter. It had been a beautiful theory — neat, convincing, satisfying. And now . . . Thanet's hand strayed in the direction of his pocket. Dare he pollute Thrall's opulent premises with clouds of unhygienic smoke? Probably not. Yet of its own volition his hand emerged from the pocket clutching his pipe.

Thrall noticed at once. 'Do smoke, if you wish, Inspector. I'm a pipe man myself. That's why the ashtrays in here are so solid.' And he leaned forward and pushed in Thanet's direction a chunk of quartz with something resembling a volcanic crater in the middle.

Thanet picked it up. 'Very nice,' he said.

'It's a piece of the Atlas Mountains. Picked it up in Morocco.'

Thanet set it back on the low table and began to fill his pipe. 'Sorry, we're disgressing. You were telling us about Mrs Parnell's visit . . .'

'Yes. Well, I think that at that point she was feeling desperately alone. She'd lost her husband and her mother within the space of three months, and either loss is enough for anyone to cope with. . . . There was her father, of course, but he lives in the Midlands, as you probably know, and there was no one else to turn to. Because of Mr Parnell's disability she and her husband hadn't had much of a social life — they could have, of course, if they'd wanted to, but they didn't seem to need other people, they had a very special relationship, a kind of mutual interdependence which was very touching. But it did mean that when Mr Parnell died, she found herself with this enormous void. She had her work in Jobline, but I think it reminded her too much of her husband — they'd built it up together . . . Anyway, when she was sorting through her mother's papers she came across an old letter from the agency which had arranged the adoption. And this triggered off what in the end became something of an obsession with her. I think she found the thought of a grown-up daughter irresistible.'

'You said she wanted you to advise her . . .'

'Yes. She wanted me to tell her how to find her child, and I don't mind admitting that I was glad that in this particular matter I couldn't help her. Adoption procedure is designed specifically to protect the child against this situation — quite rightly so, in my view. Apparently she had written to the adoption agency and they'd told her that the only way in which the natural mother can get in touch with her child is by the agency writing to tell the adoptive parents that she wishes to do so. Then, if the child is over eighteen, it's up to him or her to decide whether or not to follow up the contact. Unfortunately, in Mrs Parnell's case, this procedure couldn't be followed, because in 1972 the agency which arranged the adoption had a serious fire, and all their records up to that date were destroyed.'

'Wouldn't it have been possible to trace the child through Public Records?'

Thrall shook his head. 'Mrs Parnell had tried. The

Adoption Register is inaccessible to the natural mother. The only thing she can do is go to St Catherine's House and inspect the Index to that Register, which gives the new, adoptive name of each child, its date of birth and the date of the adoption. Mrs Parnell had done this, but the only piece of information which was of any use to her was the date of birth. I believe she made many visits to St Catherine's House to go through the Index, noting down the names of all the female children born on the correct date, but of course all she ended up with was a very long list and absolutely no means of telling which child was hers.'

So here, no doubt, was the explanation of Alicia's mysterious and erratic absences, of her absent-mindedness and lack of interest in the affairs of the agency. The search for her child had enabled her to cope with her double bereavement by providing her with a goal to work towards, a hope to sustain her. Thanet could understand the degree to which that search must have obsessed her, her growing despair as she slowly came to appreciate the impossibility of the task.

'That was why I was so astounded when she rang up a little while back to say that she'd at last actually managed to trace her daughter,' said Thrall.

Thanet's attention snapped back. 'What? But how?'

Thrall shrugged. 'I've no idea. She rang me up, early one morning. She sounded very agitated.'

'She'd actually made contact with the girl?'

'Oh no. She said she'd discovered her daughter's new identity by pure chance, that she'd tell me the whole story when she came in to see me. She said she was trying to make up her mind about the best way to contact her — she didn't want to rush in, she said, and regret it later. But meanwhile she was ringing because despite what I'd said when we first discussed the matter, she had definitely decided to make a will in the girl's favour, and she'd like me to draw up a rough draft so that we'd have a basis on which to work when she came to see me. She'd ring for an appointment in a week or two, she said, when she'd had time to think the matter over. Of course, she never came.'

'Did she ever tell you who the child's father was?'

'No.'

'Or the girl's new name?'

'I'm afraid not.'

A pity. Even though it looked as though the matter was irrelevant, a side-issue, for his own satisfaction Thanet would have liked to reassure himself that it had nothing to do with the case.

'So the original will still stands?'

'Drawn up at the time of her marriage, yes. As her husband predeceased her, everything will now go to her father.'

'I see.'

There was a knock at the door and the delectable Marcia put her head in. 'Sorry to disturb you, Mr Thrall, but there's a call for Inspector Thanet. Urgent, apparently.'

It was Bentley. 'Glad I managed to catch you, sir. Have you been to see Miss Ross yet?'

'Not yet, no.'

'Good. I thought you might like to know, before you saw her, that she was in Sturrenden on Saturday. She spent the night at the Three Horseshoes, opposite the Black Swan. Checked in at about four-forty-five on Saturday afternoon, under the name of Jennifer Rawlings. She asked for a room at the front, and left shortly before twelve on Sunday morning.'

'This is definite?'

'The landlord was positive, sir. Said the photograph was an excellent likeness.'

'Thank you, Bentley. Well done. Tell me,' he said to Thrall as he replaced the receiver, 'did Mrs Parnell have a partnership agreement drawn up between herself and Miss Jessica Ross?'

'Yes, she did. I arranged it myself, as a matter of fact.'

'Mrs Parnell retained the major share in the business?'

'Yes. It was a sixty/forty arrangement. I strongly advised it. To be frank, I wasn't too happy about the partnership. I wasn't particularly impressed by Miss Ross and I felt that Mrs Parnell should delay making such an important decision, until she had fully recovered from the trauma of a double bereavement, but I couldn't get her to change her mind. She said Miss Ross had had to carry much of the weight of the business alone during the last months of Mr Parnell's life, and afterwards too, for that matter, while Mrs Parnell was recovering, and she felt she owed it to her.'

'Was there any arrangement as to what should happen in the event of the death of one of the partners?'

'The other was to be given the first option to purchase the other's share, after an independent assessment as to market value, should the legatee wish to sell.'

'And if the legatee did not wish to sell?'

'Then the business would presumably continue under the new partnership.'

'I see. Thank you.'

Outside, Thanet decided to be extravagant and take a taxi.

'Bang goes our lovely theory,' said Lineham gloomily.

'That Penny is Rain's daughter, you mean. Yes, looks like it, doesn't it. I simply cannot believe that any reputable adoption agency would collude with the parents of the natural mother to place the child in the family of the natural father without her knowledge. Nor can I believe that Alicia's child should have been placed with the Rain family by sheer coincidence. It's just too much to swallow. No, I'm afraid that as you say, bang goes our lovely theory.'

'And it doesn't look too promising as far as Jessica Ross is concerned, either, if there has to be an independent market assessment of the value of Mrs Parnell's share of the business before Miss Ross can purchase.'

'I shouldn't be too sure about that, Mike. There are all sorts of ways of milking a business. Jessica Ross could still be in a pretty strong position now. I don't imagine Alicia's father would be anything but a sleeping partner, and a sleeping partner who's in his seventies and lives a convenient couple of hundred miles away would be a pretty attractive proposition to someone like her. Besides, I had a very interesting phone call just now. From Bentley.'

'You mean . . . Miss Ross really was in Sturrenden on Saturday?'

'No doubt about it, according to Bentley. Checked into the Three Horseshoes at around four-forty-five on Saturday afternoon, under the name of Jennifer Rawlings. Sharp's photograph came in handy. The landlord recognised her immediately. She asked for a room at the front, too'.

'Overlooking the entrance to the Swan! Terrific!' Lineham's eyes were already alight with enthusiasm.

Thanet smiled indulgently. Lineham's ability to pick himself up after disappointment and throw himself wholeheartedly into the next project was one of the sergeant's most endearing qualities.

'Four-forty-five, you say? Then she must have followed Mrs Parnell down, as we thought. I bet that's why she made a fuss when Mrs Parnell said she'd like to leave work early — she wouldn't have been able to follow her, if she had. I bet she'd been dying to know where Mrs Parnell used to go off to, those times when she left the office without telling anyone where she was going, and this time she thought she'd do a bit of detective work for herself. She'd have brought her night things with her when she left home that morning — remember the squashy bag that neighbour mentioned . . .'

'Following her out of curiosity is still a long way from killing her, Mike.'

'But it's the first step, isn't it? And you know what you're always saying . . .'

' "It's the first step that counts", you mean. Well, maybe, but . . .'

'Even if she hadn't intended killing her when she set off, even if she was just following her out of curiosity, perhaps when she saw the set-up she realised how perfect it was . . . All those people milling around in the hotel . . . it would have been so easy to slip in and out undetected, mingle with the crowd, especially around the time when Mrs Parnell got back, after the concert.'

'Maybe. But just remember, the same applies to anyone else. No, the fact remains, Mike, that what we need is some good, hard evidence.'

The taxi was pulling up and Lineham leaned forward with alacrity to open the door. 'I know that, sir. All the same, I'm looking forward to seeing her try to wriggle out of this one.'

159

SEVENTEEN

When Thanet and Lineham walked in, both Carol and Faith were busy at their desks. Carol immediately jumped up.

'Morning, Inspector.'

He was glad to see that she was looking much better today, though her shrieking scarlet and emerald green mini-dress made him blink. The orange spikes were poker-stiff and the mint-green eyes elaborately made-up.

'I'm working out my notice,' she said, lowering her voice and glancing at the inner door, which was shut. 'We both are.'

'You've definitely decided to leave, then?'

'You bet.'

'Is Miss Ross in?'

'You come to arrest her?' she said eagerly. 'See, Faith, I told you, didn't I?'

'Just to talk to her,' said Thanet, smiling.

'Oh . . .' She shrugged. 'Well, it's early days yet, isn't it? Yes, she's in. Got a client with her.'

'Will she be long, do you know?'

'Half an hour or so, I should think.'

Thanet glanced at his watch. Half past twelve.

'Would you tell her we'll be back at one-fifteen?'

In the street Thanet said, 'Thought we might as well get something to eat while we're waiting. I noticed a sandwich bar just down the road.'

The pavements were crowded with people hurrying about to make the best use of their lunch break.

'I'd hate to live in London,' said Lineham as they dodged their way along the pavement.

'Me too. Here it is.'

They had to queue of course, first to order, then to find somewhere to sit down, and it was a scramble to be back at Jobline on time. Faith was alone in the office. Presumably the

160

girls' lunch hours were staggered so that the office could remain open throughout the day.

'Is Miss Ross free now?'

Faith nodded and crossed the room to knock on the inner door.

Jessica Ross was not pleased to see them. 'I hope this isn't going to take long, Inspector. I'm very busy.'

Today she was wearing a summer dress with long sleeves and tie-neck in a silky fawn material patterned with brown scribbles. It was an unfortunate choice of colour, emphasising the sallowness of her skin.

'That rather depends on you, Miss Ross.'

'What do you mean?' She plumped herself down in the chair behind the desk and waved an irritable hand. 'Do sit down.'

'It seems you've been rather less than frank with us.'

'I don't know what you're talking about.'

'Don't you, Miss Ross? Why didn't you tell us you'd spent Saturday night in Sturrenden — and under an assumed name? And don't bother to deny it. It really isn't worth the trouble.' Thanet nodded at Lineham who flicked open his notebook and read off an imaginary script.

'Jessica Ross. Positively identified by the landlord of the Three Horseshoes in Sturrenden as having registered under the name of Jennifer Rawlings at four-forty-five on Saturday the fourteenth of July. Checked out at eleven-fifty-five on Sunday the fifteenth.' Lineham closed the notebook with a snap.

'What absolute rubbish! I told you, I was at home in bed with a migraine. . . . There's some mistake . . . how could anyone possibly have identified me as this Rawlings woman? I've never even heard of her.'

'There's been no mistake, Miss Ross, I assure you.'

'But there must have been! How could you possibly . . .?'

'Never mind how,' snapped Thanet. 'And let's stop wasting time, shall we? Or perhaps you'd prefer to come down to Sturrenden with us and take part in an identification parade. I'm sure the proprietor of the Horseshoes would be only too happy to oblige.'

Jessica Ross stared at him. Her pale blue eyes were blank,

but Thanet sensed that underneath she was desperately twist-ing and turning, this way and that, seeking a way out. He waited patiently. He had her and he knew it.

Suddenly her eyes filled with tears and she snatched at her handbag, took out a handkerchief. She dabbed at the corners of her eyes — carefully, Thanet noticed, so as not to smudge her make-up — and blew her nose. 'Oh,' she said, in a tre-mulous voice, 'whatever will you think of me, Inspector?'

So it was to be a bid for sympathy. Well, she wasn't going to get it. Thanet glanced at Lineham, who rolled his eyes and cast them up at the ceiling. Thanet said nothing, just waited.

'It was only that I was so worried . . . I mean, Alicia had been behaving so strangely. . . . And, as I told you, she had been neglecting her work, going off without warning and giv-ing no explanation when she came back . . . I was getting very concerned about her.' Miss Ross gave a final dab and then sat up with a self-righteous little twitch of the shoulders. 'And she had no one else to take an interest, no one at all.'

'So you thought it was your duty to find out what she was up to?'

'Yes. No. I mean . . . I thought I might be able to help her, if I knew.'

'How?'

Jessica Ross blinked at the staccato question. 'Well . . . I thought it might help me to take the right attitude, in deal . . . in talking to her.'

'Oh, come on, Miss Ross. We're not complete fools, you know. Why not admit it? You were intrigued by those erratic absences of hers, fed up with them, too. You wanted to find out what she was up to. So, when you discovered she was going away for the weekend, you decided to follow her out of sheer curiosity.'

Jessica Ross's puddingy face hardened, took on greater definition. Her nose suddenly seemed sharper, her heavy jaw more prominent than ever. 'Well, what if I did? There's no law against that, is there?'

'No one has ever suggested that there is,' said Thanet amicably.

'Well then . . .'

'Precisely. "Well then . . .". Why bother to cover it up?'

'Because when I heard . . . when I discovered that Alicia had been . . . murdered, I panicked. I thought that if you knew I'd followed her down there, you'd think I'd . . . I'd . . .'

'Killed her.'

'Yes.'

'And did you?'

Her head snapped up. 'Certainly not!'

Thanet folded his arms. 'Convince me.'

Her mouth gaped a little, then snapped shut. 'You'll just have to take my word for it, I'm afraid.'

'Why should I? You've already lied to us once.' Thanet leaned forward in his chair. 'Look, Miss Ross, I'm tired of all this skirmishing. It is time-consuming and time-wasting, and frankly, I can't be bothered with it. I want a clear, precise and *truthful* account of your movements on Saturday and Sunday, and if you're not prepared to give them to me, here and now, then I really shall have to ask you to accompany us back to Sturrenden, when I shall be able to question you at my leisure.'

Silence.

'Very well,' said Thanet, standing up. 'If you'd just get your coat . . .'

'No!' Her voice was harsh with anger, frustration, fear and defeat. 'No,' she repeated, less violently. 'Very well, I'll tell you.'

Slowly, Thanet sat down again.

'This is outrageous!' she began furiously, then caught Thanet's eye. She clasped her hands as if to contain her anger and took a deep breath, straightened her shoulders. 'As you said, I knew that Alicia was going away for the weekend, and I wanted to know why. I felt I had a right . . .' She faltered as Thanet shifted impatiently in his chair. 'When I left home on Saturday morning I brought my night things with me. When I got here Alicia seemed upset, as I told you, and said she wanted to get off early. Naturally I was against it — it would have upset my plans. So I said it really wouldn't be fair on Faith and myself if Alicia left early — which was true, as a matter of fact,' she added defensively. 'We were short-handed as it was, with Carol away sick. Also, there were a number of appointments already arranged and Saturday morning is always the busiest time of the week. So many people come in because it's their only day off . . . So I made an issue of it, and she agreed to stay.

'It's my job to lock up, so at lunchtime I made sure that Faith left promptly, and then I waited until Alicia came out of her front door. She took a taxi, and I followed in another. She went to Victoria and I managed to overhear her destination, when she bought a ticket to Sturrenden. There were a lot of people about and she seemed very preoccupied, so it wasn't difficult. Then I caught the same train, the two-thirty. When we got to Sturrenden I expected her to take another taxi, but she didn't. I didn't realise then how small the town was, I'd never been there before. I'd been wondering how difficult it would be to follow her without her spotting me, but I needn't have worried. There were crowds of people about and later I heard that the Princess of Wales had visited the place earlier in the day. So, there was no problem. She went straight to the Black Swan. She stopped once, on the way, to talk to someone for a few minutes — a tall man, well-dressed — but that was all. I'd already made up my mind that if she went to a hotel I wouldn't be able to risk registering in the same place, and I spotted this pub across the street, the Three Horseshoes — well, you know that already. I asked for a room at the front, and got one.' Miss Ross's large nose wrinkled in distaste and her mouth turned down at the corners. 'Scruffy place it was, too. But it did have a good view of the entrance to the Black Swan, and that was what I wanted. I settled down by the window and waited. Over two hours. Then Alicia came out. She was obviously going out for the evening. I hurried downstairs, afraid I might lose her, but once again she walked.'

'She went to a concert. Did you go, too?'

'I bought a ticket. Waste of money, the stuff they were playing wasn't my cup of tea, but I wanted to see if she was going to meet anybody. But when she sat down she was alone. The seats on either side of her were already occupied, but she didn't speak to anyone, just settled down to read her programme, so I assumed she could safely be left there until the concert ended, and I went out again. I was starving. I'd had nothing to eat or drink, not even a cup of tea, since mid-morning. On the way out I enquired what time the concert ended and well before ten o'clock I was waiting outside.'

Thanet did not glance at Lineham or betray his excitement. Jessica Ross might well be innocent of nothing more than an intrusive curiosity, and if that were so, and she had seen Alicia leave with someone . . .

'I stood there for three-quarters of an hour, until everyone had left and they were locking the place up. I'd missed her.'

Jessica Ross was too engrossed in reliving her own disappointment to notice Thanet's.

'There'd been a rush of people leaving around a quarter to twenty past ten, and it'd been impossible to check them all. I hadn't dared get too close, in case I ran into Alicia. I was furious that I'd missed her, like that. . . . I walked back to the centre of the town and hung around for a while outside the Black Swan, trying to decide whether or not to go in and enquire if Alicia was back yet, but I was afraid I might run into her. . . . In the end I went back to my room. Next morning I got up very early and was at my window by seven-thirty. As it was Sunday morning everything was very quiet in the street outside until around nine-thirty, when a police car arrived and drove into the car park of the Black Swan. I didn't connect it with Alicia, of course. Then more cars arrived, and an ambulance . . . Naturally, I was very curious by now, but I didn't dare leave the window in case Alicia came out and I missed her again.

'At a quarter past eleven, when there was still no sign of her I went downstairs. There was a woman cleaning the bar, and I asked her if she knew what was going on across the street and she told me one of the guests had been murdered. A woman from London, that was all she knew. I still didn't think it could be Alicia — well you don't, do you? You never think it could be someone you know. . . . I didn't dare go into the Swan and ask for her. If she was in I wouldn't be able to say why I'd suddenly changed my mind about wanting to see her and if by any chance it had been her who'd been murdered, I'd simply be drawing attention to myself. So in the end I waited until there were several people in the foyer, then I went in and started to chat to some of them, pretending that I was a guest there too. I said what a shocking business it was then I asked if they knew who the dead woman was. They said her name was Parnell. . . . So I went back to the Horseshoes and checked out, caught the first train back to London. And that's it.'

'I see. So between ten-fifteen and ten-forty-five you were standing outside the concert hall, waiting for Mrs Parnell?'

'That's right. Why? Was that when . . .?'

'Is there anyone who could confirm this? Did you speak to anyone, do or say anything which might make anyone remember you?'

'No, of course not. The whole point was that I was trying to make myself as inconspicuous as possible.'

'What were you wearing?'

'A navy blue summer coat and a navy and turquoise scarf over my hair.' She touched the carefully arranged blonde waves with a complacent hand. 'I thought it might be too noticeable.'

'Pity. Well, Miss Ross, you must see that this doesn't really give you much of an alibi. We'll do what we can to check it out, but it's going to be extremely difficult. I must ask you not to leave town, at present, and to make sure that you will be available for further questioning, should we need to see you again.'

'But . . .' For once she was at a loss for words, and her sallow skin was the colour of dough.

'If you are innocent, you have nothing to be afraid of.'

'Of course I'm innocent!' She thumped the desk with a balled fist.

'In that case, as I said, you have nothing to worry about.' Thanet rose and Lineham followed suit. At the door Thanet turned. 'We'll be in touch.'

They left her sitting motionless at her desk.

'She could have done it,' said Lineham. 'As I said, if she did follow Mrs Parnell into the hotel, no one would have noticed her in all that crush. And although Mrs Parnell would have been surprised to see her, she'd almost certainly have invited her into her room.'

'True. But there's still no scrap of proof and if we don't get any, she'll be a hard nut to crack. And what about that red folder?'

Time was getting on. They took another taxi back to Victoria and were in the train before Lineham said, 'That folder, sir . . .'

'What about it?'

'If Jessica Ross is guilty, and took that folder away, the implication is that there was something in it which she wouldn't have wanted us to see, right?'

'So?'

'I was trying to think what it could be. . . . Suppose she'd been trying her hand at a spot of embezzlement, while Mrs Parnell was out of touch with things . . .? Say Mrs Parnell found out, told Miss Ross she'd done so, and also told her she was going away for the weekend to think things over before deciding what action to take . . .'

'And the folder contained incriminating papers . . .'

'Yes. What d'you think, sir?'

'Within the bounds of possibility, I suppose, given the personalities concerned.'

'You think it might be worth looking at the agency's books, then?'

'It might. Let's mull it over for a while, first. In any case I think we'll get the men to show that photograph of Jessica Ross to the guests at the Ladies' Night, just in case one of them happened to notice her. She wasn't in evening dress, remember.'

'It'll be a long job.'

'That can't be helped.' Thanet shifted uncomfortably in his seat. 'I don't know, Mike, I feel we're not really getting anywhere in this case. It's not that we're not making any progress, just that as soon as we think we're getting a clear lead on one person, something crops up and we have to focus on someone else.'

They were both to remember these words when they got back to Sturrenden. Sparks was hovering, obviously bursting to impart some important information. Apparently the couple who had spent Saturday night in a room two doors away from Alicia's were now at home, their holiday over, and Sparks had

had a long telephone conversation with the wife, a Mrs Dora Brent. When asked to describe anyone she had seen in or near the third-floor corridor that evening, she had at once come up with an immediately recognisable description of Vivienne Leyton.

'You're sure?'

'Yes, sir. That hair and that dress . . . the combination is unmistakeable.'

'What time was this?'

'Around ten-forty-five, sir.' Sparks was triumphant.

'How can she be so precise?'

'Well apparently she was fed up with the noise and all the people from the dinner-dance milling about downstairs, and she suggested to her husband that they have an early night. He said it was only twenty-five to eleven and he had no intention of going to bed at that ungodly hour, so she went up alone. When she got out of the lift Mrs Leyton was just hurrying past, and disappeared down the stairs at the right-hand end of the corridor.'

'I see. Good. Where do these people live, Sparks?'

'Cirencester, sir.'

'Better contact the local police, get them to send someone round to take a statement.'

'I already have, sir.'

I might have known, thought Thanet with amusement.

'Right, Mike,' he said, when Sparks had gone. 'I think we're due for another visit to Vivienne Leyton, don't you?'

The telephone rang.

'There's a Mr Knight in reception, sir. Very anxious to see you.'

The father of Rain's fiancée. Thanet hesitated. He put his hand over the receiver. 'Mr Knight wants to see me,' he said to Lineham. He raised his eyebrows, shrugged. 'All right, send him up.'

'I wonder what he wants, sir.'

'Can't imagine, but we're about to find out.'

There was a knock at the door.

'Come in.'

EIGHTEEN

A uniformed constable ushered Mr Knight into the room. Melanie's father was wearing a well-cut track suit and expensive running shoes and his fair hair was damp with perspiration.

'Excuse my informal attire, Inspector. I needed an excuse to get away, to see you . . .'

'Please. Sit down.'

'I hope you don't mind my bursting in upon you like this, without an appointment.'

'Not at all. How can I help you?'

'I feel a bit foolish, really, coming here . . . It's just that . . . Well, to be frank, Inspector, I've come to see if you've made any progress in your enquiries.'

'Into the murder of Mrs Parnell?'

'Yes.' Knight wiped the sweat from his forehead with his sleeve. 'I know I have no right to ask, really, but . . .' His eyes pleaded for understanding. 'It's just that it's so unsettling for us all. And Nicholas, of course, is already under considerable strain, with his mother still in a coma.'

'I know. It must be a very difficult time for him. And I'm sorry to have had to add to his burdens by having to question him. Though I must say that he didn't seem to be particularly bothered by it.'

Knight had scarcely heard a word Thanet said. 'Melanie's our only child, you see, and we love her dearly. We can't bear to see her miserable, like this.'

'But I don't quite see . . .'

'They were so very happy together. And of course, my wife and I were delighted about the engagement. It seemed such a very suitable match. I know he's much older than her, but that's no bad thing in a husband, it makes for stability, and of course, they have a mutual passion for music . . . Have you ever heard them play together?'

'I'm afraid not.'

'They're both wonderful musicians, and although Melanie is still only at the beginning of her career . . . I'm sorry, you don't want to hear all this.' Knight mopped at his forehead again. 'It's just that . . . I'm trying to make you see how important this is to us.'

'Of course. But I still don't quite understand . . .'

'He's changed, you see. Nicholas, I mean. Since all this began. Well, since the accident, really. Before, he . . . well, he couldn't see enough of Melanie, but now he seems to spend most of his time at the hospital — well, that's understandable, I suppose — but even when he is with her, with us, he seems preoccupied, distant . . .'

'But as you yourself just said, that is understandable, in the circumstances, surely. I'm told that Mr Rain is devoted to his mother.'

'I know, I know. It's just that . . . well, I can't help wondering if this other thing is playing on his mind, too.'

'That he feels he's seriously under suspicion of murder, you mean?'

'Yes,' said Knight, with relief. 'And what I have really come to ask is, is he?'

'Ah, well now, it's a little difficult to answer that question, Mr Knight. You must appreciate that we have to follow up every possible lead. And we can't get away from the fact that Mrs Parnell was last seen alive talking to Mr Rain at five past ten on Saturday night.'

'And those are your only grounds for suspecting him?'

Thanet shook his head. 'I'm sorry, you must see that I can't possibly answer that question.'

'But . . . Look, Inspector, I'm only too well aware that I shouldn't be pressing you like this. But . . . have you by any chance got a daughter?'

'As a matter of fact, I have. And I can guess what you're going to say . . .'

'Nevertheless,' said Knight eagerly, leaning forward in his chair to emphasise the importance of this point, 'you must be able to imagine . . . Put yourself in my position. If your daughter was engaged to a man under suspicion of murder . . .

It's tearing her apart, Inspector, and naturally her mother and I are desperately worried in case there is anything in it. Not that we really believe there could be, of course, but all the same . . .'

'I do understand, Mr Knight, believe me. But I'm afraid that at the moment I simply cannot give you the reassurance you need.'

'You mean that Nicholas . . .'

'I mean that at the moment Mr Rain is only one of a number of people whose connection with Mrs Parnell is under scrutiny. And I really cannot tell you any more than that.'

The note of finality in Thanet's voice must finally have persuaded Knight that it was pointless to persist. He was silent for a moment and then slumped back in his chair, gave a resigned shrug. 'Very well, if you can't, you can't.' He stood up. 'Thank you for seeing me, anyway.'

Thanet watched him go and then said, 'That's the trouble with murder, Mike — or any serious crime, for that matter — the number of innocent people who are affected. We come and go in their lives, and that's it, as far as we're concerned. It's only too easy to forget the havoc we might leave behind.'

'But it has to be done, sir.'

'True. But we should always be aware of the fact that long after the case is over, these people have to go on living with the effects of the distress they may have suffered unnecessarily. I tell you, it's one of the aspects of this job which really gets me down, sometimes.'

'But if they're innocent . . .'

'That doesn't eliminate the pain of uncertainty, the days, weeks or even months of anxiety.'

'I think he had a nerve, as a matter of fact, coming here like that and trying to squeeze information out of us.'

Lineham's indignation was, Thanet knew, partly over the effect that Knight's visit had had upon Thanet himself, and for the millionth time he asked himself if he was in the wrong job. He loved the excitement of the chase, the knowledge that he was working to enforce a moral as well as a legal justice, but at the same time he was constantly aware that he himself was perhaps too sensitive to be able comfortably to tread the tightrope between objectivity and emotional involvement with the people he met during the course of his investigations. There was, he felt, a softness at the core of his nature inappropriate to the work he had to do, and try as he would to suppress it, like a many-headed hydra it kept popping up when he least expected it. Ten minutes ago he had been full of eagerness to pursue their latest lead and now . . . With an effort he forced himself back into briskness.

'Oh, I don't know, Mike. It's understandable that he should be concerned, in the circumstances. As he said, wouldn't you be?'

Lineham shrugged. 'I suppose so . . . Anyway, do you want me to give Mrs Leyton a ring before we go?'

'No. She's sure to be there at this time of day. We'll surprise her.'

It was now half past five in the afternoon and Thanet was banking on the fact that by this hour most women were at home and thinking of preparing the evening meal. Vivienne Leyton didn't have a job, so far as he knew, and Richard Leyton would presumably soon be arriving home hungry from his day's work on the farm.

But he had miscalculated, it seemed. When they arrived at the bungalow all the doors and windows were shut, and the double garage stood open and empty.

'Do we wait, sir?'

'Let me think . . . Let's enquire at the main farmhouse. Perhaps her mother-in-law will know where she's gone.'

It was a typical Kentish farmhouse, brick and tile-hung with a well-kept garden and yellow roses smothering the open-fronted porch. Mrs Leyton senior was languidly elegant in a flowered Tana lawn suit.

'She's gone to town for the day. Shopping, with a friend. Mad, going to London in this heat, but there you are . . .'

'Have you any idea what time she'll be back?'

'She hoped to catch the five-ten, I believe.'

So it would be at least another hour and a quarter before she returned.

'I see. Thank you, Mrs Leyton. We'll come back later this

evening, around seven-thirty. Perhaps you could give her the message.'

'If I see her. I could give her a ring, I suppose.'

'Some people!' said Lineham as they returned to the car. 'Give her a ring, indeed, when the house is only a hundred yards away!'

'Pity. I was hoping to catch Vivienne without her husband. He's sure to be home before then.'

'So what now, sir?'

'Might as well do something useful. We'll go and have a word with Rain, I think. We should be in good time to catch him before he leaves for evening visiting time at the hospital.'

They drove in silence for a little while and then Thanet said, 'Pull in for a minute, will you Mike?'

Lineham did as he was asked and switched off the engine. They were in a lay-by in a narrow country lane which ran along the top of a ridge. They both wound their windows right down and the fragrant country air flowed into the car, laden with the mingled scents of lush green vegetation and the faint, sweet smell of strawberries from the field below on their left. At the bottom of the slope a lorry was being loaded with the last pickings of the day, ready for its trip to New Covent Garden.

Thanet stirred. 'I've been trying to work out how this baby business fits in — or if it fits in at all.'

'We can't just ignore it.'

'I know. And I agree, Rain does seem the most likely candidate for the father, in view of the timing. But it has occurred to me that if he is innocent he really may have known nothing about the baby, still be unaware of its existence.'

'If. But if he did kill Mrs Parnell, the baby could still be the precipitating factor, whether he knew about it originally or not.' Lineham warmed to his theme. 'Say Mrs Parnell had kept in touch with him through the years, and after her husband died had hopes that she and Rain would get together again. Then she reads about his engagement, and she's furious that even though she's now free herself, he's still not going to marry her. So she comes down to Sturrenden and threatens to tell Miss Knight about the child, if he doesn't break off with her.'

'I just don't like it, Mike. It doesn't sound like the Alicia we've been hearing about. Nothing anyone has said to us has even hinted that she'd be the type to resort to blackmail in a matter like this — nor that she ever had eyes for anyone but her husband.'

'True.' Lineham chewed his lip for a few moments, gazing out of the window at the fruit lorry, which was just moving off. 'Are you saying, then, that you really think Rain is in the clear?'

'I just don't know. And I agree, we have to go on investigating this particular avenue. But we mustn't forget that it's quite possible that one of the others was the father of Alicia's child.'

'But which?'

'Who can say, at this stage?' Thanet sighed. 'It was all so long ago. A lot can happen in twenty years. People change, they forget . . . Alicia was different then — young, flirtatious, even a bit flighty, perhaps. If so, the experience of having the baby would have sobered her up considerably. And I think you'll agree that, despite the fact that she had more than her fair share of tragedy, by all accounts she became a pretty fine sort of person. I don't know . . . I suppose we'll have to see Rain, tackle him about the baby, to see how he reacts, but I honestly wonder if we're doing the right thing.'

'But why, sir? I don't see what you mean.'

'Well, remember what I was saying just before we left the office? About disrupting the lives of innocent people? If Rain is innocent, if he didn't even know about the child, and his contact with Alicia on Saturday night was limited to those few minutes in the foyer after the concert, have we any right to give him further pain by telling him that he could be the father of a child he didn't know about and will never see? He has enough troubles of his own at the moment, without our adding to them unnecessarily.'

'With respect . . .'

'Mike!'

'Sorry, sir . . . I was only going to say that although I can see the point you're making, I don't think we can *afford* to have scruples like that. This is a murder investigation, after all.'

Thanet burst out laughing and slapped Lineham on the

shoulder. 'Spoken like a true policeman, Mike. And you're absolutely right, of course.' He sat back, folding his arms. 'Well, what are you waiting for? Drive on.'

'We're going to tackle Rain about the baby?'

'We're going to tackle Rain about the baby.'

Nicholas Rain was mowing the lawn, describing slow, controlled arcs with a Flymo. He looked up as the police car pulled into the drive, cut the engine of the motor mower and walked slowly across the grass towards them. He was wearing tee shirt, jeans and walking boots. Thanet noted the latter with approval. Rain was obviously a practical man as well as an artist. Flymos should be treated with respect.

'Sorry to trouble you again, Mr Rain.'

Rain gave a resigned shrug. 'D'you mind if we stay in the garden? Then I won't have to unlace these.' He gestured at his boots.

'Not at all.'

Rain led the way around the side of the house to a paved terrace where comfortable cedarwood chairs with plump blue and white cushions were set around a slatted table of the same wood. On it stood a tray with a small flowered teapot, a single cup and saucer and, a bachelor's touch, a milk bottle. It was a pleasant place to relax on a warm summer evening. Low shrubs and variegated ornamental grasses spilled over on to the mellow slabs of york stone, softening the hard lines of the edges, and little clumps of low-growing thyme and rock plants grew here and there in spaces left between the paving stones. Beyond the terrace was the lawn, flanked by herbaceous borders, their curving edges leading the eye to a small cedarwood summerhouse with a conical roof, artfully set off centre at the far end of the garden. Behind, mature beech and chestnut trees provided a majestic backdrop.

'You have a beautiful garden,' said Thanet.

'It's my mother's pride and joy.' Rain's eyes clouded. 'She spends most of her time out here, especially in the summer. I feel I must try and keep it up until I can get someone to look after it for her.'

'How is she?'

'No change, I'm afraid.'

'And your sister?'

'Making good progress, now. Look, Inspector, much as I appreciate your asking, we both know that you haven't come to enquire about my mother's health. What do you want this time?'

Might as well be equally direct, thought Thanet. 'Did you know that Alicia Doyle was pregnant when she left Sturrenden in 1964 and had a baby the following January?'

Rain sat up with a jerk and his elbow caught the corner of the tray, knocking it off the table. The crockery shattered, scattering pieces of flower-sprigged porcelain all around them. Despite his previous determination to watch Rain's reaction to his question closely, Thanet's attention involuntarily switched to the falling tray and by the time he realised what had happened it was too late and Rain was murmuring apologies and picking up the pieces, helped by Lineham.

Cursing the accident — if that was what it was — Thanet waited until most of the fragments were retrieved and then said, 'If we could continue . . .'

Rain deposited a handful of broken china on the tray and sat down. 'Yes, of course . . . Sorry about that, clumsy of me . . . No, I'd no idea. No one knew, I'm sure of that, or I'd have heard . . . So that was why she moved away. We'd been told it was because her father had a new job, but we all assumed it was really because of Paul Leyton's suicide . . . You'd remember that, of course.'

'Yes, I do. But in view of this new information, the next question we naturally have to ask ourselves is, who was the father of that child?'

Rain stared at him. 'My God, you're not suggesting . . .?'

'Work it out for yourself. The baby was born in January 1965. Which means that it would have been conceived in April 1964. Who was Alicia Doyle's boyfriend at that time?'

Rain was still looking stunned. He was either a very good actor or genuinely taken aback, Thanet couldn't decide which. Thanet glanced at Lineham, who was sitting slightly behind Rain's line of vision, but the sergeant shrugged, obviously as uncertain as Thanet.

'I don't believe it.' It was scarcely more than a whisper.

'But it's true, nevertheless. I assure you we don't play games with this kind of information, Mr Rain.'

'I'd no idea . . . I really had no idea . . .' Rain passed a hand across his forehead and shook his head in disbelief. 'I'm sorry, Inspector, but this has . . . this is . . . It's a bit of a shock, to learn you might be a father, twenty years on.' He looked up, suddenly intense. 'What happened to the child?'

'We were hoping you might be able to tell us that.'

'Me!' Rain gave a derisive laugh and spread his arms wide. 'I assure you, Inspector, if it hasn't become obvious to you already, that I had no knowledge of the existence of any child, let alone its whereabouts. . . . Didn't Alicia bring it up, then?'

'No. The baby was adopted.'

'Was it a boy, or a girl?'

'A girl.'

'And you've really no idea where it . . . where she is?'

'Not as yet. But one never quite knows what will turn up. It seems that Mrs Parnell had been trying to trace the child for some months, and that a couple of weeks before she died she found out the girl's new identity quite by chance.'

'How do you know this?'

'Mrs Parnell's solicitor told us. Apparently she intended making a new will, in the girl's favour.'

'So she told him her name?'

'No. I gather she didn't want to rush things. She wanted to make contact with her daughter first, see how things went.'

'And you haven't found any clues to her new identity, among Alicia's papers?'

'Not so far.'

Rain frowned and then gazed abstractedly down at his clasped hands. He began absentmindedly to rub the tip of one thumb across the ball of the other. The silence stretched out until eventually he stirred, shook his head and raised it to look at Thanet again.

'I'm sorry, Inspector, but I find myself quite at a loss. As I said, it's rather a shock to learn that one might have been a father for twenty years without being aware of the fact. And at this stage . . . To be honest, I don't know whether to be glad or sorry that you don't know the girl's name, or where she is.'

'I can understand that.'

'Perhaps . . . if you do find out, in the course of your investigation . . . You'd let me know?'

'I can't promise that, I'm afraid. It would depend very much on the circumstances.'

'Yes, I can see that. But you'll bear it in mind?'

'Of course.'

There was nothing further to be said on the subject at the moment, and they left.

'What do you think, sir? Do you think he genuinely didn't know about the baby?'

'I'm not sure.'

They drove back to Vivienne Leyton's house in silence.

It looked as though she was home, this time. Some of the house windows were open and a metallic green Metro stood in the drive.

Before they had a chance to knock, the front door opened with a jerk and Vivienne Leyton stood glaring at them. She was wearing a beige linen safari-style suit, with a beige and white striped cotton blouse and high-heeled, strappy sandals. Her blazing mop of hair seemed to crackle with indignation.

'Really, Inspector, this is outrageous! It's too much! I've been up in town all day, I've only just got back, I have to prepare my husband's dinner and what do I find? An arbitrary message informing me that you will be calling to see me at seven-thirty. No "Is it convenient?" or anything like that, I'm just expected to be at your disposal regardless . . .'

'Yes, but . . .'

'It can't possibly be anything so urgent that it can't wait till morning, so if you don't mind . . .' And she started to close the door.

Thanet put out his hand to prevent it being slammed in his face. 'I'm sorry, Mrs Leyton, but I do mind.'

'Really! What right have you got, to come forcing your way in like this?'

'I am not forcing my way in. Indeed, if you would prefer not to have us in the house, that is your privilege. In which case, perhaps you'd be so kind as to accompany us to the police station, and we can talk there.'

This case was bedevilled by aggressive, recalcitrant women, Thanet thought. It was degrading to have had to wield the same big stick twice in one day, but in the circumstances it seemed the only thing to do. And the threat seemed as effective with Vivienne Leyton as it had been earlier with Jessica Ross.

She stared at him, taken aback. 'You can't be serious . . .?' She glanced from Thanet to Lineham. 'You can't possibly mean . . .' Suddenly, she was alarmed. 'You're not *arresting* me?'

'No. We merely want to talk to you. And I repeat, I do apologise for the inconvenience.'

She stepped aside. 'You'd better come in,' she said, on a note of defeat.

She led the way once more into the sitting room and perched on the arm of one of the chairs. 'If we could just get on with it, then.'

'You will recall,' said Thanet, sitting down on the long, deeply-upholstered couch, 'that the last time we were here we asked you about your movements during the interval between the dinner and the dancing on Saturday night — between a quarter past ten and a quarter to eleven, that is.'

'So?'

'You told us, if you remember, that your recollection of what you did after leaving the powder room was rather hazy, but that you thought you had probably "drifted around" chatting to people you knew.'

'If you say so.'

'Now that you've had time to think about it, can you recollect the names of any of these people?'

'I don't know what you mean by "Now that you've had time to think about it". I lead a very busy life, Inspector, and I have better things to do than spend my time fruitlessly mulling over a particularly boring half an hour during a singularly uninteresting evening.'

Thanet sighed. 'Very well, Mrs Leyton. I see you're determined to be uncooperative. I have given you ample opportunity to offer me the information voluntarily and I will, in fact, ask you just once more. Are you sure that there is nothing you want to tell me, nothing at all to add to your statement about how you spent your time during that interval?'

There was no doubt about it, his formal tone had frightened her, though she was doing her best to hide it. She put up her hand as if casually to stroke her throat, but not quickly enough to hide the involuntary swallowing movement which betrayed her fear.

'I don't know what you mean.'

'Don't you? I would remind you that it is a serious offence, deliberately to withold information from the police, especially in a case as serious as murder.'

A tense shake of the head.

How could he make her tell him, without revealing just how little he knew? 'In that case, perhaps you might change your mind when you hear that we have a witness, an independent witness at that, someone who could have no possible reason to lie . . .'

She opened her mouth. 'A wit . . .' Her voice emerged as a croak and she had to stop, clear her throat. 'A witness to what?' Her eyes were agonised.

Was it possible that she thought he meant, a witness to the murder? Had her unrelenting hostility been not merely the natural outcome of her aggressive nature but a smokescreen to hide her guilt? For the first time Thanet began seriously to entertain the possibility that Vivienne Leyton was their quarry. His eyes went to the hand which was still clutching her throat. Her nails were painted, yes, but short, very short, in fact. . . . Surely she wouldn't have had sufficient strength to overpower another woman of her own size? And yet, it was astounding just how much physical strength may be summoned up if the passions directing it are sufficiently powerful. . . . He became aware that she was still awaiting his reply.

'A witness to what?' she repeated.

'Oh come, Mrs Leyton, there's no need for me to spell it out for you.'

But still she said nothing.

It was no good. He would have to acknowledge defeat on

this point, in order to move forward. 'You were seen, Mrs Leyton. In the corridor outside Mrs Parnell's room.'

'Ah. I see.'

Was that *relief* he had glimpsed in her eyes?

'Well, Mrs Leyton?'

'Well, what?'

Keep cool, Thanet told himself. Don't let her rile you. 'I'm waiting for an explanation. And please, don't say, "Explanation of what?" To spell it out for you, I want to know exactly when you went upstairs, and precisely what you did when you got there. And,' he went on quickly as she glared at him defiantly and opened her mouth to interrupt, 'I must make it clear that I am not prepared to be fobbed off. I want answers to these questions, Mrs Leyton, and however long it takes, Sergeant Lineham and I are not going to leave until we get them.'

She glowered at him and folded her arms with a brusque, impatient movement, as if trying to contain her anger and frustration. For a full minute they held each other's eyes, locked in wordless combat. Thanet found himself willing her to capitulate. *Give in, go on, give in . . .*

Finally, recognising perhaps the degree of his determination, understanding that she could not hold out indefinitely, she gave a nonchalant little shrug and said, 'OK, you win, Inspector. Though I think that when you hear what I've got to say, you'll agree that it wasn't worth all the fuss. In fact, I can't think why I didn't tell you in the first place . . . I suppose because I thought it would save a lot of hassle . . .' She laughed. 'Big joke, in the circumstances. Anyway, it's very simple, really. I went up to Alicia's room, knocked at the door, got no reply, and came down again. And that's it. Satisfied?'

'Not quite. I'd like to take it a little more slowly. What time did you go up?'

She shrugged. 'Some time between half past ten and a quarter to eleven.'

'How did you know which room she was in?'

'Elementary, my dear Watson. I took a peek in the hotel register. It was lying open on the counter at the reception desk, and there were so many people about that no one noticed.'

'You went up in the lift?'

'Yes.'

'Then what?'

'I told you, I knocked at her door, got no reply, came down again.'

'In the lift?'

She fell straight into the trap he had set for her.

'Yes.'

'Why did you want to see her?'

'For a chat. Well, to be honest, I felt I'd been a bit off-hand with her, earlier on in the evening, and I wanted to make amends.'

'To apologise for your earlier behaviour, then?'

'That's right. Just to show there were no hard feelings.'

'Over what?'

'We parted on, shall we say, a sour note, many years ago. During dinner I kept on thinking how childish it was, to have behaved as I had, in the foyer . . .'

Thanet didn't believe a word of it. In his view, Vivienne Leyton just wasn't the sort of woman to go out of her way to apologise to a woman she hadn't seen for twenty years and would probably never see again.

'I'm sorry, I don't believe you. And I've had more than enough of this prevarication. As I told you, we have a witness who could have no possible reason to lie. And I know, I repeat, I *know*, that you are lying now.'

Vivienne Leyton's eyes flickered briefly in the direction of the door. Then, to Thanet's surprise, she burst into tears.

His astonishment did not last long. The next moment the sitting room door opened and Richard Leyton came into the room. She must have heard him arrive.

'What the hell . . .?' He hurried to his wife's side and put his arm around her shoulders, gathering her to him. Then he glared at Thanet. 'What the devil's going on here? How dare you invade my home and bully my wife like this? I shall report you to your superiors, have no doubt about that.'

'Do, by all means, Mr Leyton, but I think you will find that you have no legitimate grounds for complaint.'

'No legitimate . . .'

'Witholding evidence is a serious matter, especially in a murder case. And I'm sorry to say that this is precisely what your wife has been doing.'

'That still gives you no right to browbeat her!'

'I was not browbeating her, as you put it. I was simply informing her that I knew she was lying to me.' Thanet held up his hand. 'And before you make any further complaint, allow me to inform you that the reason why I didn't believe her story is because we have an independent — *independent* — witness, Mr Leyton, whose story disagrees with hers.'

Leyton stared at Thanet and then glanced down at his wife. Her tears had stopped now — perhaps, Thanet thought, because she wanted to be able to hear her husband's reactions to all this.

'Is this true, Viv?'

'Lend me your handkerchief, Richard, will you?'

'Of course.' He took it out and handed it to her, waited while she wiped her eyes and blew her nose. 'Viv?' he repeated.

'That's what he *claims*. I don't know what he's talking about. I just told him the truth, that I went up to Alicia's room during the interval on Saturday night, knocked, got no reply and came down again.' She was gazing up at her husband as she spoke and it was clear to Thanet that there was some kind of message, or appeal, in her eyes, but whatever it was Leyton hadn't received it. He was merely looking puzzled.

'You went up to see Alicia? But why?'

Vivienne Leyton tossed her head impatiently. 'Why not? Oh well, if you must know, because I felt I'd been a bit off-hand with her when we'd met, earlier in the evening. That's true, isn't it?'

'Well yes, but . . .'

She cut him off. 'There you are, then. I thought she might be back from the concert by then and I'd just pop up and apologise.'

'And then you went back down. In the lift,' said Thanet.

'Yes.'

'Sergeant Lineham, just read that statement out, will you?'

Lineham shuffled his papers obediently and for the second

time that day pretended to read from an imaginary script. 'Statement of Mrs Dora Brent, occupant of room number 105, the Black Swan on Saturday July 14th . . . Do you want it all, sir?'

'Just the relevant bit.'

'Ah, here we are. "My husband said it was only twenty-five to eleven and he didn't want to go to bed yet, so I went up alone. I had to wait a couple of minutes for the lift and when I stepped out on the third floor a woman passed me. I didn't see her face, but I noticed her because even from the back she was very striking. She was wearing a beautiful long, narrow, copper-coloured evening dress threaded with gold lurex and she had a mass of red hair, frizzed out in a great bush. She disappeared down the staircase at the end of the corridor": . .'

Lineham paused significantly and both policemen looked at Vivienne Leyton.

Her face still wore an expression of expectancy which gradually turned to puzzlement as she realised that Lineham had finished.

'I'm sorry,' she said, 'I must be dim, but . . .'

'The staircase!' said Leyton. 'That's what you mean, isn't it, Inspector? The statement says you went down the staircase, Viv, and you told us you'd gone down in the lift.'

'Oh. I *see*.' Suddenly she was transformed, her face vivid with relief. 'Is that *all* . . . But I made a mistake, it's as simple as that. I'd just forgotten I used the stairs, on the way back down.'

'Why was that, Mrs Leyton?'

'What do you mean?'

'Why did you use the stairs, instead of the lift?'

She shrugged. 'I just felt like it.' She gave him a pert smile. 'Exercise is good for you.'

Thanet refused to allow himself to be provoked. He was still convinced that there was more to it than that. And yet, he was inclined to believe her, when she said that she had knocked at Alicia's door and got no reply. There had been the ring of truth in her voice. So what had he missed? Missed . . . Not what she had done, perhaps, but what she had *seen* . . .

According to Mallard, the murder had taken place between

ten and eleven on Saturday night. Alicia couldn't have got back to the Swan after the concert before ten-fifteen at the earliest. Vivienne Leyton claimed to have gone up in the lift at around ten-thirty, give or take a few minutes. Mrs Brent had seen her in the third floor corridor at around twenty to eleven. Assuming that Vivienne herself had not committed the murder, what would the murderer himself have been doing at that time? There were various possibilities, the least interesting being that he had not yet arrived. But equally, he might have been in Alicia's room, talking to her; the murder might actually have been taking place; it might already have happened, and he could have been preparing to leave; or — and as far as Vivienne was concerned, these were the two most intriguing possibilities of all — he might just have been arriving at her room, or leaving it, when Vivienne appeared on the scene. *In which case she could have seen him.*

Thanet realised that everyone was looking expectantly at him. He cleared his throat, which was suddenly dry with excitement. He felt as though he himself had been given a glimpse of the murderer, an oblique, tantalising glimpse, no more than a blur of movement at the very edge of his vision . . .

'Very well, Mrs Leyton. Say I accept that you might have walked back down because you just happened to feel like it, and that until a moment ago you'd forgotten you'd done so . . .'

'Just a moment, Inspector,' Leyton cut in. 'Aren't you forgetting something?'

'What, Mr Leyton?'

'I think an apology is in order, don't you? You reduce my wife to tears and then, when you find she hasn't been lying to you after all, that it was a simple mistake in memory on her part, you just barge on . . .'

'By all means.' Apologies cost nothing and were frequently a good investment. 'Mrs Leyton, if I have upset you unnecessarily, I apologise.'

Vivienne Leyton glanced up at her husband and gave an uneasy little laugh. Richard Leyton looked mollified. He stood up. 'Now that that's settled . . .'

'I'm sorry, Mr Leyton, I'm afraid I haven't quite finished.'
Leyton frowned, took his wife's hand, but said nothing.

'You've told us what you *did*, Mrs Leyton. Now I'd like you to tell us what you *saw*. From the moment you stepped out of the lift on the third floor, to the moment you arrived back downstairs.'

On target. Thanet could tell, by the flash of terror in her eyes before she looked down at her lap, the sudden curling of her toes in those pretty, open sandals. Could he be right? Had she really seen the murderer? But if she had, why hadn't she said so? Unless . . .

Thanet looked at Leyton, who was gazing protectively down at his wife. Could it be her husband, whom she was trying to protect? If so, this would explain the unspoken message which Vivienne had tried to convey to Leyton just now. *I was there, and I know it was you*, she could have been saying. Yet Leyton hadn't understood, Thanet was willing to swear to that. Unless that misunderstanding had been deliberate, a display put on for Thanet's sake.

They were all looking at Vivienne Leyton in expectant silence. Eventually her husband nudged her. 'Come on, Viv. We're waiting.'

Again she glanced up at him with that appeal for complicity and once again there was no response.

'I'm trying to remember,' she said irritably, sliding her hand out of his grasp. She began to pluck at one corner of the handkerchief balled up in her left hand, quick, jerky little movements which betrayed her inner tension. Finally she shook her head. 'There was nothing. I didn't see anything. It was extraordinary, the contrast . . . Downstairs you could hardly move for people, but upstairs it was quiet, quiet and empty . . .' An involuntary shudder coursed through her body and she bit her lip, hard.

'So why does the memory upset you?' said Thanet. He was beginning to think that it really would be sensible to take her in for questioning. If he was right, and she really had seen her husband up there, she was never going to say so with him sitting beside her, monitoring her every word and displaying so much solicitude.

'Viv?' said Leyton. And he passed one hand gently over her head in a soothing gesture. 'Did you see something?'

Had he detected a note of warning in Leyton's voice? Thanet wondered. Or had it merely been concern?

Vivienne Leyton took a deep breath. The tension in the room was almost palpable.

She raised her head and looked straight at Thanet. 'No,' she said. Suddenly she began to tremble. 'It's just that . . . It was so horrible, to think that I was up there and Alicia . . . Alicia was . . . just on the other side of that door . . .'

She began to weep again, noisy, racking sobs which convulsed her whole body. Richard Leyton put his arm around her again. 'Viv . . .' He glanced at Thanet and said fiercely, 'There's your answer, Inspector. Now will you please leave my wife alone and get out?'

They had no choice but to comply.

TWENTY

'I still think we ought to bring her in for questioning,' said Lineham.

It was the following morning and Thanet and Lineham were arguing about Vivienne Leyton. Like Thanet, Lineham had worked out that she must have been protecting her husband — unless, of course, she was guilty herself.

'What's the point?' said Thanet wearily. 'She's obviously made up her mind that she's not going to tell us, either way.'

'But if we saw her alone . . . Obviously she wasn't going to say anything last night, with him there, but without him we might manage to persuade her.'

'I doubt it. She's a very stubborn woman, and a very determined one. Oh, I agree we'll have to see her again, but I still feel it would be best if we had some sort of evidence to confront her with, when we do.'

'If she is protecting him, I can't think why she's so set on it. They're not exactly on the best of terms, anyone can see that. And that conversation you overheard . . .'

'Maybe it's just self-interest, pure and simple. She doesn't want to lose her comfortable life-style . . . Or maybe she wants to have an extra stick to beat him with, in the future . . . Who can tell? Maybe they both enjoy the way they live. Maybe conflict is the spice of life for them — or for her, anyway.'

'I don't see what evidence you hope to get against either of them anyway. I don't see what else we can do. It's so frustrating.' Lineham thumped the edge of his desk with a closed fist.

'Looks as though you two need a referee.' Mallard had poked his head into the room in time to hear Lineham's last words.

'Come in, Doc.' Thanet grinned. 'I was just saying that for some people conflict is the spice of life.'

'As you are demonstrating, presumably. I just called in to ask if you'd had any confirmation of that adoption theory of yours.'

'That Nicholas Rain was really Penny's father, you mean? Sorry, I forgot to let you know. No, that all fell through.'

'Suspected as much,' said Mallard with satisfaction. 'In fact, the more I thought about it, the more cock-eyed it seemed. The Rains were sensible people, they'd never have gone in for some hole-in-the-corner arrangement like that. It's too risky for everyone concerned, too much could go wrong. Far better to do it properly, with guaranteed anonymity on both sides.'

'Quite.'

'So you're stuck, are you?'

'No need to look so pleased about it. But no, we're not, as a matter of fact. Just one or two temporary difficulties, that's all.'

'Pleased about it? Don't be insulting Luke. I wasn't gloating over your lack of progress, I was merely endeavouring to spread a little sweetness and light.' And Mallard gave Thanet such a hearty clap on the back that glowing flakes of tobacco from his newly-lit pipe cascaded over his lap and he leapt up, beating them out. Joan was forever reproaching him for the minute holes which appeared with monotonous regularity in his clothes.

'Sweetness and light isn't all you'll be spreading if you go on like that, Doc,' he grumbled.

Mallard was grinning. 'Serves you right. Filthy habit. Been trying to break you of it for years.' He glanced at Lineham, who was watching with amusement. 'You ought to take a leaf out of Lineham's book. Bet he could beat you hands down on fitness, any day.'

'When you've quite finished the lecture . . .'

'All right.' Mallard held up his hands. 'No need to say any more. I know when I'm not wanted.'

But he was still smiling as he left.

'He seems unusually cheerful this morning,' said Lineham.

'Hmm. Anyway, what were we saying?'

'We were talking about the Leytons.'

'Ah, yes. And you were doing a bit of table-thumping, as I recall.'

'Well it is infuriating.' Lineham was looking frustrated all over again. 'Every time we get a clear-cut lead on any of them, something crops up to stop us going ahead, or it fizzles out, or one of the others suddenly seems a better bet.' He sat up, assumed the pose of a race commentator clutching a microphone and began to talk in a rapid monotone. 'They're off! And it's Richard and Vivienne Leyton pulling away, with Bassett close behind, followed by Ross and Rain. Now, suddenly it's Rain, Rain is pulling away, but no, Ross is overtaking him, Ross is taking a clear lead. But no, Rain is coming up behind and here's an outsider coming up, it's Hollister, Hollister, no, he can't make it, he's dropping behind and yes, he's fallen, he's out of the race, it's Bassett instead, yes, it's Bassett, no, the Leytons are making headway, followed by Ross and Rain, it's going to be a very close thing . . .' Lineham made a disgusted sound in his throat and sat back, folding his arms. 'Makes you sick,' he said.

'Feeling better, Mike?' Thanet had been watching his sergeant indulgently. It had been a harmless enough way for Lineham to vent his feelings. 'All right, so at the moment it's anybody's guess. Now, let's stop fooling around and get down to it. We're both agreed, I think, that this was no casual crime committed by an outsider.'

'Because Mrs Parnell's money and jewellery were not touched, and that red file mysteriously disappeared.'

'Yes. So our chief suspects would appear to be Jessica Ross, the two Leytons and Nicholas Rain.'

'With Bassett as an outsider, sir.'

'True. All right, we won't forget Bassett. Though there's very little, so far, to implicate him.'

'He's got a possible motive, sir, if he really was as attached to Paul Leyton as we think.'

'Revenge. Yes. And no alibi, either. Perhaps we have been rather remiss, there. We'll get hold of a photograph and see if anyone who was at the Swan on Saturday recognises him.'

'If only there hadn't been that Ladies' Night, and all those people crowding the place out just at the wrong time . . .'

'No point in saying, "if only", Mike.'

'And you're still not discounting Mr Rain, sir?'

'I don't think we can.' Thanet leaned back in his chair, clasping his hands behind his head. 'As we've said before, the fact is that unless Alicia was killed by Jessica Ross, for gain, there just doesn't seem to be anyone in her present life who's even a remote possibility. In which case it seems most likely that she was murdered by someone local, for a reason connected with her past. So we have to continue to look at Rain. For all we know there's some other reason, a reason we haven't begun to guess at yet, why he might have wanted to get rid of her.'

'I still think we can't discount the possibility that he and Mrs Parnell might have kept a relationship going all these years. After all, she was an attractive woman, sir, and as her husband was incapable of making love to her . . .'

'We don't know that he was incapable.'

'But he was paralysed from the waist down! And Mr Thrall said that she had told him that her husband couldn't give her any children.'

'Not quite. He'd never *been able* to give her a child, was the way Thrall put it. And that's not necessarily the same thing at all. Anyway, that's not the point. The point is that Parnell might have been paralysed, might have been sterile, too, but he could still have been capable of making love. It depends, I understand, on the nature of the injury. If it's a spinal injury only, it might still be possible, with stimulation. You remember that furore over that Catholic couple who were initially refused permission to marry by their priest, because, he said, they would be incapable of consummating the marriage?'

'Yes. They did get permission in the end, though, didn't they?'

'Exactly. There must have been good reason, for the Church to change its mind like that. I remember that at the time I heard an item on the radio, by a doctor who specialised in the sexual disorders of paraplegics, and he seemed to think they might well be able to manage it. So I think that as far as the Parnells are concerned we simply can't take it for granted that he was incapable of making love to her, and that she would have been driven to take a lover through sexual need.

And the other thing is that from all we've heard about her, it wouldn't have been consistent with Alicia's character or with her relationship with her husband, for her to have been carrying on an affair for years behind his back.'

'Maybe. But surely we still have to take it into account as a *possibility*. In which case the reason why she would have seemed especially on edge for the couple of weeks previous to her death would not have been because she was wondering how best to approach her daughter, but because she'd seen Rain's engagement announced in the papers and was nerving herself to tell him that if he didn't break it off she'd tell Miss Knight about the affair and also about the baby. In which case, the red folder could have contained documentary evidence — photographs, love letters perhaps, even the baby's birth certificate — which she could have threatened to show Miss Knight.'

Thanet was shaking his head. 'It's no good, Mike, I still can't see Alicia as a blackmailer either. But I do agree that what you're saying all hangs together, and that we can't afford to ignore the possibility that it did happen like that. All right. We'll make further enquiries in London, see if there's anything even remotely resembling a whisper that Alicia and Rain have ever been seen together.'

Thanet made a note, then laid his pen down again. 'So much for Rain. Now, Jessica Ross. How are the men getting on with showing her photograph to guests at the Ladies' Night?'

'Slowly, I'm afraid. And with no luck so far. There were about two hundred people there.'

'They've got the description of what she was wearing?'

'Yes.'

'So we'll just have to be patient, see what comes up. Pity we didn't think of getting them to show Bassett's photograph at the same time. We slipped up there, Mike. Anyway, that leaves us with the Leytons.'

'I still think . . .'

'Mike, I know what you think. You've made it abundantly clear. And I've also stated my reason for disagreeing with you. Mrs Leyton is a tough nut to crack and before we tackle her I want some good, clear, irrefutable evidence so that I can lay it

in front of her and say, "There, explain that away." Besides
. . .' He frowned.

'What, sir?'

'Something's been nagging at me for days. If only I could think what it was . . .'

'Try thinking of something else.'

'What do you think I've been doing!' Thanet shook his head, as if to clear it, massaged his temples.

The telephone rang. Thanet answered it and raised an eyebrow at Lineham.

'Send them up.'

He replaced the receiver. 'Well, it looks as though you've got what you wanted, Mike. The mountain has come to Mohammed.'

'Mrs Leyton?'

'The same. Accompanied by spouse.'

'Really? I wonder what they want.'

'Intriguing, isn't it? A united front isn't exactly their strong point.'

'Perhaps she's come to confess, and wants him to hold her hand.'

'The trouble with you, Mike, is that you have an overoptimistic nature.'

Thanet's guess was that possibly, overnight, Leyton had managed to get out of his wife the reason for her prevarication of the previous day and had persuaded her to tell the truth at last. Thanet's pulse quickened. Vivienne Leyton had actually been there, on the spot, round about the time the murder had been committed . . .

The Leytons looked nervous, apprehensive, and Vivienne Leyton avoided Thanet's eye as they sat down. It was the first time Thanet had seen Leyton out of his working clothes and they looked a handsome, prosperous pair, he in a light grey summer suit, striped shirt and sober tie, she in an eye-opening, sizzling pink cotton dress which Thanet would have expected to clash with her hair, but for some reason didn't.

'It's good of you to see us without an appointment, Inspector,' said Leyton.

'Not at all. What can I do for you?'

'First of all, I feel I owe you an apology. I'm afraid I was abominably rude to you last night.'

Now that they had come to him voluntarily Thanet could afford to be generous. 'Forget it. It's an occupational hazard, I'm afraid. I've experienced far worse, I assure you.'

'All the same . . .'

'Please. I mean it.'

'Very well. Thank you.' Leyton shifted in his seat, glanced anxiously at his wife. 'We've come to see you because . . .' He cleared his throat, began again. 'It's just that after you'd gone, last night, well, we . . . I couldn't help feeling that you were right, that my wife was rather more upset than . . . than the occasion seemed to warrant. So in the end I persuaded her to tell me what was the matter.'

So he had been right. Thanet experienced a spurt of satisfaction, and the nape of his neck prickled with excitement.

Leyton sat up a little straighter and squared his shoulders, as if bracing himself against an anticipated onslaught. 'The truth of the matter is, that she was behaving as she did out of mistaken loyalty to me.'

'I see . . . at least, I think I do. Could you clarify a little?'

'Certainly. I . . .'

'Or perhaps we could hear this from Mrs Leyton herself?'

The Leytons consulted with a glance, then she nodded. 'All right. It was stupid of me, really. I should have realised that Richard . . . that I was mistaken. I . . . I thought, you see, that as I stepped out of the lift on the third floor that night, I saw Richard moving away from me towards the stairs at the far end of the corridor.'

Once again Thanet experienced that tantalising sensation of catching a fleeting glimpse of the murderer.

'What time was this?'

'I worked it out. It must have been about twenty-five to eleven.'

'And at the time you concluded . . .?'

'That he must have come up to see Alicia.'

'Why did you think he might have done that?'

She caught her lower lip beneath her teeth. 'Because . . . well, I don't like airing these things in public, Inspector, but I suppose . . . The truth is, as I told you, that I hadn't particularly wanted to speak to Alicia earlier in the evening, but Richard had manoeuvred me into it and I'd been . . . well, rather cross with him, all evening. I thought . . . I thought he might have gone up to see Alicia during the gap between dinner and the dancing just to . . . well, just to spite me.' She gave her husband an apologetic smile. 'I really should have known better. Richard isn't like that.'

'So what did you do?'

'Do?'

'When you thought you saw him?'

'I opened my mouth to call him, and then I thought, no, I'd wait and see if he said anything, later.'

'And then?'

She shrugged. 'The rest of what I told you was true. I went and knocked at Alicia's door, but there was no reply. I listened for a moment, but there was no sound from inside. I tried the handle, but the door was locked and I assumed she hadn't yet got back from the concert. I was still a bit shaken from seeing Richard, as I thought, and to give myself time to think I decided to walk back down, instead of taking the lift. I used the stairs at the opposite end of the corridor from the ones I thought I'd seen Richard go down, just in case he'd got held up, and I bumped into him. But I needn't have worried. When I got downstairs he was talking to someone, in the foyer.'

'And you decided not to mention this little episode to him.'

'I told you, I was waiting to see if he would say anything to me.'

Unlikely, Thanet thought. It was much more probable that she had wanted to have a weapon which she could use against her husband at a time when she needed one. And yet, there was a curious bond between this pair.

Everyone looked at Leyton and he burst out, 'Don't you see, Inspector? It's all been a terrible misunderstanding. . . . I didn't go up to see Alicia during the interval, I can assure you of that. The thought never entered my head. Why should it? I hadn't seen the woman for twenty years and I couldn't have cared less if I didn't see her for another twenty. . . . My wife was mistaken, that's all. And what's more, I can prove it.' He fished in his pocket and produced a piece of paper. 'That's why we're here. To get this ridiculous misunderstanding cleared up for once and for all. I've been up half the night, thinking back over the interval on Saturday evening, doing one of those total recall tricks — you know, you shut your eyes and take yourself back through something step by step. Here's a consecutive list of all the people I spoke to from the moment we came out of the dinner until the moment we returned to the Fletcher Hall for the dancing. I've given names, times, topics of conversation. And I think — no, I *know* you'll find that they tally with other people's accounts, and that I simply wouldn't have had time to go making social calls up on the third floor.'

Thanet took the paper. 'Thank you. As a matter of interest, Mrs Leyton . . . next day, when you heard about Mrs Parnell's death, why didn't you mention this to your husband then? If you believed that he had gone up to see Mrs Parnell at the very time when she had been killed, then this was now a very serious matter.'

'I panicked. It really was very stupid of me, I see that now. I honestly didn't think for one moment that Richard . . . that my husband could have had anything to do with Alicia's death, but . . . I don't know, I just wanted to pretend that it had never happened, that I hadn't been involved in any way, that the whole thing was nothing to do with me . . .'

All her ill-temper and arrogance were gone and two pairs of eyes, one blue and one brown, pleaded with Thanet to believe their story.

And he did. This time he was sure that she had at last given him the truth, and so had her husband. He glanced down at the piece of paper. It was all there, in immense detail. He looked up at them again and suddenly there was a pressure in his head. It was a physical sensation, as intrusive as a headache, only different. The skin of his arms tingled with excitement, as if he had received a minor electric shock. Past experience had taught him that this particular sensation of pressure usually heralded some breakthrough in understanding. He mustn't focus on it, though, or it would go away. He became aware that Lineham was watching him and that the

197

Leytons were still awaiting a response. With an effort he forced his attention back to the conversation.

'This man you saw, Mrs Leyton.' *Blue eyes, brown eyes*, 'How far away from you was he, down the corridor?'

She frowned. 'I'm not very good at distances. He was a few paces away from the top of the stairs.'

'Tell me what you can about him.' The pressure was still there, mounting as steadily and as inevitably as an approaching orgasm.

'There's not a lot to tell.' She gave a nervous little laugh.

Thanet closed his eyes as enlightenment burst upon him and a succession of images raced through his mind, like speeded-up film. Of *course*, this was what had been eluding him for days, that one crucial fact, staring him in the face, its significance recognised by his unconscious mind but submerged until now. He knew, with a complete and absolute certainty that the case was solved and he felt humble, grateful and above all exultant. He would have liked to leap out of his chair and bound about the room, shouting his triumph. Instead he opened his eyes to a disconcerted silence.

Vivienne Leyton had obviously been telling him something; her last words still hung upon the air, unacknowledged. He could tell by her face that she had thought them significant, that she had expected a positive response from him.

'I'm sorry, I was thinking. I wonder if you'd mind repeating that.'

But it wasn't really necessary. He already knew what she was going to say.

TWENTY-ONE

Thanet and Lineham led the way through the narrow country lanes and two more police cars followed on behind, sensibly spaced out. There was no desperate hurry. A telephone call had ensured that their quarry would be there waiting for them, in blissful ignorance of the real nature of their errand. The search warrant which would, Thanet devoutly hoped, set the seal on their success, was safely tucked away in his breast pocket. He was convinced that the evidence he hoped to find still existed. Lineham had been dubious.

'He'll have destroyed it, sir, surely. It would have been madness to keep it, in the circumstances.'

'People don't always do the sensible thing, Mike. I don't think he would have been able to bring himself to destroy these particular papers.'

He only hoped that he was right, that he was not about to make a monumental fool of himself. He had certainly had enough of a struggle, convincing the Super.

'You know as well as I do, Thanet, that you can't possibly be granted a search warrant in these circumstances. If you'd arrested the man, yes, or if you were applying under the Theft Act . . .'

He was right, and Thanet knew it. Desperation brought him inspiration.

'But sir, what we shall be looking for *is* stolen property. Not in the conventional sense, perhaps, but . . .'

Superintendent Parker had looked thoughtful. 'Hmm. I see what you mean.' Then he had lapsed into silence, tapping a pencil on his blotter and gazing away out of the window, as if his view of All Saints' spire would provide him with spiritual guidance.

'This is a very delicate situation, Thanet. Very delicate. The man's a highly respected citizen. If you're wrong, there could be hell to pay.'

'We have an eye-witness, sir . . .'

The Superintendent had given a contemptuous snort. 'Eye-witness! You know precisely the degree to which we can afford to rely upon eye-witnesses — not at all! And this one . . . a momentary glimpse, seen in a hotel corridor at night, with the man's back to her. . . . Defence counsel would make mince-meat of it. She didn't even identify him to begin with, though she knows the man.' Another snort. 'Thought it was her own husband, if you please!'

'I told you, sir, they're very alike. They . . .'

The Superintendent waved an impatient hand. 'Yes, yes, I know. We've been through all that once, already.'

'I'm absolutely convinced I'm right, sir.'

'You have made that very plain, Thanet, but the fact remains that you're not the only one who'd be sticking his neck out, if I let you go ahead with this. All this airy-fairy stuff is not enough. What we need is some positive evidence of the man's guilt, then we'd be home and dry.'

Thanet felt as though he would explode with frustration. Talk about vicious circles! 'But sir, the whole point of this search is to find that very evidence!'

Parker glared at him. 'All right, Thanet, I'm not a complete idiot, you know. I can see your dilemma. But you must recog-nise that I have mine, too.'

Thanet realised that anything else he said might jeopardise his chances of success. Besides, the Super was right. It would be a risk, and if anything went wrong Parker would ultimately be held responsible. And he had more to lose than Thanet.

The Superintendent took his time, tapping his pencil on the blotter again and scowling at All Saints' spire as if it were failing in its duty by not providing him with an immediate and acceptable solution. Finally he said, 'Very well then, Thanet. I'll back you. But you'd better start praying now that you're right about all this.'

The devil of it was, thought Thanet as the little procession neared its destination, he was almost praying that he was wrong. As far as his professional pride was concerned then yes, he needed that evidence, but privately . . . He couldn't ever remember approaching an arrest so reluctantly.

They had arrived. The three cars swept up the drive and parked side by side. It was a morning of bright sunshine and clear blue skies, and the garden of Three Chimneys had never looked more beautiful, nor more inviting. The cool green velvet of the lawn, the glowing swathes of colour in the herbaceous borders, the harmonious juxtaposition of foliage, shape and line which is the hall-mark of the gifted gardener, provided a visual feast enhanced by the scent of roses and by the cascade of music which flowed through an open window. Thanet stood for a few moments absorbing the almost unbearable sweetness and poignancy of the pure, liquid notes. Was this Rain's swan song? Had he guessed the reason for their visit?

By prearrangement the other men remained in their cars while Thanet and Lineham approached the front door. The music cut off abruptly in mid-phrase when they knocked and Rain was still carrying bow and instrument when he opened the door.

'Sorry, I didn't hear you . . . Come in, Inspector.' His gaze took in the other cars, the waiting men, then returned to Thanet. There was no surprise in his face, no outrage, merely resignation, a weary acceptance.

'We have a warrant to search these premises, Mr Rain.' Thanet took the paper from his pocket and presented it for Rain's inspection.

Rain barely glanced at it before shaking his head. 'That won't be necessary. I know what you've come for. You can tell your men to stay where they are.'

And without waiting for Thanet's reaction Rain turned and walked back along the passage.

Lineham raised his eyebrows and Thanet nodded. The sergeant hurried across the gravel to the cars and Thanet followed Rain into the sitting room. The violinist laid his instrument gently down in its case, then loosened the bow. He seemed completely absorbed in the little ritual, a ritual which he must have performed thousands, perhaps hundreds of thousands of times before. What was Rain thinking? Thanet wondered, as he watched him slide the bow carefully into position in the lid, lovingly folding around the mellow, gleaming wood of the violin the silk scarf evidently kept in the case specifically for this purpose. Had this little sequence of actions, no doubt as automatic to Rain as brushing his teeth, suddenly acquired a special significance, become a private farewell to his art? Once again Thanet was overwhelmed by a sense of the significance of what he was about to do. What right had he, an ordinary, humdrum mortal with no special contribution to make to society, even to contemplate depriving the world of a gift like Rain's?

Lineham came quietly into the room, shutting the door behind him. Rain closed the lid and snapped the lock, his hand lingering for a brief caress on the worn black surface of the case. Then he sat down heavily in the nearest chair, as if his legs were suddenly incapable of bearing his weight a moment longer.

'When you rang, a little while ago, to say you were coming . . . I almost told you then.'

Quietly, unobtrusively, Thanet and Lineham sat down.

'Told me what?' Thanet couldn't believe that it was going to be this easy. And yet . . .

'That I had killed Alicia.' Rain dropped his head in his hands.

So there it was. This was no false confession, made for sensational or irrational reasons. It should have been a moment of triumph and it was true that Thanet did experience one brief spark of relief that he had been proved right. But it was immediately extinguished by pity, for here was a man driven by force of circumstance into tragedy. It was true that he himself had initially been responsible for setting into motion those forces which would ultimately bring about his downfall, and also that in trying to avoid the consequences of his behaviour he had committed the ultimate crime against humanity. But despite all this, Thanet could not help feeling sorry for him and envious of Lineham who, notebook calmly at the ready, was prey to no such inconvenient emotion. At his signal the sergeant rose and spoke the formal words of the caution. Thanet doubted that Rain even heard it properly. His face was expressionless, his eyes dull.

'If we could have the folder now, Mr Rain . . .'

Rain looked blankly at him, as if he had no idea what Thanet was talking about, and Thanet experienced a brief, irrational stab of panic. What if they had been talking at cross-purposes all along? Yet Rain's confession had been specific enough . . .

No, Rain was rising, sliding aside a painting to reveal a wall-safe. In a matter of seconds he was turning, the red folder in his hands. Without a word he gave it to Thanet, then returned to his chair.

Thanet slid out the flap, extracted the slim sheaf of papers. And yes, here was the confirmation he had been seeking, the visible, tangible proof that his theory was correct. First, a list of names, sheets of them, all of female children born on the same date in January 1965, January 10th. One of those names was ringed.

Next came a birth certificate, the child's original birth certificate, naming Alicia Mary Doyle as the mother, the child as Alice; father unknown. Thanet remembered that the father's name was entered only if he had acknowledged paternity to the adoption agency. Rain, then, had probably been telling the truth when he had professed that he had originally been ignorant of the child's very existence.

Finally there was a small brown envelope. It contained the two crucial pieces of evidence. One was a newspaper cutting. What must Alicia have felt when she had picked up the paper one morning, and had been confronted with this? Thanet stared at it, Jessica Ross's words echoing through his mind . . . *She was pale, shaking, as if she'd seen a ghost.* Not a ghost, alas, but flesh and blood, her own.

The other vital piece of evidence was a faded photograph. On the back was written *Alice, February 12th 1965.* Taken, no doubt, just before Alicia had parted with the child. Thanet turned it over. The baby smiled up at him. Babies, Thanet thought, usually looked very much alike and he would have been hard put to it, to distinguish between them.

Except in this case.

For Alicia's child had had one unique, identifying feature, as individual as a fingerprint: a clearly-defined, perfectly heart-shaped birthmark on her right cheek.

TWENTY-TWO

Thanet passed the newspaper cutting and the photograph to Lineham, who compressed his lips and nodded solemnly. Rain had reverted to his former posture, knees apart, head in hands. Now, he stirred.

'I'd better explain . . .'

'If you wish. But as you have been told, you have the right to remain silent.'

Rain shook his head, ran a hand through his hair. 'No, I'd rather . . . It's been impossible, carrying this alone.'

Especially with the added anxiety over Mrs Rain, thought Thanet.

'And I can assure you, Inspector, that I would give anything, anything at all, to be able to put the clock back.' He attempted a wry smile. 'I suppose all . . . murderers,' and he brought the word out as though it were choking him, 'say they never meant to do it.'

'Far from it, I assure you.'

'Nevertheless . . . I still can't believe that I . . . that Alicia . . . I know I lied to you, Inspector, and I don't see why you should believe me now, but I was only trying to protect Melanie. No, that sounds far too deliberate, and the truth is, it all happened so fast that . . . What I mean is, I can only assume that it was the thought of what it would do to Melanie that made me lose control . . . If she ever found out that I was her . . .' and he swallowed, as if to control rising nausea, 'her father, I mean.'

'I know.'

Rain focused suddenly and fiercely upon Thanet, directing the whole weight of his formidable personality and intelligence upon him. For Thanet, the effect was as dramatic as if he had been walking along a dark alley at night and someone had suddenly shone a searchlight in his face.

'Yes,' said Rain wonderingly. 'I believe you do. I really believe you do . . . What I told you yesterday was true, you know. I had no idea that I had made Alicia pregnant, that she had had a baby before she was married. That alone was shock enough, but when she told me . . .' He ran his hand through his hair and took a deep breath. 'She rang me up, you see, on Saturday afternoon. About half past four. Said she wanted to come and see me, that it was really urgent. I was astounded, naturally. After all, I hadn't seen or heard from her for twenty years. . . . I told her it wasn't very convenient at the moment, that my fiancée and her parents were here, but if it was all that urgent she could come if she wished. But she said no, she didn't want to butt in or cause any awkwardness — I realised later, of course, that the last thing she wanted to do was meet Melanie for the first time under those circumstances. . . . Anyway, I was so tied up one way and the other that the only possible time we could manage to meet was after the concert, in the foyer.

'Even then, we had only a few minutes. Melanie and her parents were waiting — we'd arranged to go out for supper, afterwards. But Alicia wanted me to go back to the hotel with her. . . . She was so pressing . . . said she had something to show me, that it was absolutely essential I see it, a matter of life and death, almost. By now I was beginning to wonder if she was quite stable. She seemed so tense, so desperate . . . I didn't feel I could just shake her off, abandon her. She was so obviously in some kind of trouble . . . I suggested we meet the following morning, but she wouldn't be put off. She told me that the reason why it was so urgent was because it concerned Melanie, that it was a matter of Melanie's welfare . . . I still couldn't imagine any connection, but by now I was thinking that the simplest thing would be to humour her. I was afraid that if I didn't she would create a scene, there and then, in the middle of the foyer . . . and anyway by now I was becoming intrigued.

'So, I told Melanie and her parents that I'd decided to go back to the hospital after all, and I put them in a taxi. I hated deceiving them, they were very understanding . . . Then I went back to the Swan with Alicia.'

'Sorry to interrupt you, sir,' said Thanet, 'but there is just one question I'd like to ask, at this point. . . . When you left the concert hall, did you go out by the main entrance?'

'No, via a rear entrance which opens on to the small car park at the back of the hall.'

Which was why Jessica Ross had missed Alicia, despite her vigilance.

'Thank you. Do go on.'

'The Swan was crawling with people, there was some kind of function on — I suppose if there hadn't been, someone would have noticed us, but as it was we went up in the lift and when we got to her room she went straight to her overnight case and took that out.'

His eyes lingered for a moment on the red folder.

'Then she told me . . .' He dropped his head in his hands again and began to tug at his hair with tense, plucking movements. His voice became jerky, the words forced out in irregular spurts. 'She told me first . . . about the baby . . . and then she . . . she opened the folder and showed me the photograph. That, she said, was *our child*.' Rain sat up, met Thanet's eye. 'Well, you've met Melanie, you've seen that birthmark of hers for yourself. . . . To think I always liked it, thought it rather distinctive . . .' Rain shook his head in disbelief and gave a bitter little laugh. 'Anyway, when Alicia showed me that photograph, I couldn't believe what I was seeing . . . I'd known Melanie was adopted of course, she'd told me soon after we met, but this . . . I didn't want to believe it, couldn't *bear* to believe it. Melanie and I, we'd been . . . sleeping together. We were *engaged*, for God's sake . . .'

The atmosphere in the room was thick with emotion. Rain was crying now, raw, gasping sobs which tore at his throat and made him incapable of further speech. Thanet couldn't bear to sit still any longer. He rose, went to lay a sympathetic hand on Rain's shoulder, then crossed to look out of the window. Outside the garden glowed in the midday sun, its beauty and serenity a poignant contrast to the pain which filled the room. The men who had accompanied them were standing about by the cars, still awaiting orders. Thanet had forgotten about them. Quietly, he went to murmur in Lineham's ear. They could return to Sturrenden, they wouldn't be needed now. Then he sat down again.

Rain was calming down and by the time Lineham returned a minute or two later, he had regained control of himself. Eventually he said, 'I truly don't know how it happened, Inspector. One minute she was standing there, talking to me, and the next my hands were around her throat and she was . . . dead. I laid her on the bed and tried to revive her, but I could see that it was pointless. The folder had fallen to the floor and I picked it up. Then I left. I'd only been in there a matter of minutes. Minutes!' Rain shook his head incredulously. 'At times, since, I couldn't help wondering if I'd imagined the whole thing, if it was all some terrible nightmare. But I'd only have to look at that, to know it wasn't.' And he nodded at the folder.

No jury could fail to be moved by such a story, Thanet thought. Rain would get away with manslaughter. The anxiety over his mother's condition would work in his favour, too. . . . He would get a relatively short sentence, possibly even a suspended one.

And then what? What would happen to Melanie, the innocent victim of this whole sorry tale, when all this came out in court? How would she be able to cope with the knowledge that she had, all unwittingly, committed incest, how could she reconcile herself to the loss of mother, father, husband and emerge emotionally unscarred?

'Naturally,' said Rain, 'I shall plead guilty.'

It was as if he had tuned in to Thanet's thoughts.

'That way,' Rain went on, 'none of this need ever be made public.'

'You realise that in those circumstances you would get a life sentence?'

'Of course.' Rain lifted his head proudly. 'And that, I would say, seems only fair. A life for a life. Mine for Alicia's. I think, in a way, I shouldn't be able to live with myself if I didn't have to pay. If indeed I shall ever be able to anyway. But that's not the main reason why I've decided to plead guilty. As I said, if I do it this way, none of this need ever come out. Melanie need never know of our true relationship. This way, her innocence will be preserved. And my going to prison will also, I hope, have the advantage of helping her to forget me. Knowing her, she'll probably try to remain loyal. But I shall make it impossible for her to do so. I shall refuse to see her. She's young and in time she'll meet someone else, someone more . . . worthy of her. It's the best way, the only way, to salvage what we can out of this whole sorry mess. This was why, even before you rang up, earlier on, I'd already decided to make a confession.'

Nothing was going to make Rain change his mind, Thanet could see that. And he was probably right. This way would cause the least damage. The average length of a life sentence was nine years. With remission for good behaviour, Rain could be out in far less time than that.

There was nothing more to be said. He nodded. 'Sergeant Lineham will accompany you upstairs, while you put a few things together.'

While they were gone, he shut the downstairs windows and locked the back door, then went on ahead to wait beside the car. When they appeared he reached sideways and down to open the door — and found that he couldn't move.

His back had gone again.

TWENTY-THREE

Thanet lay flat on his back in bed, seething over the injustice of it all. What had he done to deserve this? It wasn't as though he had been rash, or careless . . . He squirmed at the memory of having to be manoeuvred into the car by his prisoner and his sergeant, of arriving back at the station as twisted as a corkscrew. The attitude of his physiotherapist had been the last straw.

'Been heaving your lawnmower about again, Mr Thanet?'

'No! I didn't do *anything* I shouldn't. Just bent to open the car door, that's all.'

'Well I did warn you. Once a disk has been misplaced, it can easily pop out again.'

Pop out! She made it sound so trivial, so insignificant! Not trusting himself to speak Thanet had managed to heave himself on to the couch and had once more yielded to the discomfort and indignity of being manipulated as if pain were an abstract and his body no more animate than a lump of dough.

And now here he was, his comfortable bed transformed into an instrument of torture by the planks which Joan had inserted beneath the mattress and with the prospect of forty-eight hours of boredom. He worked it out. Two thousand eight hundred and eighty minutes. Or a hundred and seventy-two thousand eight hundred seconds . . .

He reached out and switched on the tape he had made earlier, listened critically while it ran. He wondered how Lineham had handled the interview with Melanie's parents, how Melanie herself had taken the news of the arrest and whether she had already had to face the shock of Rain's refusal to see her. He wondered how Rain was taking his first night in the cells and whether there was any improvement in Mrs Rain's condition . . .

He glanced at the clock. Six-thirty. Which meant, in fact,

that his forty-eight hours was now down to forty-six; two thousand seven hundred and sixty minutes or a hundred and sixty-five . . . Was that the front door bell? He strained to hear above the muffled noise of the television from the living room below, the distant whine of the washing machine from the kitchen. Lineham had promised to call around and in Thanet's view the visit was long overdue.

There were voices in the hall. Yes, it was Lineham. Thanet listened enviously as his sergeant took the stairs two at a time.

'How are you feeling, sir?'

'Frustrated. Pull up a chair.'

Lineham complied. 'Your wife tells me you've got to stay flat on your back for forty-eight hours.'

'Another hundred and sixty-five thousand, five hundred and twenty seconds, to be precise. Comes to something, when I've nothing better to do than mental arithmetic. Which reminds me . . .' Thanet handed Lineham the tape. 'My final report on the Parnell case. Get it typed up for me, will you? How's Rain?'

Lineham put the tape in his pocket and pulled a face. 'Resigned. Quiet. Even more so since we had the news from the hospital. His mother died at five o'clock this afternoon.'

So, yet another blow for Rain, Thanet thought. The violinist must be feeling that his world had collapsed around him, his fiancée, his career and now his mother, all lost within the space of a few short hours. Perhaps worst of all, his self-respect had gone. A man at peace with himself has inner reservoirs of strength upon which he can draw in time of need, but because of those few fatal moments when Rain had lost his self-control, he had forfeited even this.

'And Miss Knight is terribly upset, of course, that he won't see her.'

'She's been into the office?'

'Asking for you, sir, yes. She wants you to use your influence on Rain, to persuade him to allow her to visit him. I told her I'd speak to you about it, but that I really didn't think there was any prospect of him changing his mind. I hope I did the right thing.'

'I don't see what else you could have done, in the circumstances. Poor kid, she must be not only completely shattered but totally bewildered by it all. It's fortunate her adoptive parents are here to see her through. The awful thing is, she'll have to live with that incomprehension for the rest of her life. If she ever learnt the truth it would make a nonsense of the sacrifice Rain is making, and the tragedy is that she can never know that that sacrifice exists, let alone that it's entirely on her behalf.'

'Let's hope she never does find out. It's pure luck that so far no one has ever mentioned Mrs Parnell's maiden name. If they did, she'd be bound to recognise it. The Knights tell me she's been shown the original birth certificate.'

'So it's true. She really was Alicia's daughter.'

'Yes.'

The news was a relief. There'd always been the niggling doubt that it had all been some terrible, ironic twist of fate, the fear that everyone might have put two and two together and come up with five, and that Melanie had not been Alicia's daughter after all.

'How are they taking it?'

Lineham grimaced. 'They're very shocked, of course. And it's difficult for them to know quite what to say to Melanie. In the circumstances they fully understand why Rain is refusing to see her, but of course they can't explain this to her.'

'They agree that it's best to keep it from her?'

'Oh yes, wholeheartedly. Though of course there's no guarantee that some nosy reporter won't dig up Mrs Parnell's maiden name and print it.'

'If that happened I'm sure the Knights would do their best to make sure she didn't see it. Though I don't know . . .'

'What?'

'It's just occurred to me . . . We're all falling over ourselves to make sure Melanie doesn't find out the truth . . .'

'Well it's what he wants, isn't it? If she did find out, it would make a nonsense of the sacrifice he's making.'

'Maybe. And we've automatically gone along with him, assumed he's right. But I don't know whether we've ever actually asked ourselves if it's necessarily the best thing for her.'

'But wouldn't any parent do the same thing, in circumstances like this? Wouldn't you?'

211

'I suppose so.' Lineham was right. Of course he would. He remembered that fierce, intense protectiveness which he had experienced in Ben's bedroom the other evening and ceased to marvel at Rain's determination to shield Melanie from the truth regardless of the cost to himself. He could imagine too the horror with which Alicia must have looked at the engagement photograph of Rain and of Melanie, right cheek with that tell-tale birthmark presented to the cameras. She must have spent a tormented couple of weeks worrying about how best to tackle Rain, when he returned from his concert tour in Canada, wondering if she was already too late to prevent incest. It wasn't surprising that she had been so distracted at work, or that she had wanted to leave early on that last morning. She must have found the prospect of even a few more hours in the office intolerable, must have longed to prevent Melanie from learning the truth at all costs, as Rain did now. And yet . . .

'I don't know, Mike. I'm not sure. Just think for a minute. If Melanie did find out she would be very distressed, yes, but she is twenty years old, after all. Her adoptive parents obviously believed her to be sufficiently mature to make a decision to marry. And yet here we all are, treating her as a child, to be protected from the truth at all costs . . . The more I think about it, the more I wonder why we're all colluding like this . . . It could be even worse for her, never to know what went wrong, and why. If she did know, she might one day be able to put the tragedy behind her, but this way I'm not sure that she ever could.'

'So what are you suggesting? That we tell her ourselves?'

'I don't think we could do that at present. But I do think that perhaps, when I'm up and about again, I might talk to Rain about this, see if I can get him to look at it differently. And talk to the Knights, too.'

'I suppose one big advantage of telling her the truth would be that Mr Rain could change his plea to not guilty. And in the circumstances I should think he might well get pretty lenient treatment.'

'Quite. Anyway, there's no immediate rush. We can think about it. Thank you for coming in, Mike.'

Lineham stood up. 'Well, I'd better be off. I told Louise I'd try to be on time for supper, for once.'

'Did you ever manage to get the matter of the house settled, by the way?'

'Oh yes, didn't I tell you? The building society agreed to the increased mortgage, subject to survey. And we have the old lady's assurance that there'll be no more gazumping. I think she felt quite guilty about it, really.'

'Excellent. Louise is delighted, I expect.'

'I should say, We're both praying, now, that nothing goes wrong for the people who are buying ours. I shan't feel we're home and dry until both sets of contracts have been exchanged.'

Lineham had been gone only a few minutes when Joan came in and plumped down on the chair he had vacated.

'Bridget and Ben are making us a surprise supper.'

Thanet grinned. 'I'm supposed to be pleased?' But he was, grim though the gastronomic prospect might be.

She returned his smile, then leaned forward, touched his arm and said, 'This case has depressed you, hasn't it?'

He'd given her a brief account of the arrest and of the reason for it, earlier.

'Yes, it has. Despite the fact that he's a murderer, I liked Rain. And I can't help respecting what he's doing. Though as I was saying to Mike just now, I'm not sure if it's the right thing.' And Thanet explained his reservations to her.

Joan was silent for a while. At last she said, 'I'm just trying to imagine how I would have felt, if I'd found myself in Melanie's situation, at her age. It would be a terrible shock, of course, but I think I'd have liked to know the truth. And yes, I think you're right. I think there'd be a better chance of her coming to terms with what's happened if she did know. Otherwise, as you say, she'll just go on and on in a fog of incomprehension and distress. Also, it would ensure that she gives up any idea of waiting for Mr Rain and marrying him when he comes out of prison.'

'Quite. Though I don't know if I'll be able to persuade Rain to see it like that.'

'I'm not so sure. You might well find that now that the worst has happened, and he's actually been arrested, he might be able to look at it differently. I imagine that up until now he

213

hasn't been able to think beyond confessing.'

'And beyond preventing Melanie from learning the truth, at all costs.'

'Yes, but if he can be made to see that this might not necessarily be the best thing for her . . . He does seem to care very deeply for her, or he wouldn't be prepared to go to these lengths to spare her.'

'Oh yes, he does, I'm sure of that.'

'Well, then . . .'

'You may be right. I'll have to see what I can do. Perhaps it's as well that I'm out of commission for a day or two. It'll give him a chance to get his breath back . . . Did Mike tell you, by the way? Mrs Rain died this afternoon.'

'Oh dear. Poor man. Not that, on top of everything. And poor Penny.'

Poor Alicia, too. It was difficult to reconcile his memories of the vivid girl he had once known with the sad, gentle Alicia of her later years, and tragic to think that her seventeenth summer, that time which had seemed so full of golden promise, had proved instead to be the fulcrum around which she had swung into the downward spiral which had culminated finally in her death.

'What's the matter, Luke?'

'I was thinking about Alicia. And how sad it was to think that an adolescent love affair could have led to all this . . . Which reminds me. Her father doesn't even know she's dead, yet. He's not due back from holiday until Saturday.'

'Will you tell him why she was killed?'

'I don't know. Perhaps. The trouble is, if I do tell him he'd be bound to feel partly responsible . . . knowing that the adoption which he no doubt encouraged eventually caused Alicia's death.'

'But he couldn't possibly think it was his fault! How could he, by any stretch of the imagination, have foreseen that Melanie would ever even meet her real father, let alone fall in love with him.'

'He couldn't, of course. But you know, as well as I do, that in circumstances like this people aren't rational. He'll tell himself that if he'd insisted Alicia keep the baby she'd still be alive today.'

'In fact, you know, it does seem the most extraordinary coincidence that Melanie and her father did meet.'

'Not if you think that they're both professional musicians. That's a relatively small world, I imagine, especially as far as soloists are concerned. She must have inherited her talent from him. They even play the same instrument.'

'Yes, that's true . . . Incidentally, talking about the adoption, you haven't yet told me how you came to cotton on to the fact that Melanie was Alicia's daughter.'

'Ah, that was a bit of luck, really.' *No, nothing as casual as luck.* 'You remember that programme on genetics we saw a couple of months ago?'

'Vaguely.'

'Well, after I met Melanie and the Knights, almost at the beginning of the case, I knew that something was worrying me. But I couldn't put my finger on it. It went on nagging at me for days — you remember? I mentioned it to you at one point. And then, suddenly, I realised what it was.'

'Go on. I'm fascinated.'

'Apparently it's not genetically possible for two blue-eyed parents to produce a child with brown eyes. Something to do with recessive genes.'

'Oh, I *see*. I gather that both the Knights have blue eyes, and Melanie's are brown?'

'Precisely. Anyway, I was interviewing the Leytons when it dawned on me. Leyton has brown eyes, his wife has blue. They were both sitting there, staring at me across my desk and I simply couldn't work out why it was bothering me so much. Then I realised, and suddenly the whole thing made sense. If Melanie was adopted, and it was she, not Penny, who was the daughter of Alicia and Nicholas Rain . . . I saw how it could all have come about. Alicia would have seen the announcement of the engagement in the papers, would have recognised Melanie by that very unusual birthmark on her cheek . . . She'd never told Rain about the child, and naturally she would have been desperate to see him at the first possible opportunity. As it was, she had to wait a fortnight, because he was away on tour in Canada. She must have been out of her mind with worry. She'd have known he was giving this concert in

Sturrenden — it was mentioned in all the engagement announcements, because he and Melanie were playing in it together — so she booked a room at the Swan and persuaded him to go back with her after the concert, so that she could show him the proof of what she was saying . . . As I say, I saw it all, and then something else that had puzzled us suddenly made sense. You see, Vivienne Leyton had been lying about her movements on Saturday evening because when she went up to Alicia's room she thought she saw her husband coming away from it. In fact, of course, it wasn't her husband, it was Nicholas Rain. They're much of a height and they both have brown hair and beards. And I remembered that the first time I saw Leyton, in the semi-darkness of the hall at his home, just for a split second I thought he was Rain.'

'But she surely wouldn't have mistaken her own husband for someone else?'

'You'd be surprised at the tricks the mind can play, where recognition is concerned. We've done tests on eye-witness credibility and the results were pretty staggering. We see, above all, what we *expect* to see. And our judgement can also be affected by a state of heightened emotion. So Vivienne was ripe for a mis-perception. What was more, both Leyton and Rain were formally dressed, her husband because of the dinner dance, Rain because of the concert. The fact that one was wearing a dinner jacket, the other tails, was immaterial. The impression was one of black and white, formal evening attire, and if you add this to the rest of what I've been saying . . . Oh no, I think her mistake was all too understandable.'

'Put like that . . . Yes, I see what you mean. So what made her realise that it had been a mistake?'

'Well, when Mike and I went out to see her last night it was perfectly obvious to everybody, including her husband, that she was holding something back and after we left he managed to get her to tell him what it was. So then, of course, they got it all sorted out. When, finally, he'd managed to convince her that he really hadn't been anywhere near the third floor that night, they decided the only thing to do was to come to me and make a clean breast of it. And once they'd cleared up the misunderstanding, the way was open for her to search her memory again and come up with a different answer.'

'She actually identified Nicholas Rain?'

'Not at first. But eventually she worked it out for herself. By this time, of course, it had dawned on me what had happened and I had to be very careful not to influence her . . . Even so, I'm not too sure how her evidence would have stood up in court. Still, her identification, tentative though it was, did support my theory and helped to persuade the Super to back me in my application for a warrant to search Rain's house.'

'Sorry, I must be a bit dim. What were you hoping to find?'

'The red folder which was missing from Alicia's hotel room. I was pretty certain it must contain proof of Melanie's real identity, and that was why he'd had to take it away with him.'

'I see. But I still don't understand why you were so sure you'd find it? Surely the first thing he would have done, afterwards, would have been to destroy it? He must have known it would be pretty damning evidence against him.'

'I know. But I was banking on the fact that he hadn't, for various reasons. To begin with, I thought he might well have been unable to bring himself to destroy Melanie's original birth certificate and the photograph of her as a baby, for sentimental reasons. The photograph, especially, was irreplaceable, I imagine. And you must remember that he was in a state of shock. He told me himself that he couldn't really believe it had happened, that he felt it must be some terrible nightmare from which he would eventually wake up. I felt he would almost have *needed* to keep that folder, partly to remind himself that it had not in fact just been a bad dream, but also to convince himself that there had been a valid reason for his having gone over the edge as he did.'

'I suppose, too, that from a purely practical point of view, he might have kept it because if ever he were arrested, it would uphold his story.'

'There's that, too, yes . . . But I'm not sure that he was ever particularly interested in saving his own skin. As I say, I think that right from the beginning he was genuinely shocked, genuinely horrified at what he had done and I think he lied to us because his first instinct was to protect Melanie. As he saw it, the only way to do that was by trying to convince us that he

217

was in the clear. And really, at the point when we applied for that search warrant, we had nothing beyond Vivienne Leyton's rather shaky identification to justify taking such a drastic step.'

'You were rather sticking your neck out, weren't you.'

'I know. If the folder hadn't turned up, I really would have looked a bit of an idiot.'

'You trusted your instinct.' Joan took his hand. 'And you were right, as usual.'

'Luck, that's all.'

'Not luck. Judgement. And there's no point in waving your hands about and trying to deny it. It's what makes you a good policeman.'

He smiled at her. 'The trouble with you is that you're biased.'

She bent to kiss him. 'And why shouldn't I be? You're my husband, aren't you?'

There were noises on the stairs and a moment later the door was flung open.

'First course,' announced Ben.

'Good. I'm starving.' Thanet eased himself into a sitting position and Joan plumped the pillows up behind him. Bridget put the special bed-tray in front of him, the one with legs, and he was touched at the trouble she had taken. She had found a pretty tray-cloth embroidered with forget-me-nots, had given him their best china and cutlery, and had poured him an ice-cold lager in a tall glass beaded with moisture. The first course was half a grapefruit with a cherry in a middle.

'This looks terrific, Sprig.'

She beamed at him as Ben returned with three more servings of grapefruit and they began to eat, Bridget and Ben sitting cross-legged on the floor. Throughout the entire meal (cold ham and salad followed by raspberry ice-cream with fresh raspberries from the garden) Thanet was aware that he was the focus of their attention, that their efforts were being directed solely towards comforting him for his misfortune. By the time they had finished eating he was thoroughly ashamed of himself. This was only a temporary injury, after all. In a couple of days he'd be up and about again. Why didn't he make the best of the enforced break, instead of mumping and moaning about it? He could read, listen to music, talk to the children, have leisurely conversations with Joan — do, in short, all the things he never normally had time to do. He reached for Joan's hand.

'Sorry I've been such a bear.'

She smiled back, leaned forward to ruffle his hair. 'Good. You're beginning to look human again.'

'Food always does that for me. Congratulations, you two. That was a really delicious meal.'

Bridget and Ben looked gratified and Ben, ever the opportunist, said, 'How about a game of scrabble, Dad?'

'We've got to wash up first.' Bridget began clattering the dishes together.

Thanet saw Joan wince. It looked as though their best dinner service wasn't going to last the night.

'I'll do that,' she said hastily. 'Fair's fair. You prepared it all. Now it's my turn. Though I don't know if your father can manage scrabble. He's supposed to be flat on his back.'

'I could keep the score,' said Thanet, reluctantly sliding down in the bed.

Bridget fetched paper and pencil and they set up the scrabble board on Thanet's stomach.

'Hey!' he protested. 'I won't be able to move.'

Ben grinned. 'You're not supposed to anyway. I heard Mum say.'

They perched on either side of him and the game began. They were half way through when Ben's face lit up with excitement. Then, frowning with concentration he laid out his counters on the board, pausing twice for readjustments. 'Thirteen letters!' he said at last, triumphantly.

'Let me see.' Bridget swivelled the board around. 'That's not how you spell it,' she said. And then, reproachfully, 'Oh Ben.' She glanced at Thanet, then back at her brother and there was an amused complicity in the look they exchanged.

'What's the joke?' said Thanet. 'What's the word?' And he craned to see, wincing as pain immediately stabbed at the base of his spine. 'It's no good. I can't lift my head far enough. What is it?'

They grinned at each other and Bridget said, 'It doesn't count, anyway. He's spelt it wrong.'

'I haven't!'

'Yes you have. There should be a "y" there, not an "i".'

'There shouldn't! You're making it up.'

'No I'm not!'

'When you two have quite finished squabbling, perhaps you'd tell me what it is. Then I can decide whether Ben's spelt it wrongly or not.'

'Yes, go on,' said Bridget. 'Ask Dad.'

Silence.

'Well?' said Thanet, beginning to wonder what on earth Ben could have put.

Ben gave him an assessing look, and then, in a tone which begged him to share the joke, said, 'Physiotherapy.'

With a straight face Thanet spelled it for him and then, unable to contain his amusement, began to laugh.

Scrabble counters flew everywhere as the children joined in.

ABOUT THE AUTHOR

DOROTHY SIMPSON, winner of the prestigious Silver Dagger Award, is the author of seven Luke Thanet mysteries, most recently ELEMENT OF DOUBT, LAST SEEN ALIVE, CLOSE HER EYES, and SUSPICIOUS DEATH. A contributor to *Ellery Queen's Mystery Magazine* and *Alfred Hitchcock's Mystery Magazine*, she lives in Kent, England.

THE MYSTERIOUS WORLD OF AGATHA CHRISTIE